I0721113

Secrets

By: Mary Reason Theriot

Dedication

Without the love and support of my family and friends, I would not have pursued this new path in life. I would especially like to thank those that have proofread copy after copy, to give me their honest opinion of the books.

Theresa, thank you so much for your continued encouragement. Without you, some of the characters would not have "come to life."

To my wonderful husband, Mat, your continued love and support mean the world to me. I don't know what I would do without you in my life. One of these nights I'm sure you will be able to sleep with both eyes closed. Eventually, I should run out of ideas... or maybe not. These books wouldn't be what they are without you pushing me forward.

To Little House of Edits for all of the wonderful work.

To Don Reason and Malcolm "Phil" Theriot for sharing your knowledge and experience of Law Enforcement protocol.

To my fans, I would like to offer a special thank you for your continued support.

This book is a work of fiction. Names, characters, places and incidents are the product of the author's imagination and are used fictitiously. Any resemblance to actual persons, living or dead, events or places are entirely coincidental.

This book has been professionally edited by Little House of Edits and proofed by Proofreading by Katie.

Copyright © 2014 by Mary Reason Theriot

ISBN-10: 1-945393-42-4
ISBN-13: 978-1-945393-42-6

Also Available by Mary Reason Theriot:

The Hideaway
The Traveler
Dr. Frankenstein
Above Suspicion
Horror in the Night
Echoes on the Bayou
Seven Deadly Sins
A Kiss So Deadly
A Deadly Combination
Seduced by Voodoo
CarnEvil of Souls
Redemption
Haunted Visions
Love's Embrace

www.maryreasontheriot.com

Chapter 1

Her husband was looking for a fight this morning. This time, however, Chandra planned on facing her husband's anger head on. Lately, he stayed angry at her. She couldn't do anything right. She had finally had enough of his attitude towards her. She was sick and tired of the way he treated her.

This morning as he once again complained about the money she spent in a day, she felt as if she was having an out of body experience. His mouth was moving, but no sound reached her ears. Although, in all honesty, after six years of marriage, she knew how to tune him out. Instead of replying, she waited for him to lose steam.

If only he put as much effort into their sex life as he did in his money "speeches". Perhaps if he left her well satisfied, or at least satisfied, in that department, she wouldn't find other ways to spend her days. At least with shopping, she received some instant gratification.

No, when it came to sex, all Andrew cared about was his needs being met. "Chandra. Chandra!" Hearing her name being called broke her from her musings, she turned her focus on him.

"I'm sorry, honey. What did you say?"

"Oh, just forget it!" Andrew exclaimed as he turned to storm away. "You don't give a rat's ass about how I feel anyway, at least not anymore." His cold tone shook her to the core. Did he feel as neglected as she did?

After Andrew had left, she went to her room to prepare for her new job. The money had started coming in, but if this continued it wouldn't be long before she had her own money to spend however she wanted.

Bored one morning, she was perusing the classifieds until one in particular caught her eye. Curious as to what the job entailed, she set up an interview and was hired on the spot.

What started out as a simple way to show dominance over men had become extremely lucrative for her. Most of the clients had strong sexual fantasies. She never knew so many men wanted to be dominated by a woman. Hell, she didn't think she had it in her, but it turned out she was good at this. Perhaps being an outgoing and ambitious woman made it easy to fall into this particular role, or maybe the way Andrew treated her caused her to do this job well. Recently, some of the men had started giving her gifts to show their appreciation.

While most of the men wanted nothing more than to be a "slave" who would "serve" and "follow" her, several had peculiar fantasies for her to act out. At least none had been too outlandish where she was uncomfortable performing the requests.

These men enjoyed being all but ignored to even being treated poorly. They reveled in the chance to impress a woman, even if it was an anonymous woman online. A few requested she verbally abuse them, while some were eager to do whatever she asked. But, most of the men were lonely and sought a beautiful woman to dominate them.

More surprisingly, some of them were clueless when it came to anonymity. They didn't even bother to hide their real identities, which made blackmailing them easy.

As she signed on under her stage name, Mistress Aurora, she wondered how many men were waiting for her to control them. A shiver of pleasure ran through her when she saw the clients hankering to be commanded by her. The role as a Virtual Dominatrix was such a new and exhilarating experience that she spent her free hours practicing various personas.

As she moved into view of the camera, she let her Dominatrix persona take over. She cracked a small whip through the air to get their attention. Once she had their full attention, she let her hands wander over her body, enticing the men. "If you were man enough, you wouldn't have to watch me please myself. No, you would be out there pleasing a woman yourself."

Without thinking, she adjusted the feathered mask she wore, the only thing she never removed in her shows. The mask allowed her the freedom to perform without worrying about her reputation being ruined. Besides, this was safe and harmless fun. She didn't have sex with these men; all of her contact was over the computer.

Today she wore a black leather bustier, matching thong and thigh high leather boots with a black lace garter adorning the top of the boot. She moved her hips to the sultry music of *"If"* by Janet Jackson playing in the background. Tossing her head back, she let her long black hair with red highlights float around her shoulders.

She cupped her breasts with both hands and gave them a gentle squeeze. Next she ran her palms over her nipples until they stood taut.

While she continued ordering the men around, she kept her eyes on the camera. This way the clients felt as if she were looking directly at them while giving them orders. She planned on encouraging a few more men to request private sessions. While the money was good in the open forum, the one on one sessions were more lucrative.

She needed this release after her fight with Andrew earlier. If only she could dominate him the way she dominated these men. She found it thrilling to order these men around. It made her wet and hot, hotter than anything she ever experienced.

She had one client, though, that she particularly liked. She allowed herself to be submissive to him, and him alone. Not only did he tip well, but he made her feel special, as if she were the only woman he desired. She envisioned him in her mind. Strong, manly, and rough. Just what she craved lately.

About to give up on her fantasy man joining her online today, an instant message flashed across her screen, "You are a very naughty girl. How dare you touch yourself without me being present!"

Her knees nearly buckled as she thought about what he would command that she do to herself. As he gave her detailed instructions on what he wanted her to do, a realization washed over her. She was tired of self-gratification. If her husband refused to have sex with her, she would find a man who could satisfy her like she craved. Surely one of these eager men would be happy with a personal, one on one meeting with their Mistress.

Chapter 2

Lucas Stevenson sat at his computer desk and watched the Dominatrix slowly move her fingers up her thigh. He was anxious for her to reveal more of that delectable body of hers.

She was the only woman he allowed to berate him the way she did. Normally, he wouldn't stand for a woman to talk down to him, yet he paid this woman to do just that. There was something erotic about her being in control of him. However, as their relationship progressed, she became the submissive. So far, she has done anything he requested.

He reveled in the pleasure of getting off to her almost as much as she enjoyed the thrill of having him as a customer. She told him numerous times that he was her favorite.

It could be difficult to drag her away from the other viewers, but today it had been easy to get a private session with her. Was she waiting for him, keeping herself available? It had been too easy to capture her attention and lure her away for an exotic private session that would more than likely cost him a small fortune.

She mentioned once before that she didn't do this for the money, but for the attention. At home, her husband was the dominant one, but here, in this online fantasy world, she controlled the men.

Although she had included this tidbit of information in her profile, on several occasions she mentioned to him that her sex life was non-existent. Her husband was at work more than at home. He paid little attention to her needs. This was how she added spice to her life and obtained attention from men, attention that she craved and needed.

Lately, she has offered him more and more private sessions, almost as if she was seeking him out. With him she revealed a little more about herself. Did she look forward to seeing him just as much as he looked forward to seeing her? He'd wanted a woman such as her for a while now. He found her mentally stimulating and physically exciting.

As he watched her touch herself, he rubbed his rock hard erection, stroking his hand over the smooth skin while admiring her now naked body.

He pleaded with her to show her face, but so far she refused this command. She promised him that soon she would reveal herself to him. He anxiously waited to find out just what she looked like without the mask.

She had long, black hair, with red highlights. By the look of her skin and voluptuous breasts, he put her in her mid to late twenties. From what he saw she was an attractive woman, and he did not understand why her husband had no interest in her.

His heart rate quickened as she stroked herself even faster. Desire filled him. He should be the one pleasing her.

Online, she was far from a passive lover. She was very vocal about how she wanted him on top of her, inside of her.

As she inserted two fingers slowly inside of her, she urged him on; talking about how she wished it was him touching her body. Just hearing those words sent him over the edge. His body ached for what she did with her hand.

If only he could reach inside of the screen and please her. As she continued to talk about her fantasizing it was him there with her, his body moved in response. He wanted her to feel the power of his body thrusting deep into her.

His eyes feasted on her body, the way her hand moved inside of her, and the way her breasts bounced up and down. He couldn't contain himself anymore. Her dirty talk had the desired effect on him; it always did.

Chapter 3

Detective Derrick LeDoux was thirty-five years old, tall, muscularly built, good looking and a transplant from New Orleans. Living there for so long gave him a streetwise skepticism that his partner for six months now, Detective Stephen Riley, had yet to develop. He had been told several times he was too blunt, hard-nosed, brusque, and his manner overly aggressive. He always came across as a tough guy where his partner came across as laid back. However, Detective LeDoux learned that was nothing but a mere cover for his partner. Detective Riley may appear laid back and easily fooled, but he was nothing like that.

While still in the honeymoon phase, so far, they seemed to get along. These last few months, LeDoux learned that Riley just sat back and absorbed everything before making a move. With his dark, coal black hair, and bedroom eyes women fell for him with one look. Riley had a confidence about him that surprised LeDoux. Even now, his sense of humor took time to get used to.

The air outside was hot, stifling. The humidity was so thick that your clothes seemed to stick to you. LeDoux took a long drink from his iced tea, trying to cool off in this oppressive heat as Riley devoured a double bacon cheeseburger. "Bon ami, I have no idea where you put all the food that you eat."

Wiping his mouth as he finished the burger, Riley replied, "I have a high metabolism is all. Besides, Allison was a nympho last night. She couldn't get enough of me."

LeDoux shook his head, "I don't want to hear how good your sex life was last night."

Shrugging his shoulders, Riley said, "Not my fault that it has been a while since you got laid."

Before LeDoux could respond, his cell phone rang. "LeDoux."

The dispatcher's voice came across loud and clear for a change, "Detective, we have a homicide. A husband came home to discover his wife dead."

"On our way."

Looking at Riley, he told him, "Got to go, husband came home to find his wife dead."

Quickly throwing away their food, they headed to the police cruiser. Turning on the cruiser lights, the two detectives sped down the road. Riley said, "Just when I thought we would have a nice quiet week."

As they approached the crime scene, they saw several black and whites already on scene. A young officer was busy cordoning off the area with yellow crime scene tape to keep any trespassers and gawkers away. A small gathering of curious neighbors watched with extreme interest as to why the police were in their quiet neighborhood.

Riley stated, "Not your typical neighborhood for a murder."

The large two story home had a light brown stucco façade and hurricane shutters adorned the windows facing the street. He also noticed that the black, wrought iron torchieres which flanked the front porch had been inadvertently left on.

LeDoux replied while shaking his head, "No. Let's go see what happened."

Just as they headed up the drive, the medical examiner's van pulled up behind them. Officer Stansbury greeted the two detectives. "Officer Stansbury, what do we have?" Riley asked.

Officer Alan Stansbury looked back towards the house before responding, "The victim is Chandra Guidry, age twenty-seven. The husband came home to find her tied up on the bed with her throat slit." Leaning in closer, Officer Stansbury stated, "This one, though, may be harder to believe when you see the victim."

"What makes this case so different?"

With a sly grin, Officer Stansbury said, "Oh, I think you need to see it for yourself sir."

LeDoux looked around the house on his way to where the body was located. "It doesn't appear that robbery was the motive for the murder. The living room has more than enough electronics to make a robber happy."

The décor of the house was a little too modern for LeDoux's likings. The spacious, ultra modern house had soaring ceilings and was decorated in black and white with splashes of red here and there. The focal point of the living room was a baby grand piano.

Riley stated, "My whole house would fit inside the downstairs of this house."

As they neared the murder scene, the coppery smell of blood permeated the air. The victim's hands and feet were bound to the bed and blood covered her upper body and bed. "Something is in her mouth," Riley stated. "It appears to be a rubber ball of some kind with straps around the face."

Officer Gary Chauvin stated, "They call it a ball gag, sir."

LeDoux laughed, "It would be the young officers who know about these kinds of kinky toys."

Shaking his head, Officer Chauvin stated, "All you have to do is watch television nowadays, and you can learn what these items are."

Shaking his head, LeDoux put on latex gloves and observed the knife wound. He stated, "There doesn't appear to be any hesitation marks. Our killer had no qualms about what he did."

Riley pointed out, "I would say that our victim here met up with a lover, unless she dressed like this all the time for her husband."

"Maybe the husband discovered his wife was getting some on the side and had enough."

Riley found a large suitcase tucked under the bed. He carefully pulled it out and opened it. Letting out a whistle as he removed a dog collar, he stated, "Our victim was into some strange stuff."

As LeDoux looked at the body, he feared this wasn't done by a jilted lover or an outraged husband, but instead, by a killer who was just getting started.

Chapter 4

Denise Mahoney flung her tiny silver clutch on the couch with such force that the clasp sprung open, spilling its contents onto the floor. She never had a submissive misbehave as this man had. But it annoyed her even more that she didn't know how to handle such a man.

As she bent down to pick up the money, she caught her knee on the corner of the coffee table. Nursing the welt on her knee, she shoved the money back in her clutch. She would put it away later. Right now she needed to release some of the stress that held her body hostage.

She straightened the sapphire blue silk dress that molded sensuously to her curvy body. She ran a hand through her wavy, auburn hair and let out a deep sigh. Clients like tonight have her longing to get out of the business. If he had done this to an actual date, he would be in jail.

She massaged her temples with her slender, well manicured fingers to ease the stress building. She should have gone to college and made something out of her life. Instead, at the age of sixteen she ran away from home and started wandering the streets. At least on her own, people couldn't order her around, telling her what she could and couldn't do. She had been woefully naïve, believing it would be easy to make it on her own. Back then she wore rose-colored glasses, but not anymore.

If it weren't for her baby girl, Denise would still work at a strip club. When she found out she was pregnant, she stopped doing the drugs and quit working at the club. After the birth of her baby, Mike Johansen approached her about making a little side money.

His offer came at the right time. She did not realize babies were so expensive. However, since dancing was all that she knew, she jumped at the opportunity to work as an online dominatrix girl. Just thinking of her baby's infectious smile made everything she did worthwhile. She would do anything for her.

She had no problem showing off her goods to the masses and performing for the horny men dishing out obscene amounts of money just to watch her. The minute she stepped on the stage; she became a sex goddess. The men believed she danced for only them.

She brought that same concept to her new line of work. She looked into the camera as if she were looking directly at their desperate, lonely faces. Mike had two rules to obey for this job. The first was never to lose control of the situation, and the second was never to have sex with the men, unless he arranged the appointment. However, when a few of the men requested personal sessions, the money was too tempting to refuse. Besides, she considered these rules Mike implemented to be more of a guideline than anything else.

While working for Mike paid well, the men whom she saw gave her extra spending money that Mike knew nothing about.

What she needed right now was a long, steamy bubble bath, with all the works. After looking in to make sure that her daughter was asleep, she started to fill the tub up with water. She walked into the kitchen and poured herself a glass of wine. Once back in the bathroom, she turned her *Pandora* station to some soothing sounds of jazz. Waiting for the tub to finish filling, she rolled her neck to loosen the muscles.

As she went to step into the tub, her phone rang. Walking back to the bedroom to grab her phone, she knew there was only one person that it could be, and if she didn't answer, he would keep calling.

"Hello, Mr. Johansen."

"The client was impressed with you. He asked that you be his regular."

Groaning inwardly, she replied, "Well, I am glad he was satisfied." Her voice purred out of her, hiding the bitterness she felt towards her boss and the client.

Mike Johansen didn't even pick up on the hidden message in her statement as he continued, "He will be in town the same time next month."

She bit her tongue to keep from screaming. She kept telling herself to think of the money. No other job paid a couple of grand for a few hours work. "Words can't explain how much I look forward to seeing him again." She forced enthusiasm into her voice.

After confirming the standing appointment, she hung up the phone. It took all of her self-control not to flush the phone down the toilet. She dreaded their next appointment already. While most men were easy to control when they requested a Dominatrix, this man was not. He wanted her to be the submissive. Remembering the inviting bath, she headed back to the bathroom. She stepped into the marble tub and let the steamy water work its magic. The aromatic scent of the bubble bath helped to relax her tense body.

One bottle of wine and several hours later, she curled up in her living room reading a thriller. She almost ignored the knocking, but a female voice called out, "Come on, Denise, I know you are in there."

A smile formed across her face. Amanda must be on her way home from a "date". Amanda Benoit and her had been friends and confidants for about five months now. They were closer than most sisters, having forged and cultivated their friendship with extreme care.

She laid the book on the coffee table and went to welcome her friend. The blonde haired bombshell was a complete contrast to Denise. Amanda reminded Denise of a Barbie doll; with her dark tan, blonde hair, blue eyes, and standing a good six inches taller than Denise.

"I didn't wake you, did I?"

Laughing Denise answered, "No."

Putting her hand to her chest, Amanda said, "Oh, good. Do you want to go to the gym in the morning? I need to work off the extra calories from tonight's meal."

"What's wrong? Your date didn't give you a workout."

Shaking her head, she rolled her eyes, "Girl, that was the easiest three grand I ever made. Talk about a minute man. All I did was look at it, and he went off."

Wiping the tears from her eyes, Denise said, "I wish I could say the same for my date."

"Uh-oh. What happened?"

Shuddering at the mere thought of tonight, she confided in her friend, "Let's just say he was a piece of work. He may have requested a Dominatrix, but he really wanted a submissive."

"Oh honey, I'm so sorry." Leaning in closer to her friend, Amanda confided, "You do know that there are ways to control temperamental clients."

Intrigued, Denise asked, "What do you mean? Some clients aren't into bondage and freak out at the mention of handcuffs."

"Oh, there are other ways to handle clients. Ways to bring a man to his knees quick."

Now her curiosity was piqued. "And just how do you do that where they won't come after you afterwards, or worse, tell Mike," Denise asked.

"Trust me, honey, they won't tell and you don't have to worry about them again."

"Tell me what to do then."

Grinning as she recalled the first time she used this technique, Amanda explained in detail what her friend needed to do. "It takes some practice to get the technique right. You cannot let your client notice something is off."

"Now I am even more curious. What do you do?"

"You carefully open a condom wrapper so that it can be resealed. Remove the condom and add a little cayenne pepper juice to the inside of the condom. Once done reseal the package, and you will be ready to bring him some serious pain."

Amazed, Denise asked, "And the cayenne pepper juice will work?"

Nodding her head, "Oh, honey, it works really well. It will blister him so bad that he won't ever forget you. While he is rolling in pain, though, take a picture or two of y'all together so you can have a picture handy for blackmail. That way, if he threatens to tell Mike you have your own ammunition."

Letting out a whistle Denise laughed, "Damn woman, remind me never to piss you off."

Amanda shrugged her shoulders, "Unfortunately, there are always a few clients who are difficult to control."

"Do you remember when we first met," Denise asked.

"I still think Mike thought we would be instant enemies instead of becoming the best of friends."

Laughing, Amanda agreed, "That was my first threesome, and I was so nervous."

"The guy was definitely surprised by the turn of events." Sighing, Denise asked, "Do you ever think of getting out of this business?"

Amanda looked at her friend in disbelief, "I know the customers can sometimes be overbearing, but remember that you are only with that person for a few hours. Keep reminding yourself of the money you make." Grinning, she added, "Besides, there is no other profession where a woman can dominate a man like we do."

Sighing Denise said, "I have to admit that the money is nice, but sometimes I get tired of spreading my legs for complete assholes."

"True, but then again, not every client wants sex. Look at it this way, even with a regular job you deal with assholes, and you still don't make the kind of money we make."

"I know. It's just... I wonder what it would be like to get out of this business." Slumping back with a frown, she sighed, "Maybe I need a vacation."

Standing up to leave Amanda said, "Well, we may not be able to take a vacation right now, but I say we go shopping after the gym tomorrow."

As Denise walked Amanda to the door, she said, "Now that sounds like a great idea. Maybe we can even fit in lunch."

Chapter 5

He raced through the house, hoping he wasn't too late. The Dominatrix always started promptly at noon each day, but she informed them the previous night there would be no sessions for today. Curious why she didn't have one today he rushed home to find out. Seeing her was what kept him going. All he wanted to do was sit in front of his computer and watch the love of his life.

In his room, he wasted no time in switching on the computer. After the system came to life, he quickly typed in the codes that turned on her web camera. Most nights he watched her sleep, wishing he was there worshipping that body of hers.

Once the camera was active, he waited for the love of his life. *Where are you my sweet, tantalizing mistress of my heart?* He entertained so many fantasies about her; most prevalent was the one in which he had a future with her. He wanted to be her protector, the love of her life.

Soon he saw Mistress Desiree. Even though she hid her face behind a half-mask, he knew it was her. This time she came on screen naked, in all her wondrous glory. Seeing her naked was almost too much for him. Her body was made for pleasing a man. It was tanned, toned, and oh so shapely. Her lean torso, fabulous legs, an ass to die for, and breasts that made any hot blooded man drop to his knees.

His blood ran cold as he watched in part disgust and part exhilaration. He couldn't believe his eyes. The woman he adored was with another man. She was so seductive, so beautiful, and such a whore.

He never imagined his temptress would allow a stranger to use her body in such a vile way. He wanted to avert his eyes, but he couldn't take his eyes away from the sight in front of him. Her body moved fluidly against the man's, welcoming him with complete ease. Her breasts bounced with each thrust as her rosy nipples grew taut with excitement.

It should be HIM thrusting into that enticing womanly juncture between her thighs. Even though she was betraying him, his body hardened as she pleasured the other man. It should be him running his hands over her body, sucking those perfect breasts, and enjoying that delectable body of hers. He could not believe the woman he dreamt of, wanted to be with, was such a whore.

He closed his eyes and imagined she was mounting him, instead of this stranger. His breath quickened as he felt her moving over his toned body. He imagined himself ramming deep inside of her, spilling his seed into her womb.

As he opened his eyes and fixated on the computer screen once more, he knew this man was to blame for her betraying him. He must be eradicated from her life.

***

This was the only solution. He stood up and stretched his honed muscles as the anticipation of what was to come swept over his body.

He walked into his closet and dressed in black. Next, he sorted through the various military weapons he'd collected over the years. He had an extensive collection to choose from; hand grenades, various knives, guns, silencers, and even a pea shooter with poisoned darts. After he had found the perfect knife, he grabbed a couple pairs of latex gloves.

He was ready. He stepped out of his house and into the darkness of the night. Night had long since fallen. Not a star shone in the black velvet sky. Darkness clutched the bayou in its cold grasp, as fog slithered along the land reminiscent of ghostly snakes.

Hiding in the dark, being one with the night, he patiently watched the cabin before him. HE would no longer be a temptation for her. She would finally be his.

As he closed his eyes, he saw her standing before him. Shoulder length hair the color of midnight and eyes the color of liquid chocolate. She was the one. His hands clenched into fists at just the thought of her with another man, the sinewy muscles in his biceps grew taut.

Inhaling the night air gave him strength. His sinister eyes looked up and down the road to confirm no one was nearby.

Sounds of the night filled the air. With movements as stealthy as a cat, he slipped a pair of gloves on, sneaked into the cabin, and waited. His muscles tensed in anticipation as he prepared to make his move. He tucked the serrated knife into his waistband. The icy steel against his bare skin gave him a sense of raw power. He could hardly wait for the cold steel blade to slice through the man's flesh, spilling his blood. Life and death lay in his hands tonight.

Blood pulsed through his body, pounding in his ears. Crimson fluid filled his eyes, giving the night a red haze. He could already smell the scent of spilled blood.

Soon a life would no longer exist. Soon, she would know that she belonged to him.

***

Denise Mahoney, aka Mistress Desiree, laced up the black leather corset and slid on the sheer black hosiery. She dabbed gold dust powder on her skin and pulled her hair into a ponytail high on her head. Her eyes were lined in black, and her brows darkened. Next she slipped on her thigh high three inch, spiked heel, black patent leather boots.

Glancing in the mirror, she confirmed that she looked smoking hot. Long black gloves and her black trench coat completed the ensemble. Before leaving, she kissed her baby on the forehead, "Be good, baby girl. Momma will be home before you know it."

She called out to Charlotte, "Thanks again, honey. I owe you big."

"Just be careful. We will be fine here."

As she left the house, Denise grabbed her bag from the closet and took off. As she checked her watch once more, she let out a soft curse. She refused to be late. In her line of business, she depended on referrals and word of mouth. One bad reference could cost her numerous clients.

Despite the fact that the fog outside was as thick as pea soup, she stepped on the gas. Her 2013 Camry leapt forward with complete ease. She swerved into the other lane to avoid hitting a slow moving pickup in her lane. The idiot didn't even have his lights on. She blasted her horn as she passed him.

She typically met clients at hotels, but this client insisted that she meet him at his hunting cabin. When he sensed the hesitancy in her voice, he doubled his original offer. An extra four thousand dollars was too enticing to refuse.

As she drove in the moonless Louisiana night, she reconsidered her decision. She checked her GPS once more as she traveled through the swampland. When he said a hunting cabin, he wasn't joking. She had not envisioned anything like this. The entire area appeared to be in complete disrepair. She prayed this man could afford to pay her and wasn't looking for a free ride.

Up ahead, she made out a faded No Trespassing sign nailed to a tall pine tree. It had definitely seen better days.

As she turned down the overgrown road, she said a prayer that this wasn't a scam, or worse, that he lured her here to kill her. Ruts plagued the overrun road, and the gravel appeared to have been washed out years ago. Her car shuddered and bounced over the potholes as she crept along. A rusted gate hung haphazardly on one hinge, and the old cattle guard was missing a few bars causing her car to jump as it tried to rumble over the entrance.

Mais, it is dark back here. The setting reminded her of the horror movies she watched as a teenager.

She shook her head, trying to figure out why she was driving around in the middle of the swamp at night. A shudder ran through her as she thought about which creatures lurked in the darkness. She picked up the cell phone and groaned when she noticed there wasn't even cell service out here in the boondocks. When she caught a glimpse of the cabin, she let out a sigh of relief.

***

His heart raced when he saw her headlights shine in the night. This was the moment he'd anxiously awaited. Every nerve in his body was stretched to the breaking point as his body trembled in anticipation.

Tonight was perfect for what he planned. The moonless night was heavy with a dense fog. Even better, no one would hear her cry out in anguish over her lover's death. Tonight she would discover that he was the only man she needed.

The metallic scent of spilled blood filled the air. She must see what he did for her.

He listened for the sound of a car door closing. All that greeted him was the stillness of the night; no frogs croaked, and no crickets chirped. All that could be heard was his racing heartbeat and his short, rapid breaths.

His body was still very much alive from his recent kill. Oh, how exquisite it felt when the blade sliced into the soft tissue of his throat and his warm blood oozed from the gaping wound. He couldn't wait to show his Desiree what he did in the name of love.

His eyes flew open at the sound of her car door. His blood heated as he waited for her. Her footsteps echoed in the night as she made her way up to the old wooden front porch.

She knocked on the door before opening it. "Hello?" She called out.

He caught a whiff of her intoxicating perfume as soon as she stepped inside. She smelled better than he ever imagined. It took all of his self-control not to jump from the shadows and pounce on her.

His heart kicked into overdrive at just the mere sight of her. He drew in a shivery breath as he envisioned her writhing underneath him. He immediately hardened.

Calling out once more, she asked, "Hello? Is anyone here?"

***

Denise let out a long sigh as nothing but silence greeted her. She should have known the money was too good to be true. It pissed her off that she came all this way for nothing. "If this is some kind of game it really creeps me out. I hate these kinds of games."

A noise near the back of the cabin caught her attention, and she ventured deeper to see just what it was. Her heart pounded in her ears as she chastised herself for not leaving. "I am done with this game. If you don't show yourself, I am leaving and will never take another request from you again.

I will also tell all of my friends, who will in turn tell their friends."

Irritated, she turned to leave when a movement in the dark living room caught her eye. He turned on his flashlight. Denise jumped in fear and put a hand over her heart. "You scared the crap of me."

He extended a hand out to her and said, "You are so beautiful, mon cher." Taking her hand in his, he led her to the bedroom, "Come, I must show you just what I did for you my love."

As Denise followed him to the back of the cabin, she wondered what he was blabbering about. What she saw in the soft light of the flashlight sickened her. Dark, black blood was everywhere and coated the bed.

Terror clawed at her insides as bile rose in her throat. Instinctively, she took a step backwards in retreat as a scream bubbled to the surface. "What have you done?" Tears streamed down her cheeks as she stared at the dead man. Glaring at the man she yelled, "He didn't do anything wrong. This man didn't deserve this."

Waving the knife in front of her, the man exclaimed, "Yes! Yes, he did!" She could sense the anger seething from his pores. "He didn't deserve you. You are mine!" His eyes narrowed. He regarded her solemnly as his gaze dropped to her delectable body. "I have forgiven you for your depraved past. I will show you that I am the only man for you." He yanked her to him, bruising her mouth with a punishing kiss.

Panic welled up inside of her. This guy was a lunatic. Why was he acting this way? She tried to push him away. "Why did you kill him? He meant you no harm?"

"Just the mere thought of you made me hard." Running his fingers through her hair, he said, "I wanted you all to myself. I am supposed to be the one pleasing you, not this man. I watched your every move, knew exactly what you did. How could you degrade yourself like that? You were not supposed to sleep with any of those men!" He gazed at her with barely disguised contempt, "Let me show you how much you mean to me."

Her stomach rolled with nausea. If she intended to get out of here alive, she had to put on the performance of a lifetime. She looked up at him, trying to keep the fear from showing in her eyes, "How do you plan on showing me that we are meant to be together?"

He stared down at her and explained, "You don't have to degrade yourself by selling your body to these men. You will be the submissive now, abide by my rules. If you do as I say, you will want for nothing." He looked into her eyes before continuing, "Abiding by the rules isn't an option. If you want to please me, you must obey my every command."

Keeping any emotion out of her voice, she said, "Those men meant nothing to me. It was just business, never personal. I needed money to pay the bills. I have a daughter to provide for. Sometimes you need to do whatever it takes to survive. I'm sorry if I disappointed you."

As he went to touch her once again, she stepped back. Grabbing her by the shoulders, he gave her a shake. "This man had to be punished. You were falling for him." Fear crawled up her spine as he continued, "It was revolting to watch you. Each time I saw you with another man it took away a little more of my soul."

She tried to free herself from his grasp, "What punishment do you intend for me?"

Adrenaline, fueled by horror, took over her body. Revulsion rose from deep inside of her. When his grip loosened, she freed herself from his grasp and ran out of the room. Acting quickly, he grabbed her hair, jerking her back. White hot pain exploded through her head as he wrenched her neck backwards.

When she swallowed, the sound was so loud that you could hear it. She finally grasped how much danger she was in. With a shaky voice, "Please, you don't have to hurt me. I will do what you want."

***

As he looked down at her, he smelled the sharp, tangy aroma of fear emanating off of her. He ran his finger along her jawbone before moving down her arms to the upper part of her breasts. Her dark hair was silky, shiny and cascading. His hands itched to get lost in that luxurious mane of hers.

He saw the terror in her eyes. He breathed in the very scent of her fear as it oozed out of her pores. Her body shivered underneath him. "My love, I don't want to hurt you. I did this for us. So we could be together, forever and always."

She swallowed down the fear and said, "But you didn't need to kill him."

Shaking his head, he explained, "Oh, but I did. You would have never stopped seeing him otherwise. I could tell you were falling for him."

She reached up and caressed his face, "No, I wasn't. If you had asked I promise, for you, I would have given it up."

He felt her tense underneath him; she was lying. He caressed the cold steel of the knife's blade behind his back. He pressed his lips against hers. Before she could react, he moved the knife across her neck.

As her body dropped to the floor, he looked down in disgust. He thought he had found the one, but now he knew he had been wrong. After making sure he removed any evidence of his recent visit, he left.

Once at home, he dropped the knife into the sink. As he looked down at the bloody knife, he could not believe what he did. With this knife, he killed the woman he thought he loved.

He watched in fascination as the blood of the two lovers mixed with the water as he washed his hands. He should feel remorse for what he did, but he felt nothing.

Once he finished cleaning his hands; he moved onto the knife. The water in the sink turned crimson red. He closed his eyes and visualized what his perfect woman looked like.

Once done, he laid the knife on the counter to dry. He would return it to his arsenal of tools after his shower.

He placed his dark clothes in a black trash bag. There was no sense washing them. He would burn the clothes later on to ensure no evidence was left behind.

In the bathroom, he turned on the shower. Steam filled the room as he stepped in and let the hot water run over him. He lathered the soap on his body repeatedly until the water ran clear.

Stepping out of the shower, he towel dried and dressed. Sitting in front of his computer, he began his search for the perfect woman, one who would love him until the end of time.

Chapter 6

Karen Miller didn't set out to be a high priced prostitute, but certain circumstances led her to this job. She may tell herself that she was merely a Dominatrix, but in truth, she sold her body for money, and a lot of it. The job had started out as a virtual dominatrix, but she soon grew bored with even that job. She wanted something more, so while her husband was away, she invited clients into their home. Having the men come here was her way of humiliating her husband. While he may not know what she did in their marriage bed, she did and that was what mattered.

She should be content as a mother and wife, staying home to take care of her children while her husband went to work every day. When her children were both at home, she kept busy. There was always something to do. But with them in school, her days became lonely, and she grew bored.

No one needed constant attention any longer. Her day consisted of cooking and cleaning. A person could only clean so much before the whole process became obscenely monotonous. There was only so much shopping one could do, unless, of course, you had an endless bank account, which she did not.

While drinking her morning coffee one day, she saw the ad. It appeared harmless enough, work from home, make your own hours. It sounded too tempting, so she made the call. That was six months ago.

Her time in front of the web camera became her escape from reality, even if it was a few hours each day. She saw nothing wrong with dominating these men; everything took place online with no physical contact. That was before she started receiving the "gifts" and then the requests.

She never thought she had it in her to be a Dominatrix, but she had proven herself wrong. For once in her life, she was in control. She gave the orders, instead of having a man order her. It also gave her a chance to explore her own hidden desires.

Standing in front of the mirror, she stared at her image. When she landed this job, she scheduled a Brazilian wax along with a new haircut and color. Her long brown tresses were transformed into cascading waves of auburn locks.

Even with having two children in the last ten years, her body was still curvaceous and her stomach nice and trim. Gravity had yet to take its toll on her body, so her breasts were still high and firm. While she wanted to increase them by a cup size, her husband told her that more than a handful was a waste. Still, she wanted to fill out a swimsuit like those models he ogled over.

Her stomach caught as she thought of her newest client. He was older than most of her other clients, but even for his age he was handsome. Unlike her other clients, he was outgoing and full of confidence. There was something else, though, hiding just below the surface, something dangerous. He had yet to learn his place; he wanted her to be the submissive.

As she thought about him, she slipped on the black spandex dress. Her next client had rather peculiar fantasies, but she shouldn't complain. He paid her very well to be humiliated and abused on a weekly basis. He also tipped her well to ensure that she kept his dirty little secret. However, if you asked her he should go to confession rather than come to her.

Her "sessions" with Marvin Sargee lasted an hour, but it was the longest hour of her life. In that hour, he cried, sucked his thumb, and let Mistress Kara insult him as much as she desired. In her eyes, he was a pitiful excuse for a human being.

For the president of one of the largest banks here in Louisiana, he had some strange fantasies. Most days he preferred for her to treat him like a naughty child, spanking him with the crop. He especially enjoyed verbal humiliation. Whatever she said to him turned him on further.

Chapter 7

"Yes Mistress Kara. I have been a bad boy and must be punished." The Honorable Judge William Bradford looked up at his mistress, waiting for her punishment with great anticipation.

A respected judge in this community for over ten years now, he stepped away from his office once a week for his "appointment" with his newest mistress. She never complained when it came to fulfilling any of his fantasies.

His wife of twenty years would die of embarrassment if he ever asked her to do half of what this luscious woman giving him a blowjob did.

An attorney friend, who shared the same tastes as he, referred her. Even though her fees were a little exorbitant, she was well worth it. Plus, she had just as much to lose as he did if her extracurricular activities became known. No, she would be discreet about his visits and fantasies.

He grew even harder as she slipped the black silk stockings on his legs. Now, he understood why women loved wearing the silk underwear; it felt divine against his skin. This was the only time he ever allowed himself to wear women's underwear, in the presence of this woman.

After attaching the stockings to the black garter belt, she looked at him, "Now, tell me what terrible things you did so that you can be punished?"

He took in her whole body. From the scarlet red corset that pushed her breasts up, down to the crotch-less scarlet lace panties, all the way to the black silk stockings.

"I'm a bad boy, Mistress. I like to wear women's underwear. Please, I beg of you to punish me."

***

It took extreme willpower not to laugh at this man. Every week it was the same thing. He wanted her to dress him up in silk underwear and then punish him for it.

She grabbed her breasts and played with the nipples through the material, "You want this you bad boy?"

Crying out, he said, "Oh yes, Mistress. Please, I beg of you to give me what I need."

She leaned over and whispered in his ear, "And what will you do for me?"

"Anything you command my Mistress."

She lay down on the bed and spread her legs wide open. "On your knees now! I want you to please me with your tongue."

***

Just as she walked back downstairs, the doorbell rang. Her next client had arrived right on time. As she opened the door to greet him a chilling realization came over her, she swore he had been hovering nearby awaiting his appointment.

She liked her side job, but the last thing she wanted was for a customer to become romantically attached to her. Walking inside, he took her hand in his and kissed it, "My love, I've been waiting for you."

She looked at him with indecision. Normally, he was her favorite client, but something about him today had her on edge. Pulling her into his arms, he told her, "You look even more ravishing today."

As he looked down on her, she pushed him away from her, "I'm not your love. You can't love me. You can never love me!"

"But why? You must know how much you mean to me?" He grabbed her trembling hands as she tried to move away from him.

Her heart pounded in her ears, "No, I can't mean anything to you. I'm happily married."

Pulling her close to him, he whispered in her ear, "You can't be happily married if you seek out love from other men, cher."

"I'm not seeking out love from other men. It is merely sex."

His voice became thick with emotion, "No! What we have is more than sex. You must feel the same way as me!"

The intensity of his gaze caused her to step back from him involuntarily. She saw the anger taking over his body. He reached for her as she tried to escape from his grasp. "No! You are mine. We are meant to be together."

***

As he dragged her upstairs to her room, he didn't understand what went wrong. This sweet, tantalizing woman turned into the epitome of evil. She was the keeper of his heart. He told her how he felt. Why didn't she reciprocate the feelings?

He must convince her they were destined for a future together. He would love her, protect her, and make her realize that he was the only man for her. She didn't need to keep up this façade anymore. He saw the person she truly was beneath this icy demeanor she portrayed.

Once in the room, he threw her onto the bed. Just looking at her, seeing the fear in her eyes brought a change in the air. Something sudden and mysterious moved through him.

He watched her, calculating his next move. He had to prove to her that he was her one true love. His life was cold and empty without her.

His heart skipped a beat at the thought of being with her. He wanted her to touch him, caress him, and let him take her. All he thought about up until now was her, and now he found out that she saw him as she did the others.

Could he make her understand that he needed her desperately, needed her love? He looked at her curvaceous body outfitted in the leather bustier and crotch-less panties. It crushed him to find out she was like the others, a whore.

She captured him with her beauty. Yet she did nothing more than tease him with her body.

Tonight he had planned to show her he was the lover she dreamt of. He wanted to worship her, partake of her body, and love her. He has desired a woman such as her for a while. He couldn't wait to smell her, feel her body beneath his, and make sweet love to her. He sought nothing more than for her to experience his love's sweet embrace. Love was always on his mind; he missed that sensation when desire coiled inside of you and begged to be released in ecstasy. He wanted true love and passion. He wanted the happily every after.

His heart raced in anticipation. He wanted her so bad that he was about to lose control. His manhood twitched in anticipation as his body trembled with need. Could he bring himself to forgive her and make sweet passionate love to her?

"You mustn't fear me my love. We are meant to be. You are mine. All I want is to please you."

He gathered her in his arms, unable to wait for her to take him inside of her. His blood coursed through him like molten lava. Once in his arms, she would feel the passion they have for each other.

She was the one; he knew it. Then, as she struggled to escape from his grasp, his blood ran stone cold. Anger ripped through his body; rage consumed his very being. He moved swiftly, his vengeance final as the knife slit her throat with complete ease.

Chapter 8

As Detective Derrick LeDoux drove home, he couldn't wait to pop open a beer and relax. As he walked into the house, his phone rang. When he saw the number on caller ID he knew that this phone call meant a new case, "LeDoux."

"Detective, you have a new case. A husband came home from work and found his wife murdered."

"I'm on my way. Have you called Riley yet?"

The dispatcher responded, "Yes, sir. He will meet you there."

Without even bothering to go home, he turned around and drove to the crime scene. When he arrived, the coroner was already there. There was no denying Dr. Lacy Chauvin's presence. She was a statuesque brown haired beauty. Her eyes reminded him of a blue sky, but he had seen them turn a stormy gray when fired up. He had never met anyone as passionate as her when it came to a case. When this no holds barred woman first started working in the coroner's office, he considered asking her out, but then he thought better of it. He had seen her cut a man to the quick, and he had no desire to be the next man emasculated by her.

LeDoux took his time and absorbed the crime scene. Each one had a story to tell; you had to be patient and let the story unfold before your eyes.

He overheard Detective Riley attempting to calm the distraught husband once more. "So, you came home and found her like this? You didn't move the body?"

The man tried to stop the flow of tears, "No, I didn't move her. When I saw the blood on the mattress, I knew she was dead." Wiping at the tears, he added, "I don't understand who could do this to her."

Taking out his notepad, Riley asked, "What time did you get home from work?"

"Traffic was pretty light, so it was almost six thirty when I walked in the door." Letting out a loud wail, the husband cried, "Please don't tell me that if I had come home a little earlier I could have saved her."

Looking down at the body, LeDoux knew that the victim, Karen Miller, had been dead for a while. Trying to pinpoint when the killer may have entered the house, LeDoux asked the husband, "Is this what she had on this morning?"

Shaking his head, he answered, "No, I have never seen this outfit before."

Damn LeDoux hated hearing that. Trying to be tactful, he asked, "Mr. Miller, do you think that your wife was having an affair?"

"Absolutely not! There was nothing wrong with our marriage."

As LeDoux listened to Mr. Miller, he came to the conclusion that the good husband was protesting a little too much. Looking around the house, he noticed the furnishings. They were more than a cop could afford on his salary, unless he was on the take. Even the cars in the garage were more than he could afford.

He told one of the crime scene techs, "Make sure you search the computers, especially the laptops. Maybe we can get lucky, and she talked to her boyfriend on one of them."

"Yes, sir."

LeDoux walked through the house cautiously, taking notes of anything out of the ordinary. He walked back into the room in time to watch the medical examiner's assistants place the deceased into a body bag.

She had dressed for someone special.   The scarlet red corset and thong were not something a woman wore for comfort. "Who did this to you, cher?" He mumbled to the lifeless body.

As far as murder victims went, Karen Miller on the surface didn't seem a likely candidate to be on that list. By all accounts, she was happily married, nice house and car, loving husband, and no criminal record. She led what some considered a charmed life.

That was on the surface, when he dug deeper he learned more about the victim's life that she kept hidden.

After several hours, LeDoux and Riley left the crime scene while the techs continued to photograph and gather evidence. Looking over at his partner, LeDoux said, "Let's find out if the neighbors noticed anything out of the ordinary."

"Let's hope they saw something that will help us. The bodies are piling up."

They knocked on the next door neighbor's door. A Hispanic woman wearing a black dress and white apron opened the door. She raised her eyebrows when she saw the two men. "Can I help you gentlemen?"

"I'm Detective LeDoux and this is my partner, Detective Riley. We need to ask you some questions about the couple next door."

"I don't know much about them. I come in at nine in the morning and leave at six o'clock."

"What about your employers?"

Shrugging her shoulders, she answered, "I'm not sure. Mr. and Mrs. Carlson are seldom home when I am here." Looking around, she added, "I know it is not my place, but I am not surprised the police are asking about the neighbors."

LeDoux asked her curiously, "What makes you say that?"

"I come from Mexico. Although I try to mind my own business, sometimes I noticed the traffic that came and went over there during the day."

Riley asked, "Did you see who it was by chance?"

She shook her head, "No sir. All I saw was the constant line of cars during the day." Lowering her voice as if someone may hear her, "Cars came and went at all times of the day."

LeDoux figured those must be the days when the husband was away on a business trip, such as this weekend.

Crossing her arms over her chest, she continued, "Sometimes I saw that woman on her balcony, dressed so trashy, lots of makeup and barely any clothes. She didn't care who saw her." Sighing, she said, "If you ask me, she dressed no worse than a common whore."

After thanking the woman for her time, they walked back to their cars. Standing by his car, Riley stated, "Sounds like our victim let the guy in."

LeDoux agreed, "It is more than likely she let the wrong client in."

Chapter 9

Mike Johansen cringed inwardly at the sight of Frank Marcel walking through the door. Why did he get involved with one of the largest mafia families in Louisiana?

Without wasting time, Frank slammed the newspaper on his desk. "Just what are you doing about these murders?"

"My sources inform me that the cops haven't figured out the connection with these women."

"I'm not worried about that. Our clients pay handsomely for our services, and someone is killing off some of our most prized women. The last thing we need is someone knocking off the girls, or worse our customers getting scared!"

As Mike listened to Frank Marcel talk, he still couldn't believe this businessman was a cold blooded killer. People saw him as a good Catholic and a prominent member of the community. But, he wasn't someone you wanted to cross. Those who witnessed his true nature could attest that even the prince of darkness would fear him.

He kept his true nature hidden, even from his wife. She saw him as a loving husband who spent every evening with the family.

Mike, however, knew what this man was like. He didn't care who he maimed or murdered. The only thing you would never see Frank Marcel do was kiss someone's ass. That was far beneath him.

No, this man was a master puppeteer. Mike learned the hard way that Frank Marcel was someone you never wanted to owe money to. Mike would be six feet under if Frank had not stumbled upon the "escort" operations he ran.

His only saving grace was that Frank did not know the full gamut of his affairs. As far as Frank Marcel knew, he was strictly involved in the "escort" business.

If Frank discovered that Mike deceived him, his life would be over. If he hadn't owed Frank Marcel well over a quarter of a million dollars in gambling debts, he would never have become involved with him. Unfortunately, Frank saw potential in his business and offered to forgive the debt in exchange for the business, which, of course, would be run by Mike.

"Relax; I have it under control."

Glaring at him, Frank demanded, "You better! These girls don't grow on trees. Not only are they beautiful, educated, and classy but these particular women will fuck whoever we tell them to. They have no qualms about performing all sorts of debauchery. The sexual know how these girls possess and dispense is not something easily acquired."

Mike nodded his head in agreement. Most of the women would never even consider doing what they did if they didn't owe money to Frank.

"This business is very profitable, and I don't want anything, or anyone, messing it up. If you find whoever is doing this handle it. Do not bother calling and asking for my permission. Also, handle this yourself. I don't want any extra links in the chain with regards to this. Just be sure to leave no traces. Understand?"

Nodding his head, Mike answered, "Yes, sir."

"Don't disappoint me. You don't want to see me upset."

Mike let out a sigh of relief as his boss left. He continued to stare at the computer monitors in front of him, as he thought about what Frank had said. He had to hire a new girl to fill the vacancies. Even with a large share going to Frank Marcel, this was indeed a profitable venture. However, finding a replacement would not be as easy. While most of these girls performed any sexual fantasy a client asked of them, it took a special kind of woman to be a Dominatrix.

His legitimate business, KJUN Bonds, was the perfect cover for his side business. From the storefront, it appeared to be a bail bonds business, but he had used it as his headquarters for several years. It was the nerve center of his nefarious activities. The computer system could easily be explained as a much needed security system for the various dregs of society that walked in his door. However, in truth, it allowed him to keep a close watch on his girls. He has not only tapped into each of their computers, but their cell phones as well, both personal and those he provided. He knew everything that they did and he watched it from his computer with a few simple keystrokes.

Each of his employees had been issued their own disposable cell phone and personal laptop, of course, each with a camera, so that he could reach them when needed. He also videotaped the "sessions" for blackmail purposes. The whole reason Mike Johansen entered this line of business was for the sole purpose of making money, and lots of it.

So far each of the girls he recruited understood the rules and there were no issues. If a problem arose, the woman was quickly "terminated" and never heard from again. Though these women were just as interested in the money as he was. He paid them well for their complete discretion, regardless of the circumstance.

Frank Marcel had mentioned several times that he wanted to expand. However, a bigger company meant a greater chance of exposure. Mike had no desire to spend his life inside a prison cell. Besides, in this economy the market for high priced call girls has decreased. The number of clients willing to pay for the services he offered has declined. Which was the main reason he ventured into the Virtual Dominatrix business. It was easier to get these fools to pay a few measly dollars to see flesh rather than pay thousands to live out their fantasies.

Chapter 10

Bree LaFleur looked at herself in the mirror, closely inspecting the tiny crow's feet starting to show. If there was enough money in the budget this month, a quick trip to the spa was in order for a few injections to erase the wrinkles.

As she ran her hand through her chestnut hair, the caramel highlights shimmered in the light. She also saw the telltale signs of her roots showing and cringed. She detested not having highlights at her next appointment, but she couldn't allow her gray to show either.

For forty years old, she was still attractive. She kept herself in shape even after giving birth to two children. Running her hands down her body, she noticed that, even at her age, her breasts were still nice and firm.

She was one of the fortunate moms who after the birth of her second child, her breasts increased another size, instead of shrinking down to next to nothing. She was a plump 36DD and at times she looked a little too top heavy.

Turning around, she inspected her derriere in the mirror. It also had remained nice and firm. Gravity has been kind to her, but time would soon catch up and she would start to sag. She feared she'd already lost her attractiveness; she couldn't recall the last time her husband had noticed her. Lately, she found herself hungry for the things he ignored. She tried to convince herself that it was because he worked so hard, but still the self-doubt was there. She couldn't shake the fear that he no longer found her desirable.

When she married Tom, it had been a dream come true for her. He was not only breathtakingly handsome, but one of the kindest men she had met. His being well off didn't hurt either.

Even though they have been married for fifteen years now, she still remembered their wedding like it was yesterday. The church had been standing room only. White satin ribbons streamed from pew to pew. Pink and white rose petals were scattered down the aisle. Her hair piled high on her head as a cascade of ringlet curls framed her face. The wedding gown hugged her body like a glove, showing off every curve of her body and flowed like an ocean of satin. Her tanned, bare shoulders gleamed against the glittery white of her dress.

Tom looked so handsome standing at the alter in his tuxedo. The wedding had been planned to perfection. She and Tom even wrote their own vows. Bree became weak in the knees when Tom slid the two and a half carat diamond wedding ring onto her finger.

It had been a beautiful ceremony. The happiest moment was when they were pronounced man and wife. During the limo ride to the reception hall, they could not keep their hands off each other. At the reception, they danced every dance, holding each other tightly. She felt like a princess as she floated around the dance floor.

When they were first married, they were inseparable, spending as much time as they could together. He even came home from work early to help her with dinner, and their weekends were spent in bed.

They made it over the seven year itch, but with each passing year she noticed that their marriage had become stuck in the same rut. Hell, most nights she was lucky if he even made it home for dinner.

She did the same chores, day in and day out. She cooked breakfast every morning for her husband and children, before sending them off to work and school. As each left, they gave her a peck on the cheek, including her husband, and then the next several hours she had to herself. Once they left, she cleaned up the breakfast dishes, made the beds and picked up the house. On nice days, she went for her morning run outside, but most days she preferred to run inside on her treadmill. Living in Louisiana, half the time it was too hot to run outside.

Once a week she did yard work, making sure to do it early before the heat of the day became too much. Tending to the weeds was a never ending task, and one that she didn't care for either. She wished they could afford a gardener to tend to the yard work. She swore the blasted things grew overnight just to taunt her. They seemed to litter her garden and multiply before her very eyes.

By lunchtime, she had completed her household chores and was bored to death. In reality, she spent most of her time alone, trying to figure out something to fill that time. Her friends were on various committees or had other things, like work, to occupy their days. One of her closest friends, Ava Guidry, tried to convince her to join a few of the committees she was in. However, she didn't fit in with the same crowd Ava hung out with. Most of those women were older, matronly women, which was the last thing Bree would ever be.

Around three o'clock every afternoon, she started dinner, so that when her family came home supper was ready. Most nights she kept Tom a plate in the microwave. When he came in late at night, he didn't even bother eating what she had cooked for him. Lately, he had come home and gone straight to sleep, with no hello or kiss.

While she understood that he was stressed about their current financial status, she wished he would pay a little more attention to her. Going back downstairs, she walked into her kitchen and looked around. The kitchen was a chef's dream. It was large, spacious and had almost every amenity one could want. The floors were done in a beige terrazzo tile, and a richer beige accentuated the walls. The deep, mahogany cabinets, copper backsplash tiles and granite countertops compliment the room. In the center of the room was an island perfect for a chef's workspace. She spent hours in this kitchen learning how to cook extravagant meals to please Tom.

Perhaps that is where they went wrong. From the beginning, they had to have the best of everything and now that the money wasn't coming in as it had been they were paying for that mistake.

Chapter 11

LeDoux cringed when he saw Mr. Miller walk into the precinct and from the look on his face he was not happy. Without knocking, he barged into LeDoux's office and stated, "Detective LeDoux, I have some questions I need to be answered."

Closing his office door, LeDoux replied, "Mr. Miller, I'll try to answer all of your questions, but please realize that the investigation is still ongoing."

"I want to know if the rumors I am hearing are true. Was my wife involved in some kind of kinky prostitution ring?"

LeDoux shook his head. He could kill whoever released that information. "Mr. Miller, currently all we know is that your wife's murderer has killed before. We have no proof that your wife was involved in any kind of prostitution ring."

Anger clearly registering on his face as he said, "Well, whoever spread those rumors needs to be dealt with. This is bullshit! She was not having an affair; I would have known." Slamming a fist into the palm of his other hand, he continued, "I want this man caught. If you need reward money, just let me know. Also, I want whoever is spreading these rumors silenced."

Trying to calm the man's rattled nerves, LeDoux replied, "Mr. Miller, a reward isn't necessary. I just need you to bear with us for a little longer. Investigations like this take time."

"Detective, answer me honestly. Are you searching for my wife's killer or do you also believe that she was a whore?"

"No, Mr. Miller, I do not believe your wife was a whore. Even if she were, she was also a human being, one whose life had been cut short. It is my job to find her killer. When I am done with my investigation, your wife's secrets will be revealed, but are you confident of her innocence?"

"I knew my wife and she was no prostitute."

LeDoux shook his head. "Mr. Miller, I never said she was. There was no sign of forced entry, so now, I have to ascertain just how the killer entered your house."

Standing up to leave, he glared at LeDoux, "Detective, I am sure you are aware that I am a very powerful man in this community. I have been known to be vindictive towards anyone who has wronged me. You may want to pass that word along to whoever may be spreading rumors about my wife."

Without another word, he stormed out of LeDoux's office. He hoped whoever spread those rumors was prepared to deal with Mr. Miller's wrath. LeDoux did not doubt he would honor his threat.

Chapter 12

Candi Boutin walked into the dark night with nothing to illuminate the sidewalk but dim streetlights. A light breeze lifted her midnight black wig away from her face, sending a chill down her spine. A cold certainty washed over her; someone was watching her. Her gut clenched as she looked around. Seeing nothing, she continued to her car.

Her stilettos click clacked on the pavement. Two more blocks to go, but tonight it felt like two miles. She tried to calm her nerves, reminding herself that she had an aerosol container of pepper spray on her key chain if she needed it. She kept her shoulders square and chin up, forcing herself to maintain a steady stride in spite of the wobble in her ankles.

A flicker of movement in the shadows startled her, and her heart thumped wildly against her chest. She let out a sigh of relief when an alley cat showed its head and laughed at her silliness.

Still, the knot in her gut told her not to let her guard down just yet. As she walked to her car, she thought about the way her life turned out. If not for a stroke of luck, she may never have found this job. She had been born poor, never knowing when her next meal would be. Growing up, most nights she went to bed so hungry that the rumblings of her stomach kept her awake. It wasn't until she started working for an escort agency that she learned what it was like to never go hungry. When she moved up to Dominatrix, she found the perfect job for her. No longer did a man control her, she controlled men.

At five feet nine inches, narrow face, natural DD cup breasts, red hair, and green eyes, she always drew looks from men, wanted or unwanted. Those looks are what kept her fed. Amber Brady, who ran one of the most lucrative escort businesses in Louisiana, pulled her in off the streets and away from the clientele she serviced. After a while, Amber saw a real potential in Candi and taught her how to be a Dominatrix.

However, no matter how nice Amber was to her, Candi could never bring herself to trust her, or anybody else. No, Candi knew what it was like to be used by people. She found it hard to become attached to anyone. She had been used all of her life. Perhaps that was why she made a good Dominatrix. It was easy to control these clients. For once she had complete control. She was without it.

At the age of ten, her own dad saw her as nothing more than a place to put his cock in. Afterwards, he shared her with his friends. By fourteen, Candi had tired of constantly being hungry and pimped out for drugs and cigarettes. If men were going to use her body, it would be on her own terms and not someone else's.

Touching the bruise on her cheek, she regretted leaving the agency and branching out on her own. This was the first time that a submissive had become physically abusive with her and it wasn't a performance she wanted repeated. She wondered if she went crawling back on her hands and knees if Amber would take her back.

As Candi reached her car, she looked over the area to make sure no one lurked nearby. Growing up on the streets, she learned to be aware of her surroundings at all times.

Not a soul could be seen, although several other cars were in the lot. Satisfied, Candi unlocked her car and opened the door.

"Excuse me," came from behind her, causing her heart to jump into her throat. She heard the man chuckle, "I'm sorry. I didn't mean to scare you."

Candi looked at the tall man standing near her Porsche 911 Carrera. "You scared the hell out of me," she laughed nervously.

He told her, "I saw you leaving the hotel and couldn't stop myself from following you. I apologize for not saying something earlier, but it took me a while to build up the nerve to talk to you. I was wondering if, perhaps, you would care to join me for a drink."

Candi planned to go straight home, but a drink with this handsome man sounded far better than sleep. She couldn't even remember the last actual date that wasn't business related. Holding out her hand, she introduced herself, "My name is Candi Boutin."

A charge of electricity ran through her body as soon as their hands touched. "It is a pleasure to meet you Candi. The bar isn't far from here, would you care to walk?"

"A walk sounds lovely. Besides, if it is anywhere near here, finding a parking spot would be a miracle." He took her elbow and escorted her to the bar.

It wasn't too crowded, and they spent several hours getting to know each other a little better. Before they said goodbye, they made plans to go out for dinner Friday night.

Chapter 13

All he thought about was his date tonight. He couldn't remember ever being this nervous. His stomach tightened in exhilaration at seeing her again. She was all he thought about lately, and he finally had gathered enough courage to ask her out.

As he went to ring the doorbell, he wiped his sweaty palms on his pants. He fidgeted as he held the bouquet of red roses. As she opened the door, he handed her the bouquet. "I saw these and thought of you. Their beauty holds no comparison to your beauty. You look simply ravishing tonight."

Bringing the bouquet to her nose, she breathed in the fragrant scent and replied, "They are lovely, thank you."

"Are you ready to go out to supper," he asked.

"I am famished."

"I made reservations at Riverside Inn."

Candi laughed, "That is one of my favorite restaurants."

"I have never been there before, but the reviews are fantastic."

"You won't be disappointed, the chef is unbelievable."

The ride to the restaurant was quiet, both unsure of what to say. After parking his car, he opened her door and escorted her to the restaurant. Once they were seated, a young woman introduced herself, "Hi, I'm Jasmine. Can I get y'all something from the bar?"

He looked up at her and answered, "Bring us a bottle of the house wine, please."

The waitress asked, "Would you like an appetizer to start out with?"

Nodding his head, he replied, "We would like an order of the seafood fondue."

"Very good, sir. Tonight's special is Chicken Rockefeller with a mushroom risotto. Do you know what you would like or do you need a few more minutes?"

He perused the menu once more, "I would like the Crawfish Acadian, over blackened redfish."

"Yes sir and you, ma'am?"

Candi handed her the menu, "I would like the special."

"That's an excellent choice. Would either of you care for a bowl of our gumbo? I sampled it earlier, and it is very good tonight."

"That sounds excellent. Thank you."

The waitress collected their menus, "I'll be right back with your drinks."

As they talked about their day, the waitress arrived with their drinks and appetizer. Over wine and food, he listened as Candi talked about her childhood. He inwardly cringed at the thought of growing up so poor. "My childhood was

nowhere near as traumatic as yours. I was a nerd in school;
the one nobody wanted to hang out with."

Whenever she let out a soft little laugh, it sent chills down
his arms. Dinner was going so well. They talked and
laughed for hours, as if they were old friends. The night
passed by quickly, and before they knew it, the waiter came
over to inform them that they would be closing soon. Candi
gasped in surprise, "I didn't realize we talked this long."

As they walked back to the car, he placed his hand on the
small of her back. As she leaned into him, she said, "It has
been such a pleasant evening. I hate to see it come to an
end."

"Would you like to get together again," he asked

"I'd like that very much."

Looking into her eyes, he said, "I can't remember the last
time I enjoyed such a pleasant evening. I must admit that I
almost lost the nerve to talk to you that night."

Candi reached over and touched his arm, "I am so glad that
you did."

When they arrived at her house, he went around and
opened the car door for her. He took her hand in his and
escorted her to the front door. Placing a finger under her
chin, he tilted her face up, bent down and kissed her gently,
"Good night Cher."

***

The gentle kiss left her speechless.   She looked into his eyes and anxiously waited for him to kiss her again. Instead, he took the keys from her and unlocked her door, "Thank you for the company tonight, mon cher. We will definitely do this again."

As he drove away, she hoped she heard from him again. Her mind still reeled from the good night kiss. The chaste kiss caught her by surprise. A date not ending with sex was a pleasant experience for her.

Chapter 14

Candi walked in the door, kicked off her high heels and started to remove the confining clothes. This was her first week at "The Cave", and today had been a trying day. She was beginning to enjoy her new job at the S&M club. However, a new client proved to be quite difficult and didn't want to follow the rules.

From her bedroom, she heard her cell phone ring and rushed back to the living room where it was charging. Disappointed to see that it was only the club, she let it go to voice mail. She was hoping that he would call. She thought the date had gone well last week, but maybe she misread the signals.

Perhaps it was for the best that he didn't call. After all, she wasn't the kind of girl you brought home to meet your mother. She sure wasn't the type of girl a man dreamt of marrying, but still a girl could dream.

After changing into something more comfortable, she went into the kitchen to cook herself a quick bite. The lack of groceries in her house depressed her, but she wasn't in the mood to go shopping. Instead, she settled for a grilled cheese sandwich. Once it was done, she grabbed her plate and headed to the living room. She curled up on the couch and flipped through the channels until she found a movie she hadn't seen in ages.

No matter how hard she tried to concentrate on the movie, her mind kept going back to the man she had recently met. As she finished supper, the phone rang.

"Hello?" she asked as she answered.

"I didn't catch you at a bad time, did I? I wanted to call you for the past few days, but I also didn't want to scare you off either."

She responded quickly, "Oh no, I am so glad you called."

"Would you like to get together for supper Saturday night?"

Hoping she didn't answer too quickly, she blurted out, "Yes, that would be great."

***

She didn't think tonight would ever get here. She was falling hard for the man she just met. She even put clean sheets on the bed this morning in case she did get lucky.

She took an extra-long time getting ready, wanting to knock his socks off. She forgot to ask how she should dress when he called to finalize plans, so she dressed for an elegant evening out.

A shudder of anticipation ran through her. Butterflies fluttered around in her stomach as she waited for him. She didn't want to appear overly anxious, but she couldn't wait for him to arrive.

Watching out the living room window, she opened the door before he had the chance to knock. When he bent down and kissed her lightly on the lips, the simple kiss left her craving so much more.

Candi chatted nonstop on the drive to the restaurant. She hoped she wasn't talking the man's ear off, but from the smile on his face, she believed she still had his full attention. He looked completely enamored, not bored, as he listened to her every word.

When they arrived at La Madeleine, she noticed the long line. "This place is popular tonight. I'm not sure we will ever get a table."

Instead of answering her, he gently took her elbow and escorted her to the front door. When he gave the hostess his name, the maître de appeared, "Right this way, sir. We have everything ready."

Candi looked at him with genuine surprise in her eyes. He looked down at her and smiled, "I wanted everything perfect and reserved a special table."

The maître de escorted them to a private room near the kitchen that was bathed in candlelight. "Oh my," she gasped, "you outdid yourself. This is absolutely beautiful."

He informed her, "I wanted a nice, cozy table where we can sit and talk."

She was actually relieved to be dining with him in seclusion. Several of her clients enjoyed this particular restaurant, and she didn't want to run into any of them. She had not told him about her occupation, because she feared that he might not approve of what she did for a living. Smiling up at him, she said, "A girl could get spoiled being around you."

He smiled over at her, "I'm so glad you agreed to go out with me again."

As they ate their dinner, she couldn't take her eyes off of him. He looked dashing in his suit and tie, and was unbelievably handsome as well.

She moaned in ecstasy as she ate her food. Her taste buds came to life with each bite. "I wish I cooked like this. I do good not to burn a grilled cheese sandwich. What about you? Are you a master chef?"

"I can cook a few good dishes. My mother didn't take the time to cook so if I wanted to eat, I either asked the surly housekeeper or made it myself."

She replied, "That was the first time you mentioned your mother."

"I've never been comfortable talking about myself. Besides, I would much rather listen to you talk."

"I tend to talk nonstop at times, so you don't want to give me free rein."

Once again, Candi didn't even realize the time until the lights began to turn off in the dining room. Looking at his watch, he told her, "It's well after midnight and something tells me they are ready to close. I hadn't realized how long we talked. I guess I need to take you home so that you can get some rest."

She didn't want to see the night end. Should she ask him in for a nightcap? As previously, once they arrived at her house, he escorted her to her front door and kissed her lightly on the lips, "Good night Candi, sweet dreams."

"Good night."

Candi's heart sank as he drove off. She chickened out at the last minute and did not ask him in for a nightcap, and now, she regretted it. She wouldn't get much sleep tonight; all she could think of was him. Letting out a sigh, she went to bed.

Lying there, she worried that he didn't find her attractive. Perhaps no man found her attractive. The only men who slept with her were the ones who paid for sex. At first, the fact that he was such a gentleman turned her on, but now it had become annoying. If they did go on another date, she would make sure he found her sexy.

Chapter 15

Candi just walked inside her house from the club when the doorbell rang. Wondering who it was, she looked through the peephole and her heart swelled when she saw him, "This is a pleasant surprise. I figured you were busy at work."

Holding up the grocery bags, he answered, "I thought I would show off my cooking skills. I hope you don't mind."

Candi smiled up at him, "I would love for you to show me how well you can cook. I just made it home from the gym though and need a shower." She prayed that the smell of sex did not emanate from her body.

Sensing her reluctance, he asked, "Are you sure this is okay with you? I don't want to impose. It never occurred to me you may not like surprises."

"No, not at all. This is a pleasant surprise. I just need a hot shower."

Candi reached up and kissed him on the lips before dashing off to shower. As she entered her room, she called out to him, "Make yourself at home. I won't be long."

***

He walked around the small house, trying to get a better feel for the woman who had him completely intrigued. He couldn't get his mind off her lately. An overwhelming urge came over him to make sure she was home instead of seeing another man. Could it be that she gave up her occupation for him? Perhaps he had found the love of his life.

As he set up in the kitchen, he heard Candi leave her bedroom. She took his breath away standing there in the doorway, "You look absolutely breathtaking tonight."

She blushed from the compliment and asked, "Was there something I can help you with?"

He shook his head in response, "I have everything under control."

"I have never had someone cook a meal for me before. You are spoiling me way too much."

As he cooked supper, she opened a bottle of Chardonnay for them to enjoy. He told her, "I wanted a chance to enjoy your company, and this allows me to spend all of my time with you."

While he cooked, he took in how she looked tonight. She had changed into a pair of skinny jeans and an emerald green peek a boo shoulder top with gold flecks woven into it. The top made her eyes seem to be a vibrant green and the gold brought out the copper highlights in her hair. The whole outfit showed off her assets nicely.

"So, Chef, what is on the menu tonight?"

Shrugging his shoulders, he informed her, "You have to sit back and watch to find out what it is."

When he took out the stock pot to boil the noodles, she commented, "Okay, I am fairly sure that you are making spaghetti, but I'm not positive."

Giving her a wicked smile, he answered, "It is my specialty, chicken spaghetti with andouille sausage." Using his fingers, he blew a kiss. "This will be the best spaghetti you ever ate."

She peeked into the other container and asked, "Is that bread pudding?"

"Mais, of course. White chocolate bread pudding with a rich amaretto sauce."

She leaned back in her chair and let out a soft moan, "You can come over and cook for me anytime you want."

Walking over, he gave her a quick kiss on her lips, "I am so glad that we met. I have waited my whole life for you."

"Well, I am glad that you introduced yourself that night."

The last thing for him to cook was the french bread. As she refilled their wine glasses, he prepared two plates for them. He took his time and arranged everything expertly on the plate. "You pay special attention to detail don't you?"

He simply replied, "I just want to make sure that everything is perfect for you."

The night went by quicker than he wanted. He enjoyed sitting this close to her and talking in such an intimate setting. Looking deep into her eyes, he confessed, "I don't know if I can wait until the weekend to see you again. Would you like to go out to supper on Wednesday?"

"Why don't I cook for us this time?"

He picked up her hand and tenderly kissed it, "That's not necessary; I can take you out to eat."

"Nonsense, it's really no problem. Don't worry, I won't give you food poisoning or anything, I promise."

He reluctantly stood up, not wanting the night to end, but knowing that he would see her again sent a thrill through him. At the front door, he pulled her into his arms and kissed her a little harder than the previous times, "Until Wednesday night, then."

"I'll be counting the minutes."

"I'm not sure what time I will be over here, but it will likely be sometime after seven o'clock."

Candi told him, "I will be here."

As he pulled away, he was tempted to turn around and spend the night, but something kept him from taking the next step in their relationship.

Chapter 16

Candi looked at her watch and grimaced. She threw on a loose fitting dress over her outfit and rushed out the door. She enjoyed her role as a Dominatrix, but tonight's date meant more to her. Being a Dominatrix helped satisfy something deep inside of her that craved this. There was a release when she caused a man pain instead of him causing her pain.

She made a quick dash into the Café near the club and picked up a boneless chicken breast stuffed with crabmeat dressing and a sinfully decadent chocolate mousse pie. She worked off enough calories earlier to justify eating this dessert. Everything else was ready at the house for the green salad, and she even had a bottle of Blackberry Sangria chilling.

She also stopped by the bakery and picked up a fresh loaf of bread. Her car smelled so good that her mouth watered.

As soon as she arrived home, she had just enough time to put everything in the oven to keep it warm while she took a quick shower. She couldn't wait for him to get here. She enjoyed having him eat at her house. The setting was more intimate, plus, she didn't have to worry about running into any of her clients.

As she dressed, she wondered if she could convince him to stay the night. When she walked into the kitchen, she heard the doorbell ring. She hollered out, "Just a minute." She rushed to the door to let him in. "Come on in. I was about to take everything out of the oven."

***

As he walked into the house, he forced himself to control his anger. When he drove by earlier, he had discovered that she wasn't home. He expected her to spend the whole day dedicated to pleasing him. After all, he took time out of his busy schedule to shop for ingredients and cook.

Trying to keep his voice steady, he said, "It smells delicious in here."

She smiled at him, "I have a pitcher of Sangria chilling in the fridge if you want to pour us a glass. Would you prefer to dine al fresco or sit in the dining room?"

"It's a beautiful night; let's eat outside." Hopefully, the night air helped calm the anger building inside of him. As soon as he noticed the trash he saw red; she had purchased him prepared food. The supper they were about to eat wasn't even something she cooked with her own two hands. Perhaps she didn't care about him.

"That sounds good to me." Candi carried their plates while he carried the wine glasses.

Over dinner, he remained quieter than normal. After dinner, they moved to the swing to finish the wine and enjoy their dessert. The moon and stars shone brightly, giving the night a romantic atmosphere. But, no matter how hard he tried, he kept thinking about her lack of enthusiasm in cooking him supper.

Even now, as he talked to her, she seemed to be staring off into space. Instead of answering him, she informed him, "I'm sorry, my mind must have drifted off."

"I was just saying that it's getting late. I should get going."

If he didn't leave, he might do something he regretted. He wanted to cry out in disappointment; he thought she was the woman of his dreams. He believed that she loved him. It was time to watch her closer to see if she had given up her career.

When he leaned down and kissed her, she wrapped her arms around his neck and pulled him in closer. As the kiss deepened, he pulled her closer to his body.

Her touch ignited something deep inside of him. He battled with his conscience, wanting to know more about her first. However, the longer they kissed, the harder it became for him to walk away. He was tempted to throw it all away and drag her off to the bedroom. He had to know if she was still sleeping with the other men.

"I better let you go before this goes any further."

***

She wanted to ask him once more to stay, but found it difficult to find her voice. Her body trembled with desire for him. She didn't know if she could stand the humiliation of rejection again if he said no.

As soon as he left, she felt cold from where his body had been. She missed his arms wrapped tightly around her. She wanted him to stay so bad, but the words never made it out of her mouth.

As he drove away, she waited until she no longer saw his taillights before closing the door. She hoped that he would change his mind and drive back, carrying her straight to her bedroom. When she realized that wouldn't happen, she closed and locked the door.

Chapter 17

In the darkness of the night, he watched the woman of his dreams. He observed her every move this past week. He sat in front of his computer night and day, not moving a muscle.

Now he knew the answer; she was a whore. She must pay for betraying his love this way. His body grew tense in anticipation of spilling her blood. His palms became sweaty, and his heart pounded as the thrill of the kill over took him.

***

The music that filled the club vibrated through her body tonight as Candi made her way to the room where her next client waited. This was her third month working here, but she was starting to enjoy her new job. It was the one place where she could be herself.

On the outside, the club was unremarkable, but once inside you found that it was a cross between a brothel and an adult fantasyland. Seductive lighting illuminated cozy sitting areas; various erotic artwork adorned the walls and the staff dressed seductively.

The clientele here ranged from various ages, colors, and sizes. Several dressed rather conservatively for this type of club while others dressed downright outrageous. All around you slaps, moans, and grunts could be heard.

There were several "dungeons" here with chains and whips along with various other devices. Candi's favorite was the whipping bench, but, unfortunately, that was not on the menu for tonight.

For a Tuesday night, the club was extremely busy. Trepidation moved through her as she went over what her next client wanted. Normally she was the Dominatrix, but this next client requested her to be a submissive. She still did not like being the submissive in the relationship.

Once inside the room, she went to the far corner and kneeled, eyes facing the floor as she waited for him. Just how long she stayed in that position she wasn't sure, but she knew he was taking his time on purpose. Making her kneel there and wait for him, it was as if he were daring her to break the rules, urging her to be a bad girl and look up. It was extremely difficult for her, but she continued to look at the floor like a good girl.

As she heard him walk around her, her pulse raced. She ached for his touch, for his dominance. This was a new experience for her, one that made her nervous.

He snapped his fingers, "Come to me on your knees."

She crawled on all fours over to where he waited; her body actions suggestive of a sexy feline. She slinked over to her Master, keeping her eyes on the floor. She noticed the fine leather and detailed stitching of his shoes. Just the size of his shoes had her purring as she nuzzled up against his pant leg, the soft material of the suit pleasing to the skin of her cheek.

He assisted her in the "swing of screams". At first glance, the swing looked intimidating, but once you became used to the feel of it you fully understood just why it was called the "swing of screams". The amount of pleasure it brought you was incredible.

Her long, lean body was bent forward from the waist and her wrists were bound. She watched as the shadowy figure moved around her. He secured the ball gag in her mouth and reached for a flogger on the wall. Moving slowly behind her, he raised it and lashed her exposed buttocks. The flogger came down harder than she anticipated. By the sixth lash, she was struggling against her restraints, but they wouldn't give way. She bit down hard on the gag, but nothing eased the pain. Her muscles tensed as each new stroke became more painful than the last. How much more would she be forced to endure?

Tears stained her cheeks and her throat was raw. She wasn't sure just how long the beating lasted, but the pain had become excruciating. She tried to catch her breath when she felt a hand running across her welted skin.

Before she realized that something was terribly wrong, it was too late. Everything happened in slow motion. It was as if she was watching from afar. Sinister orbs glowed from the dark mask as fear paralyzed her.

The man in front of her wore a full black leather mask that only allowed his eyes and mouth to be visible. When he slipped off the mask, she let out an awkward gasp. Standing in front of her was the man she loved, except this time his face was distorted in a mask of rage. The eyes staring down at her were as cold as ice.

She didn't even see the flash of the blade as he brought it up against her neck. Her body quickly turned cold as blood poured from the huge gash in her neck. Her eyes rolled backward in her head as her body went limp.

***

He walked out of the club, calmly and deliberately. Soon the body would be found, but he would be nowhere near. He was careful to keep his face hidden beneath the mask. He had made sure to dress as the other patrons. His knife moved against his ribs as he walked, keeping perfect rhythm with his movements as if they were in sync.

He wished he could be here when the body was discovered, but he needed to find another woman to take the betrayer's place.

Chapter 18

By the time LeDoux and Riley arrived at the crime scene, the club was cordoned off, and the patrons were being held in the main part of the club. LeDoux asked the young officer at the door, "What do we have?"

"A worker was killed in one of the private rooms. From the amount of blood, the room is the crime scene."

This was LeDoux's first time in the club, and it was not what he expected. It looked similar to a medieval torture chamber. Shackles hung from the ceiling and suspended along the walls were various whips, paddles, and other instruments of pain. The smell of freshly spilled blood and sex permeated the air.

The room was a hive of activity. However, everyone who entered was taken back by surprise. Riley stated, "This place gives me the creeps. I don't see how people get turned on by this."

LeDoux could only stare. He felt as if he needed to be the one wearing a Tyvek suit and not just the forensics team. "There are no words to describe this room." Snapping his latex gloves, LeDoux said, "Come on, let's get to work."

In the middle of the room was the murder victim with her most intimate parts on display. She was in some contraption he would never have even imagined pleasurable. Who considered something like that enjoyable?

He tried to maintain a professional demeanor, although it was difficult. As he looked around the room, he envisioned the various "punishments" that must go on here.

LeDoux shook his head as he looked over the victim. Even in death you could see that this woman had been beautiful. As he moved around her, he grimaced at the pain she endured.

LeDoux found Dr. Chauvin kneeling over the body and asked, "How bad is it?"

"It looks as if your killer made another appearance."

LeDoux pointed to the marks on her back, "He's never tortured the women before."

Nodding her head in agreement, she replied, "No, but he took full advantage of one of the floggers readily available here. From the striped markings, she was repeatedly lashed with a flogger." She pointed over to an area on the wall and said, "Crime scene techs have already removed the weapon they believe caused the marks. It appeared to have fresh traces of blood."

LeDoux nodded his head in agreement. As he walked around the crime scene, the forensic team scoured the scene for clues. This place was a nightmare for evidence; too many people had been in and out of this location for useable prints.

"Who found the body?"

Officer Hinkle responded, "Another couple wanting to use the room. They didn't hear any noises coming from it, so they figured it was empty."

LeDoux bent down, carefully moved the blood soaked hair to one side, and stared at the gaping knife wound in the victim's throat. "It sure in the hell looks like our killer."

Dr. Chauvin nodded her head, "Yep, another left-handed stab wound. He didn't even hesitate when the blade came into contact with the right ear lobe. As with the others, he severed the carotid arteries bilaterally when her throat was cut."

Officer Hinkle informed LeDoux that the media vans had arrived. LeDoux walked over to one of the young officers guarding the scene, "Make sure everyone working this case knows not to talk to the media. Inform them that I will have their heads if anyone is caught spouting off to a reporter or appears on the evening news. Also, try to keep them far away from the scene."

"Yes, sir."

LeDoux pulled a packet of antacids from his pocket and popped one in his mouth. The coffee from this morning churned in his stomach. The media would soon put the notion in everyone's mind that a serial killer was on the loose. When that happened, this would turn into a full three-ring circus. They needed to find this guy quick.

Outside, the reporters assembled on the street like a pack of wild dogs ready to attack, merely waiting for the signal to lunge forward and annoy the officers with questions.

LeDoux never figured out how the reporters knew the exact time to move in and start their feeding frenzy.

Before he could make it to his car, he was spotted.

"Detective, can you tell us if the victim has been identified?"

"Now you know that we will not release any names until the victim's family is notified," he answered honestly.

"Any suspects?"

"No comment at this time."

Another reporter called out, "Was this murder related to the previous women murdered?"

"No comment."

Yet another reporter called out, "Could this murder be mob related?"

LeDoux looked around for the reporter, wondering why she suspected this killing was mob related. The reporter's voice sounded calm and collected; the question was not rushed, as if she thought about her questions. He looked for the reporter and groaned when he noticed that it was Cassandra Evans. Standing at only five feet, two inches with long, auburn hair, she was a firecracker who could be hard to dismiss. "As I said previously, no comment."

Walking toward LeDoux, she continued, "She was murdered like the previous women, am I correct?"

"No comment. You can speculate to any conclusion you wish. This is an active murder investigation, and we are still sorting through the evidence."

On the way back to the station, LeDoux kept wondering why Cassandra Evans asked about the mob. Could it be that the club was owned by the notorious Frank Marcel? He wouldn't be surprised; the man had his hand in everything. However, it would be hard to prove since he kept everything in his company's shell name with no paperwork leading directly to him. Besides, just about everyone in town believed that he was an affluent member of society.

Riley interrupted his train of thought, "I know what you are thinking, and you can forget about it. I have no desire in talking to Mr. Marcel without proof that he is involved in a prostitution ring, especially one that involves an S&M Club. I don't think he would appreciate the accusation one bit."

LeDoux laughed, "Relax, I have no plans on even talking to one of Campton's most prominent citizens until I am positive of just what questions I need to ask."

Riley ran his hands through his hair and asked, "Any idea how we find what the man's connection to the S&M Club or these escorts may be? I mean this man is not only a prominent citizen here, but he is also married and a huge supporter of the local Catholic Church. He will never openly admit being involved in anything like this."

LeDoux nodded his head in agreement, "This is a delicate situation. Even in this day and age, no one wants to admit to infidelity, especially when you have to pay for the sex. Besides, I don't see Mr. Marcel readily admitting to the fact that he likes it when a woman dominates him in the bedroom." Shaking his head, he added, "And I doubt his wife wants to find out that he pays for kinky sex."

Riley looked at his partner, "I don't think my wife would even give me the chance to apologize. No sooner than she found out, bon ami, you would be saying my eulogy."

This was definitely a touchy situation. Mr. Marcel was not only well liked by the citizens, but he was friends with the mayor and some of the very elite here. While some people state that they are laissez-faire about certain subjects, infidelity was not one of them.

"So how do you want to play this?"

LeDoux responded, "Let's play this one close to the vest right now. There's no sense in ruffling feathers, especially the wrong ones."

"We need a list of members to the club."

LeDoux let out a short laugh, "That's easier said than done. Most of the people in there wore masks which means they want their anonymity. The owner of the club won't turn over a list to us."

"Then we subpoena them and force the matter."

"No judge in town will sign that subpoena. Besides, even if they did, the club still won't hand over a list."

"Come on, they can't ignore a subpoena."

LeDoux looked at his partner, "I have a feeling some very prominent members of society are involved in this business.

People who will do anything to keep their names from being released.”

Chapter 19

Amber Brady ran one of the most lucrative escort businesses in Louisiana. Her clientele included some prominent people from across the country.

By the age of thirty, she'd earned more money than she ever dreamed she would. The escort business gave her the opportunity of a lifetime. She took several luxurious vacations across the globe; most paid for by clients. While the money was good in the escort business, she soon learned that it was far more profitable in the Dominatrix business. Certain men paid generously for a woman to dominate them.

Amber had been lucky in that Jacqueline, her former Madam, saw potential in her and trained her well. Jacqueline taught her how to scout girls for the service, pick up payments, and, more importantly, how to put out any fires started. The most important lesson, though, was to never mix business with pleasure and to keep the two lives separate.

Lately, Amber had let her emotions come into play; she was worried about her girls. She heard through the grapevine that Candi had been murdered. She should never have left to venture out on her own. *How many times have I told these girls just because they are a Dominatrix, to be cautious about whom you see?* Just because a man hired a Dominatrix didn't mean he was docile.

She stepped onto her deck for a breath of fresh air. While outside, she looked over her house. It was the house of her dreams; a lot of thought and consideration went into it when she designed it. The entryway was large and airy. The kitchen was a gourmet chef's dream. Everything was top of the line. The master bedroom was downstairs and upstairs consisted of several bedrooms for guests, each with their own bathroom. The back of the house had one large window that overlooked the Mississippi River.

The master suite was her retreat from the world. It was spacious with a king-size four poster bed. The bathroom had a whirlpool tub and a massive walk in shower. Her closet was as spacious as one of the upstairs bedrooms. It was big enough to house her clothes, along with her handbag and shoe collection. She also had an area designated for her sunglasses. After all, a girl could never have too many accessories.

In the backyard, massive oak trees canopied the yard. Spanish moss dripped from the branches. Snowy white egrets and great blue herons flew over the brackish water, dragging their feet to create a soft ripple in the once calm water. Near the river bank were a few giant cypress trees, their gnarled knees rising out of the shallow water.

When she first started out it had been a real struggle. She learned quick that it was a dog eat dog world out there. If she wanted to be more successful than anyone else, she had to be the pièce de rèsistance. Now that her business was successful, she could indulge herself.

She began as an escort in the company, but when Jacqueline retired Amber wanted to take over the business. While she seldom entertained anymore, she enjoyed her position as not only Madam but a Dominatrix. She taught her young charges to treat each man as if they were a sugar daddy. That very practice helped her land some of her most prominent clients.

She grabbed her glass of Moscato and took a sip of the wine. It had a nice flavor, light and clean, with just a hint of apples. The hot, thick air blowing off of the Mississippi River carried with it the pungent smell of the river. The humid air weighed down on her like a hot towel. She watched as ominous clouds formed to the south. Hopefully, the rain brought some relief to this oppressive heat wave. Thunder crackled in the distance. A bolt of lightning flashed across the darkening sky. The storm had moved in fast. Grabbing her now empty glass, she moved back to the house to get ready for her date.

Chapter 20

Bree LaFleur looked at the ever growing pile of bills as a shudder of fear moved through her. Depression had her feeling sick to her stomach.

By eight thirty in the morning, she had already received three phone calls from bill collectors. These last few months had been extremely challenging. No matter how hard she tried to catch up, she kept getting further behind.

Tom had been under an extreme amount of pressure, so she had not mentioned how far behind they were but soon, she would have no choice. The electricity company threatened to cut off their service by the end of the week and the phone company graciously gave her until Monday.

The mortgage company offered to work with her on refinancing, but first she had to catch up on the three months they were behind. The same was true for their car payments.

With tears filling her eyes, she looked at the almost nonexistent bank account once more. They had already drained the retirement accounts and she didn't have any luck when she tried to pawn her jewelry.

Unable to take the stress anymore, she fell to her bed sobbing. She turned forty this year, and this was not how she pictured her life would turn out.

Tired of feeling sorry for herself and needing fresh air, she changed into her running outfit and hit the pavement.

Maybe a run would clear her mind enough to where she could solve their money problems. Even though Tom opposed her returning to work, Bree didn't see any way around it. However, since she dedicated her life to her husband and family, prospective employers might consider her past her prime.

Tom liked having her home for the children, and to take care of any errands he may have during the day. Still, that left her with five or six hours to herself. With money tight, she should be earning a paycheck. Unbeknownst to Tom, this last month she had sent resumes to the help wanted ads in the paper, except for the adult entertainment ads. However, she still had not received any replies. With things as tight as they were, working in a strip club may be her only choice.

On her run, trying to keep her mind off her worries, Bree observed the other houses in the neighborhood. As many times as she passed each of these houses, she never took the time to inspect them.

As she continued to pass by, she noticed how empty the neighborhood was during the day. This would be the perfect time for a robber to strike. Even if he walked in on an unsuspecting housewife, no one would hear her scream. No one was home during the day, which instead of cheering her up, depressed her even more. Everyone in the neighborhood, except for her, had something to do.

While she cooled down from her run, Bree fixed herself a strawberry and banana smoothie with the Greek yogurt she loved so much. As she drank it, she perused the want ads once more. One ad in particular caught her attention. It merely stated that a web consultant was needed for a small, but growing business. It was as if the job had been made for her. She could work from home and chose her own hours. Anxious to beat anyone to the job offer, she called the number.

It surprised Bree when the man informed her that he could meet with her in the next hour if she was available.   Bree quickly showered, dressed, and left. When she arrived, she noticed that the office was barely bigger than her master bedroom closet with very few windows. When Bree saw the empty receptionist desk, she had second thoughts and considered backing out of the interview.

A silent alarm must have sounded in his office because no sooner than she opened the door he stepped out of his office.

"Ms. LaFleur?"

Taking the hand he extended, she answered, "Yes, sir. Thank you for fitting me in this morning."

She watched as his eyes traveled up and down her body before settling on her wedding band. "Why don't you come into my office and we can discuss the job in detail."

***

Mike Johansen couldn't believe his luck. He found himself drawn to the gentle sway of her hips as he showed her in. This woman definitely fit into his plans. What brought a woman like her into his office?

She looked as if she could be a model. He would never guess that she was forty. She would fit in well, and he had no doubt that the men would follow her. He needed someone who would bring in the business, increase sales, as well as attract new clientele and she could do just that.

He watched as she made herself comfortable in the chair across from him. He took in her legs, from the tip of her Jimmy Choo shoes to the hem of her skirt, up to her full breasts, and ended at her gaze. Her body screamed sensuality. She would control these men with no problems whatsoever.

Her navy blue suit fit her like a glove and left nothing to the imagination. What he wouldn't give for just a preview of those sensuous curves hidden under her suit.

Even walking in heels came naturally to this woman. Hiring her would be beneficial for him and the company's future.

She was a gold mine for his business. He must snare this hot little number. The clients would definitely be impressed, men and women alike. Clearing his throat, he stated, "As I am sure you are aware technology has come a long way. What we do here is make it safer for men to seek out various pleasures without certain risks. It is safe for the women we employ, as well."

"I am almost afraid to ask what you do here."

"It is not what you think. My business started out as a phone sex company. However, now with the internet I have started the newest form of sexual satisfaction for men, hiring women to be a Virtual Dominatrix."

"Just what is it these women do?"

"I have several girls in my employment who basically sit in front of the camera and order men around, for a fee of course."

"What all is involved?"

"Some of the girls take off their clothes, tease the men, and masturbate all while live on air. Sometimes you have a request for a private viewing which means more money for all of us." He paid close attention to her facial expression before continuing, "However, most of the time you will order these men around. Have you ever heard of a Dominatrix?"

Bree nodded her head, "I've heard of a Dominatrix, but I'm not exactly sure what it means." Sighing, she added, "I'm not sure if I can do this. I just don't know."

"Ms. LeFleur, if you want to earn a lot of money in a fast amount of time, this is one of the best ways to do it. You have a nice body, and the clients will go crazy over you. You can make a fortune dominating these horny men and women. You will have complete anonymity, and there is no sex involved with these customers." Looking into her eyes, he added, "Besides, you mentioned that your hours are limited and with this job you can choose the hours you do work."

The mention of money caught her attention. "Just how much money are we talking about?"

"I have one girl who makes almost two thousand a week, sometimes more. If you build up a fan base and get regulars, the money will start to come in for you." Looking up and down her body, he said, "You would be surprised just how much money people are willing to pay for the privilege to have you talk down to them. I think you will be perfect for the job. You can start as soon as you like."

Extending her hand, she said, "Thank you so much. I promise I will try to meet all of your requirements."

As he shook Bree's hand, he was impressed with her firm grip and business attitude. She would lure the men in and keep them intrigued. Hell, even he would give her a chance to degrade him.

***

When she got back home, Bree couldn't believe that she accepted the job. She still had doubts about it, no matter how innocent her new boss made it sound.

At least she didn't have to have sex with these men. It would be just her in front of the camera, performing. She didn't have to work hard for the money; it was a bunch of horny guys paying her to control them, all online. No harm, no foul. This was probably the closest some of these guys would ever come to a woman.

Bree in no way could be considered a prude. She had been wild when she was younger, but that was before she met Tom. Before she met Tom, she considered sex as a fun pastime. She saw no shame in exploring her sexuality and lost count of the men she slept with over the years. Until Tom, love and passion never entered her mind. She didn't see sex as a taboo activity or let emotions come into play.

By the time she graduated high school, she was well versed in various sexual techniques. During her college years, sex was just something she enjoyed partaking in, never a way of expressing affection.

In the beginning, the main reason she married Tom was for his money. She loved him, but it was not an all-consuming, passionate love. She was tired of her life, tired of having to work two jobs just to make ends meet. Tom's proposal would get her out of the slump her life was in. However, with each passing day, month, and year she found herself loving him a little more. He became not only her husband, but her confidante, her best friend.

She wondered if he felt the same for her now or if he still looked at her just as a trophy wife. She tried her best to be everything Tom wanted.

The oven timer went off; reminding her that the lasagna she made from scratch was done. As she removed the bubbling pan from the hot oven, Tom walked into the kitchen. She smiled warmly at him as he returned her smile.

As she placed their supper on the stove top, Tom smelled the air, "Supper sure does smell good."

"I made lasagna for tonight. The kids should be home soon. Jonathan had football practice and Gracie cheerleading practice."

As he nodded his head in approval, Bree watched his every movement. She longed for him to come over and give her a kiss hello. It caught her by surprise that he had come home in time to eat supper with them as a family. She wished he would sweep her into his arms and kiss her passionately. Even if he only gave her a simple kiss on the cheek or a pat on her derriere she would be satisfied. Any small act of affection would do.

She looked over at Tom and felt guilty about taking the job. But they needed the money. She hoped it would be as good as Mike said. It sounded almost too good to be true.

She arranged her hours where she worked during the day while her children and husband were away from the house. The last thing she wanted was for one of them to walk in while she "performed" for a viewer. She even went as far as purchasing a different comforter set to use while "working" just in case her husband stumbled upon the chat room. She didn't want anyone to recognize the bedroom.

Chapter 21

LeDoux had just made it to the restaurant when his phone rang. *Crap, dispatch.* His parents were waiting at the table for him. *So much for a quiet evening, or he should say listening to his mom tell him it was time he settled down and gave them some grandkids.* "LeDoux."

"Sir, I hate to ruin your evening, but we've got another dead body."

As LeDoux jotted down the address, he informed the dispatcher, "I'm not too far away. I'll be there in a few."

At his parents' table, he bent down to kiss his mother on her cheek and shook his dad's hand. "I hate to do this, but I have to go to a crime scene."

His mom responded with her typical self, "But you just got here. Can't you stay for a minute?"

He patted her hand; he loved her – even if she was trying to be manipulative. "I wish I could, but duty calls."

LeDoux went back to his car and headed to the crime scene. A haze of activity confirmed that he was at the right spot. Half a dozen cop cars lined the street and the ambulance to carry the body away. Blue and red flashing lights lit up the night sky. Forms shifted through the lights before merging with the darkness once again.

LeDoux surveyed the scene. Even after all these years, it still surprised him what man was capable of doing. With everything he witnessed in his lifetime, he should not be surprised at the amount of pain another individual could inflict upon someone, but it was still bothering him.

Before entering the house, he closed his eyes and erased the images of the previous crime scenes from his mind. He wanted to look at this one with fresh eyes. Maybe this murder wasn't connected to the others.

Steady now, images and emotions gone, he stepped inside. Forensic technicians were busy collecting evidence and processing the scene. He didn't need to examine any evidence. If this case was like the others, there wouldn't be much to bother with. He tried not to focus on anything but the overall feeling that lingered in a room after a murder, as if the victim's tortured soul was trying to tell him something. He still felt the rage the killer had for the victim.

With the first murder, he had hoped it was simply a crime of passion, but now he feared they were searching for a serial killer. This was not a scorned lover who lashed out. He had a purpose to killing.

Upon walking in the house, LeDoux could smell why he was called. Death hung heavy in the air. From the smell, the body was well into decomp.

As he walked through the house, he took notice once again that robbery was not the motive. The house was full of expensive furnishings, electronics, and art that remained untouched. If anything were stolen it was only small items, but his gut told him that was not the case. It wouldn't be long before he investigated another murder involving a woman killed in a compromising situation.

As Riley walked into the room and looked at the victim, he asked, "Do you ever get tired of that deja poo feeling?"

"Deja poo?"

"Yeah, same shit, different scene."

Nodding his head LeDoux agreed, "Yeah, I suppose I do."

Chapter 22

In the police station, detectives and uniformed officers bustled about. LeDoux made his way to the conference room which had been converted to their work room. Around the room were several whiteboards, each with diagrams and pictures. He saw that Riley was already studying several photos.

Riley turned to greet LeDoux with a grimace on his face, "Captain called a brief meeting soon."

LeDoux took a sip of his coffee as he stared at the pictures of the victims. As soon as Captain Fontenot walked in he informed everyone, "Let's not waste any time. We all know that another woman was murdered. This guy is pissing me off." Looking at LeDoux, he asked, "What do you know about our recent victim?"

"Gretchen Weston, age thirty-two, was found by her husband, bound and throat slashed at their residence. She had been dead for approximately forty-eight hours. He was away on a business trip and came home to her dead."

Officer Wilson asked, "Didn't he wonder why he hadn't heard from her in a few days?"

"Apparently, it was the norm for them not to stay in contact while he was away."

Captain Fontenot looked over the pictures of the crime scene once more, "How did the perp get in? I'm sure a house like this had a security system."

LeDoux nodded his head, "It appeared that our victim let the perp in. There were no signs of forced entry."

Captain Fontenot asked, "Could it have been the husband?"

LeDoux played the 911 tape. A man's frantic voice filled the room, "You have to help me. My wife, she's dead. Oh my god, Gretchen is dead!"

"Sir, please try to remain calm. I need your address."

"Please, come quick!" the voice pled, "There is so much blood."

The operator tried to calm the frantic man, "Sir, help is on the way. Have you touched the body? Are you sure she is dead?"

"There is so much blood."

LeDoux stopped the recording. "The husband was obviously distraught when he called. On top of that, he feels extremely guilty. After questioning him, it turns out that he has an airtight alibi. He was busy servicing his mistress all weekend. There was no time to call his wife."

For the next hour, they compared the similarities and differences between the crime scenes. "According to the next door neighbor whenever Mr. Weston was away, there was a constant flow of traffic around their house."

Officer Daniels stated, "I know the Westons are well off, but I did a little digging into some of the designer labels that the late Mrs. Weston had in her closet. This woman liked to spend money, and a lot of it, on shoes and clothes. She had numerous "toys" and lingerie that her husband had not seen as well."

Captain Fontenot stated, "Okay, so we know that the Westons were well off. It shouldn't be surprising that she had clothes and shoes that most people couldn't afford."

LeDoux shook his head, "No, what we are saying is Mrs. Weston was a pro. A high class pro to be exact. From the items she had hidden, it appears that she was another Dominatrix."

Captain Fontenot had to wipe the surprised look off of his face. He may have to pay a visit to a certain friend to see if the deceased worked for her. "Although this wouldn't be the first time a wife stepped out on her husband for a little side business. We need to make damn sure your assumptions are correct before we even consider approaching the husband with this."

LeDoux agreed, "I have NO desire to tell a grieving husband, who already feels guilty about cheating on his wife, that she had a side profession."

Officer Wilson threw his pen down on the table, "What I don't understand is why we are spending all this time on these women. They were hardly innocent; they were hookers – albeit high paid hookers."

LeDoux looked at the young officer, "Officer, you need to get your head on straight. These women were human beings and deserve to be treated as a victim of a heinous crime, despite their vocational proclivities."

Holding up his hands, Officer Wilson said, "I am only implying that we are spending a lot of manpower on these murders and have nothing to go on."

LeDoux glared at the young officer, "Right now his sights are set on women who he believes are readily available. However, in my experience, serial killers tend to escalate right before they screw up. Now, how long before that happens, none of us know. We do know that this guy is just getting started. He has extreme control in the amount of time he can wait between kills. These women more than likely knew their killer; they let him into their homes. This guy could be the guy next door. The possibilities are endless."

Chapter 23

The next morning, after her husband and children left for the day, Bree walked back into her bedroom for her workday to begin. The master suite was the epitome of luxury. The large room had dark bamboo floors, a massive four poster California King bed and posh furnishings. It took some ingenious work on her part to keep the room from being recognized on the website.

Of course, the bathroom was her favorite part of the room. There was a whirlpool bathtub, large enough for two, as well as a double shower. Both were surrounded with Italian marble tiles. The shower had a built in bench seat, along with jetted showerheads on either side, as well as nozzles on top that simulated rain.

She changed into her sexy lingerie, applied a generous amount of makeup, carefully fixed her hair, and slipped on the mask. As soon as she saw the mask in the store, she knew that she had to have it.   It was perfect for her. It was made of black feathers, lace, and embellished with bling. It covered the top part of her face, framing her face, leaving the lower half of her face free. With this mask, she easily slipped into her role as Mistress Azaria. The mask completed her dark, mysterious persona.

It took her a little while to learn how to control all the chat windows on the computer because of all the people talking all at once, but once she figured it out it was a breeze.

She took a deep breath in and prepared for her first show. She still had some time before she started and wanted to familiarize herself with the role she came up with. There were also a few "toys" she was unfamiliar with. Even at her age, she never found the need for vibrators or toys.   They never appealed to her. She always preferred the real thing inside of her, something that pulsed with a live heartbeat.

She picked up the first item the sales girl told her was a must have and stared at it. Shaking her head, She realized she was way out of her league with these toys. *Just what exactly are you supposed to do with this?* It had some weirdly spaced appendages that promised to give the woman a perfect orgasm. As she studied the directions, she came to the realization that this particular one may have to wait. She didn't want to look like a complete novice on her first day.

As she moved her body to her favorite music, she was ready.   Her first step was organizing the massage oils and toys that she planned on using for today's show. She wanted to keep them out of view, but still within easy reach. She gave herself a pep talk when she started to doubt herself once again for embarking on this new venture. She needed this job if they were going to try to keep their head above water. Besides, this was her chance to be the dominate one in the relationship. She would be the one controlling men, talking down to them.

Standing nearly naked in front of the camera, soon she would be visible to anyone in the world with an internet connection. Her profile had already been added to the other available girls. Men would have a chance to select her profile and then enter "her room". Once there, they would be able to view her and send her messages. If they liked what they saw, they could even tip her.

She was told that some requests might be as simple as her talking to them in her lingerie, to a striptease, to using the sex toys. The more she met their demands, the more money in tips she could earn. But her ultimate goal was to coerce these men into private shows.

Once the camera was running and she was in position, she started off by cracking her whip. She was putting on a show for these men and wanted to make sure that they got their money's worth. She rubbed her dark pink nipples, giving them a slight tweak to become taut, waiting to be lavished with a mouth.

While one hand played with her breasts, another moved down ever so slightly to her soft folds. All the while telling these men if they were any kind of a man they would be pleasing a woman instead of seeking her out. She could just imagine the men watching, waiting to see what she did next. It brought a slight shiver of power to her, knowing that their eyes watched her every move.

As she worked the well oiled vibrator in and out of herself, she found that she liked the friction of the device and turned it up a degree. It made her a little more sensitive than she realized, and she found herself pushing it deeper inside of her as she rubbed herself faster.

She adjusted her toy to where it rubbed the ridges of her g spot and felt the orgasm building up inside of herself.

Over the next few days, she performed several strip teases, showed her body, and played with herself. By the end of the week, she learned just how to please her viewers. She also purchased several lace, push up bras, thongs, and even a few more toys to add to her show. Her breasts were in no way small but when she wore the push up bras they looked enormous. She also practiced on makeup techniques and colored contacts. When she first saw herself in the mirror, she was surprised. Even her own mother wouldn't recognize her with the blue eyes and dramatic makeup, especially with the new haircut and highlights. It hurt her when Tom didn't notice the haircut or that she had changed her hair color. She told herself that he was tired, but in her heart of hearts she suspected that he didn't find her attractive anymore.

If she wanted her viewers to stay online for as long as possible, she needed to be a little bolder in what she did. As the money started to come in, she began to believe that this may indeed be the answer to their problems. The number of viewers increased and she began to receive several requests for private sessions. The men loved being talked dirty to; some begged her to belittle them even more.

Tom still had not asked how she managed to catch up on some of the bills. The money went into a private checking account, and she transferred what they needed to the joint account. Tom hadn't even noticed that the bills were being paid. Right now, the only big bill looming over their heads was the mortgage. While the money was good with the webcam business, she hadn't worked there long enough to earn enough to pay the overdue mortgage bill. The bank agreed to accept minimal payments, but she feared it wouldn't be long before they demanded full payment.

She did learn a few tricks to tempt more men into requesting private chats, but she needed to pull in some serious money if she wanted to keep from losing her house.

Several of the men had requested that she sell them her unmentionables, offering thirty dollars for a pair that she had worn. A few more of her regulars had asked if she would consider meeting in person for some private one on one time. One viewer even offered her five hundred dollars an hour if she would walk him around the bedroom on a leash; no touching needed, but he required that the "lesson" be done in person. The money was tempting. If a few others made offers like this, the mortgage would be caught up in no time.

While she was still contemplating if she could see any of these men in person, she didn't see any harm in selling the men her undies. If this kept up, she would need to look into buying panties at a wholesale price. Just today alone, she had a request for ten pairs.

One viewer even asked Bree if he purchased something for her to wear, would she wear it. As more and more requests like this came in, Bree went out and obtained herself a post office box. Lately, the gifts rolled in.

Chapter 24

When Bree checked her mailbox that morning, she grew nervous. There was a rather large package for her, but the return address was from a nearby city. Once in the car, she opened the package to find an outfit and a letter asking if she would wear it for him in person. The letter went on to state that he would gladly pay her $500 for an hour of her time.

On the front seat lay scattered past due utility bills, maxed out credit card statements and also a certified letter from the bank. It stated that if they didn't receive $1200 by next week they would start foreclosure proceedings. There was no other way out of this dismal financial situation they found themselves buried in. Most of the problems could be blamed on this damn economy, but also the lifestyle they chose to live. She wanted nothing more than to bury her head in the sand and hope that the problems disappeared, but they wouldn't. If she didn't do something fast, they would be out on the street.

She looked down at her Lady Datejust Pearlmaster Rolex and wished that the pawn shops would pay top dollar for these items, but they were overloaded with jewelry and watches. Everyone was pawning and not buying. Building up the nerve, she decided to accept the man's offer. Besides, there was a chance he didn't want sex, but to have the Dominatrix performance in person. If he did indeed want sex, she would cross that bridge when the time came. She hoped that this man found her desirable and did not want his money back. Lately, her own husband hadn't looked at her with desire in his eyes so she questioned whether a stranger would.

After sending him a confirmation email that his date and time were acceptable, she decided to accept the other man's offer as well. This gave her an easy thousand dollars that she desperately needed.

***

As Bree slipped on the hot black leather mini skirt, kinky fishnet thigh high stockings, leather halter top, and some super sexy pumps, she instantly began to feel desirable. She purposefully didn't wear any panties, and it made her feel completely wicked. The outfit pulled in all the right places and pushed up her breasts until they threatened to escape from their confines. The miniskirt showed off her legs to perfection.

She took a lot of time with her body this morning. She was defuzzed, buffed, and moisturized to perfection. Her skin glistened with tiny little sparkles of glitter which shimmered as they caught in the light. Her hair and makeup were perfect. She took the time to polish her fingernails and toenails a bright blood red. She even found a lipstick that matched the nail polish. Her lips looked full and pouty, something that she found she liked.

She had serious doubts until she gave herself a once over in the mirror. The woman looking back at her was someone she hadn't seen in a long time. She looked pretty damn hot, actually smoking.

She wondered if her husband saw her now if he would find her desirable. What she wouldn't do to give him a raging hard on. She wanted him to find her sexy again.

As she waited for her gentleman caller, she began to wonder what he looked like. If a man was willing to pay this for an hour of her time, she feared there was something seriously wrong with him. Images of unattractive men flooded her brain. She shook her head to dislodge the unwelcome sight.

While she knew that she shouldn't have these men come to her house, she wanted to make sure that where they met she would have the utmost privacy. With the neighborhood being dead during the days, no one would be around to notice her having any visitors. Besides, with money being as tight as it was, there was no way she could afford a hotel room and something told her these men would expect her to pay for the room.

Remarkably, he arrived right on time. As soon as she opened the door, she was surprised to see an attractive man waiting for her.

Once inside, his eyes went directly to her breasts and erect nipples. It felt good to see a man appreciate her body once again. She started to relax a little and began to feel as if she may indeed enjoy this. After all, she'd always had a healthy sexual appetite.

As she led him to the bedroom, she felt herself getting wet just thinking about him ramming in and out of her. It felt good to have someone look at her as if they wanted to devour her. It had been a long time since she was the center of attention for a man, not counting those who watched her on the webcam.

Once in her bedroom, she pushed him onto the bed. Standing in front of him, she decided to play the dirty slut that he paid for and began to caress her breasts through the leather material.

As he looked at her with lust in his eyes, she fell into line with his fantasy and asked, "Do you like what you see?"

Nodding his head, he said, "You are even more beautiful in person. I love watching you play with yourself, Mistress."

She looked down to see that his erection bulged in his pants. "Do you want to have your way with me? Do you think you can handle a woman like me?"

Getting into the fantasy now, he asked, "Mistress, I am not sure I am worthy of you?"

She never felt as horny as she did right now. She got into the part, wanting him to believe that he received an absolute bargain. She found it alluring that her pleasure was entirely irrelevant. She could give all her attention to this man and his body. If he came too soon, then it was his dime not hers. She felt like a temptress right now.

Bree enjoyed her new role and wasn't ready for this to end. She pulled her skirt up to show him her bare, wet womanhood. "Do you like what you see, slave?"

She'd hoped that last night her husband would appreciate that she had a Brazilian wax, as normal, though, he climbed into bed and fell sound asleep.

She had even worn an exquisite nightie last night in hopes of catching Tom's attention. It was a rich emerald green satin with matching lace panties. Tom used to like it when she wore nighties to bed. He told her he liked the way it felt against his skin. Half of her nighties no longer had the matching panties because he was in such a hurry to get them off that he ripped them off.

As her client's eyes took in her smoothness, his fingers traced bare skin as he sent shivers of desire up and down her body. As his hands traveled to her womanhood, she slapped them away, "I did not give you permission to touch. Now you must be punished for being a bad boy."

It was the most enjoyable five hundred dollars she ever made in her life. As his lips touched her bare skin, there was no denying that this was not her husband. The scent of his aftershave was different from what Tom wore. He smelled of a potent mixture of excitement, allure and sensuality. She found herself intoxicated just from the smell of him.

As her hands ran up and down his body, she found no fault with his physique. His chest was well defined by hard muscles and his chiseled abs rippled under her touch. For the first time since she said "I do" to Tom, she contemplated having sex with another man.

Chapter 25

As Bree prepared for her next show, she adjusted the leather straps to the complicated outfit. She coated her lips with lipstick and combed her hair until it shined. Smiling into the mirror, she touched up her mascara.

She rolled on the thigh high stockings reveling in the way they felt against her skin. The black leather and silk stockings contrasted nicely against her skin. She looked damn hot today and would have the men begging for more.

There was always a rush of excitement as she started her show. She anxiously waited to see how many men wanted to see her. While she performed a slow strip tease, a list of perverse messages started to come in, detailing every fantasy.

The more you wore, the more you had to remove and that is what drove the men wild. She propped her leg up on the bed and slowly ran the whip up and down it. She could see the dollar signs as the men spent their hard earned money in the hopes of catching a glimpse of something more.

***

This woman was too pretty not to know it. She must be the kind of woman whose life was defined by her good looks. If he closed his eyes, he could imagine what she smelled like. It would be a purely seductive scent of sandalwood and golden opium. He had no doubt that her laugh would linger in a room long after she departed. It seemed almost unfair that one woman could be so well endowed with such good looks and a body that left men wanting more. Yet here she was in front of him, performing as if for no one but him.

He must know where she lived. More importantly, he must know if there was another man in her life when it should be just him. Clearly older than the twenty-something girls he watched, but he was drawn to her.

He watched the way her hips moved. How he wanted to feel those hips move in rhythm with his own thrusts. He wanted to tangle his hands in her lustrous hair. He could already feel the silky tendrils against his skin.

Her sweet smile played around her full lips. As she pleasured herself, he couldn't help but wonder if she was one of those women who only ate salads, or something equally as healthy. No, not her, she was the type of woman who gave into forbidden temptation.

He would make her his. He must patiently wait until they could meet in person, for now he had to share her.

When they met, their joining would be perfect. It would be the moment in which her life changed forever. Nothing would stand in his way from possessing all of her. She would be his. It was all a matter of timing. Timing was crucial; he couldn't be reckless. He must wait.

This woman was special. He could tell that she wasn't like the others he watched. When she performed, it was only for him. She knew that he was there watching her. Her eyes penetrated his very soul.

She felt his want, his need for her. His blood rushed through his body as excitement and anticipation washed over him.

Oh yes, she was very special to him. As he watched her, he felt her sexuality exude from her pores. She was a temptress, begging him to come taste her forbidden fruit. She was his destiny.

She must have sensed his lusting for her. She looked into the camera and parted her lips ever so slightly, as if begging for him to kiss her. He saw the desire for him etched clearly on her face. "Soon, my love, we will meet. I will be your everything, your whole world. I will make you mine."

Chapter 26

Monday morning, Bree took the cash she recently earned to the bank. For now, the mortgage was caught up. She was surprised when both men asked if they could have a standing date for the same day and time next month. Realizing that this was a chance for her to make next month's mortgage as well, she readily accepted.

At first Bree feared Tom would catch her, but her fears were unfounded. As usual, he never even called both times to check in on her. He never called or texted her during the day to see how she was. Lately, she was nothing more than a doormat for him.

Perhaps that was why she found work as a Dominatrix exciting. Men actually desired her, sought her out. This job awakened so many feelings in her, feelings that she thought died a long time ago.

This was a new journey for her, one that helped her find her true self once more. She was not just an unwanted housewife, but a desirable woman. These men, even though they were in cyberspace, helped her to realize that she had needs, secret needs that she wanted to fulfill.

The job turned out to be exciting. The possibilities were endless in what she could do. There were times when she wished she could talk to someone else about her new liberation, but she doubted her friends would see this job in the same light as her. Most of the women in her clique would be appalled at what she did. They would be even more appalled to learn that she thoroughly enjoyed herself.

At first it had been about the money, but now it was so much more.

As she waited her turn in line, Bree found herself watching the security monitor above the teller. She noticed how many people standing in line today looked grim. Towards the entrance doors, a man caught Bree's attention. He appeared to be filling out a deposit slip, but for a moment Bree swore that he looked directly at her, watching her every move. She shook her head, telling herself that she was being silly.

When it was her turn, she deposited the money and headed outside. Afterwards, she decided to do some window shopping. Before she knew it, the time was nearing two o'clock. When she opened her car door, the scorching heat of today had invaded the car's interior. It may be ninety-five degrees outside, but inside her car it was well over one hundred degrees. She turned the car air conditioner on high and blasted the heat out.

On the way home, she couldn't shake the feeling that someone was following her. No matter how many times she told herself that it was her imagination in overdrive, her gut instinct told her that a danger lurked in the shadows.

Chapter 27

Bree looked at the clock on the microwave and wondered if he would keep the standing appointment. She had not heard from him and was too nervous to send an email confirming the appointment.

From what she ascertained about her client, he made a fortune in the oilfield and broadened his investments to various types of energy. Normally, Blake Covington was in a good mood, but on several occasions she saw a slight temper and even some resistance. During their online sessions, he could turn on a dime and anything could set him off. She suspected he could be bipolar from the way he had his mood swings. As long as he kept his temper in check during their in person meetings, she saw no reason to stop his weekly dose of discipline.

If anyone asked her what she liked about the job, she would tell them with complete honesty that it was the power. She was one of the few women who would ever experience complete dominance over some influential men. However, she must also remember that while these men were obedient sex slaves in the bedroom, it didn't mean they were pushovers either. Most of them found their appointments with her helped to maintain control in other areas of their life. Abandoning their egos once in a while was a way to release the tensions of their day to day life.

This morning before her appointment, she sat down at the kitchen table with her laptop and paid various bills. Even though they were catching up on the delinquent ones, they still spent an exorbitant amount of money. The money disappeared just as fast as she made it. At the rate they spent money; she needed more clients to entertain if they would ever get everything paid.

She breathed a sigh of relief as the doorbell rang. When she opened the door, he simply stared at the beauty in front of him. She was dressed in black leather spike heeled boots and a tight black one piece latex dress that looked to have been poured on her. Various shiny metal chains were wrapped around her body. "Good evening, Mistress."

As he stepped inside the house, Bree smelled his aftershave, something spicy and dangerous – just like him. No sooner than they were in her bedroom did he ask, "May I touch you Mistress?"

"Not yet, assume the position." Cracking the whip in the air, she ordered him, "Face the wall."

"Yes Mistress." With his hands against the wall, he spread his arms and legs as if waiting to be frisked by the police. Bree took her time, starting with the firmly muscled arms and worked her way down.

"I see you didn't bring any toys with you today?"

"No Mistress." Looking deep into her eyes, he asked, "May I touch you now, Mistress?"

With the nod of her head, he pulled her to his chest, kissing her hard on the lips, lightly biting her tongue while slowly removing the latex dress. Once free of her confines, his hands explored her breasts, pinching her nipples.

"Slave, you will obey my orders. You will take me. I want it
to be long, slow and very thorough as you spread my legs
and fill me with your cock. I want you to ride me hard."

"As you wish, Mistress."

Bree unfastened his belt and pushed his slacks down to the
ground. As he pulled her closer to the bed, he expertly
stepped out of his slacks.

Once on the bed, his mouth slid down to her breasts, kissing
and licking first one then the other. She moaned in delight
as his warm mouth sent a mixture of sensations down her
body. Desire moved through her as shivers of anticipation
snaked down her body.

As soon as he flipped Bree over, she took advantage of her
new position. She trailed hot kisses all the way down to his
erection, reveling in the salty, sweet taste of him.

When he was unable to take the torture from her mouth,
he pulled her up to him. She straddled him and moved over
him, slowly at first. Once he was deep inside of her, they
found a steady rhythm. Thrust after thrust he went deeper
and harder.

She spread her legs wider so he could bury himself inside of
her. She felt the orgasm stirring deep inside, building with
each new thrust, "Don't stop," she ordered.

"As you wish, Mistress."

Chapter 28

He watched her house from the protection of his car. The beams of the sun ricocheted off the hood of the car, yet he kept watch intently. *I see you. Do you see me? Do you know that I am here, watching your every move? We are destined to be together.*

Sneering as rage filled him. She hugged this man with open arms, as if she were welcoming a lover.

He took a quick picture of the couple before the door closed. The two believed that their secrets were hidden in the confines of her house. There was no hiding from him, though. She would never be able to escape him.

His next few moves must be done with great deliberation and calculation. He knew for certain what she did in that house. He knew she was up to something when she cut back on the number of performances she did in a day.

She thought she had been careful keeping her daily activities hidden, but he knew what she did. If only she knew that he reveled in the time he watched her on the computer screen. He believed that she performed just for him and no one else.

Even now, being this close to her thrilled him. He had waited for her to check her P.O. box and then followed her home. So many times he considered knocking on her door, but the timing was never right and now this. Now she entertained men in her house and she never once extended the same offer to him.

He didn't understand why not though. He told her over and over that the very sight of her took his breath away, every single time. If only she would tell him that she loved him back, even if it was a fraction of the same love he felt for her.

It took extreme willpower not to rush into the house and throw the man off of her. He should be the one satisfying her, not this stranger whom she knew nothing about. How could she be so close, yet so far away?

This woman was perfect for him, the woman he had been waiting for. He wanted nothing more than to ravish her body. Every time he saw her, his eyes greedily took in every inch of her.

Why was she with this other man instead of him? That question kept playing over and over in his mind. It crippled him, crushing his confidence. Just knowing that another man's hands touched her body drove him crazy. He felt a deep seated hatred for the man and even her. How could she let another man touch her when it should be HIM pleasing her, bringing her to the brink of ecstasy?

The hatred was so pure that he wanted to make her pay for not loving him the same way she loved this man, this stranger. Soon, though, she would know of his love for her and how she wronged him.

His fingers gripped the steering wheel even tighter as he thought of this man on top of her, worshipping her body. His pulse quickened, hammering wildly in his chest.

Chapter 29

Bree looked over the costume one more time, wondering what this man's fantasy was.   The red cape draped over her shoulders, and the hood hung seductively over her head. The white cotton blouse was hard to button, revealing her luscious cleavage with the lacy white bra peeking through the fabric. The plaid skirt barely covered her bottom, and when she moved the white cotton undies were noticeable. The costume also came with baby doll socks and black Mary Jane's. As she looked in the mirror, she groaned. Not only did she feel foolish, but she looked it as well.

He arrived on time, dressed head to toe in black leather.

She no longer felt guilty about what she did. There was something so satisfying about this. These men reminded her that she was still desirable, even if her husband no longer touched her body. As she took his money, she reminded herself it was the only way to make ends meet. They had a mortgage to pay, and she had to put food on the table. Her husband tried his best, but the amount of money he brought in wasn't enough to cover all the bills.

She pushed her client onto the bed while she began to order him around. He admitted to her last time how he liked to be humiliated by her. Well, today she needed to release some stress, and she planned on doing just that.

As he waited patiently for her to make the first move, he watched her every move expectantly. His eyes traveled over her body as they feasted on her; she felt desire building inside of her.

She ordered, "On your knees slave!"

"Yes, Mistress."

She started by spanking him gently at first, but with each stroke of the leather strap the blow became a little harder. Once the whipping reached a feverish pace, his bottom showed several bright red welts.

He enjoyed turning his head so that he could get a good view of her whipping him. She reveled in watching as the muscles in his body tensed with each lashing. The whole time he succumbed to the spanking his face had a deadly serious look.

"Finish undressing for me, slave. I want to see your naked body."

Once undressed, she brought out the black leather collar and handcuffs. She placed the collar on her slave, making sure that it was tight but not overly tight. It satisfied her immensely to see his welt reddened bottom and collared neck.

After handcuffing him to the bed, she asked him, "Are you ready to please your Mistress or must you be punished more?"

"I'm ready to please you, Mistress."

While she started to undress, she teased him by giving him quick glimpses of her nipples, before unhooking her bra and letting it fall to the floor. Next, she teased him by pulling her panties down slowly over her hips. His breath caught when he saw that she was bare.

Bree could tell that he liked the Brazilian wax. Several of her clients preferred her this way. She read online that most men prefer women completely bare and that it heightened the sexual pleasure.

As she removed her panties, she turned around and made sure he got a full view of her from behind. She knew he liked what he saw because he let out a low moan. When she turned around, she saw that his eyes were taking her all in. She grew wet just from the way he looked at her.

She also noticed he had become very hard for her. That mere fact brought a smile to her face. With one of her hands, she curled her fingers around him and began to stroke him, teasing him.

She ran a finger slowly over his body and watched as goose bumps appeared on his skin from her touch. With her other hand, she continued to stroke him.   Without ever taking her eyes off his face, she maneuvered her body around.

She ordered him, "You are to watch me as I take you in my mouth."

He obeyed her, with his eyes wide as he watched her. He inhaled sharply as her tongue teased the head of him. As her lips slid over his swollen head, he moaned loudly.

She bobbed her head as she sucked him tightly. Her lips traveled up and down his shaft as her hand slid down to cup his balls. She gave them a gentle squeeze while she continued to torture him.

Up and down her mouth went, driving him closer to his climax. As his moans turned into groans, she knew that he was almost there. Her tongue teased his shaft as his muscles began to twitch. His hands tightened in her hair as he teetered on the edge. Just before he was about to cum she moved to his ball sack, gently sucking it.

He asked, "Mistress would you please turn around? I want you in front of my face." A bubble of pleasure moved through her body. She never expected one of her slaves to take her own pleasure into their consideration. She assumed it was all about them.

She quickly removed the handcuffs and straddled him to where her back was to him. Bending her knees, she lowered herself down to his face. His mouth hovered over her as his tongue teased her. She was completely exposed to his gaze and touch. She moaned against his cock as his tongue explored her intimately, lapping deep and then pulling back to nip at her.

His tongue and lips were everywhere at once, licking and sucking at her delicate flesh. She couldn't remember the last time she was this wet, the last time someone paid this much attention to her.

Using one of her hands for support, she moved the other hand to her breast, pinching and pulling on her nipple. Shards of pleasure slivered down her body as his tongue worked its magic. As his tongue made circles around her, she felt the orgasm rising up inside of her. Her breathing became ragged as the orgasm pushed through her like an exploding volcano.

As her client was leaving, he informed her, "Mistress, you are better than I ever imagined. If only you could give my wife lessons."

Bree tucked his comment in the back of her mind. Should she consider giving wives lessons? Then again, if she did, it might cut into her income, the income she desperately needed right now.

Chapter 30

He rubbed his hand over his crotch as an urgency hummed through him. Just watching her sent a rush of desire through his body.

The foolish woman never put away her laptop during the day. It was so easy to tap into the feed of her web camera. He could control it from his house whenever he wanted without her knowledge. Even better, she synced her phone to the laptop. Now he had access to her whenever he wanted. He knew what she did day in and day out.

****

As her latest client left the house, she heard her home phone ringing. She rushed to answer it, laughing to herself at how she spent a couple of tireless hours with this man and not once did her phone ring. Now with him gone, someone found it important to call her. She snatched at the phone wondering who might be calling her at home. Most of the people she knew called her on her cell phone. No one called the home phone anymore.

"Hello."   At first there was no response, when the laugh crackled over the line a shiver ran down her spine. The laugh was full of malice.

"Who is this? What do you want?"

"You are a dirty whore."

Before she could respond to the insult, the connection broke. Her hands shook as she hung up the phone. She looked over at caller ID but the number showed as "blocked". She dialed *69 only to hear a recording informing her that the callback service was unavailable for this number.

Fear began to fill her as she tried to steady her racing heartbeat. Who could have called her and why would they have called her a dirty whore? Who could possibly know what she was doing?

She didn't dare call 911. The last thing she needed was for police involvement. She sure didn't want anyone snooping around, especially with what went on in her house during the day. She could never let it be known how she made ends meet. She could lose everything she had.

This had to be nothing more than a prankster, some bored teenager dialing random numbers.

Chapter 31

As Bree looked over her private checking account, she was surprised to see just how much had been deposited into her account this last week. Lately, she had gathered quite a following of fans and her client list kept increasing. Several of her clients referred new customers; most were married men who wanted someone to perform acts that their wives would never even consider.

She had to pay some of the bills from her personal account so that Tom didn't ask where such a large deposit came from. The cash her clients paid her during the day was tucked safely away in a small safe at the bottom of their closet. She withdrew small amounts as needed, but even that sum was accumulating.

She never suspected that degrading men the way she did would pay so well. At times she felt guilty about what she did, but it was, after all, hard earned money; money that they desperately needed. Besides, these men brought fun and excitement back into her sex life, something that she had seriously been lacking lately.

So far, each man she encountered had his own unique kink or fetish and, thankfully, none of the men had been a psycho or a cop. However, there was something exciting about the risk factor involved too.

Most of the men she met on the website were kinky, unpredictable. She had a few normal callers, and those were usually referrals. She often wondered if these men knew about their friend's kinky side.

A few men wanted to play some strange submissive fantasies. She found it enjoying as the Dominatrix. There was something tantalizing about making a man crawl to her on her command, kissing her feet before being allowed to stand. Some of their role play fantasies bordered on ludicrous, particularly those who wanted to be called "daddy".

A few men fantasized that they were an extremely dominant man, being a little too extreme in their role play. She reminded each and every man that came through her doors to be mindful of any bruises they may leave on her body. Bruises were too hard to explain, especially if they were frequent and in some rather conspicuous spots.

She had come to love the exhibitionism of the website. She enjoyed showing off her body to excite strange men who were safely tucked in their own rooms. She could just imagine the pleasure showing on their faces as she controlled them. Each day she became a little bolder with her role. There was a control factor that she never even realized was there at first. Little by little she learned how to empower her own inner sexual liberation.

Her boss also noticed just how well Bree acclimated to her new job. She brought in more clientele than any of the other girls working for the company, although none of them met in person. He made sure she knew just how well he appreciated her by the bonuses he gave. He believed she was a true moneymaker who had the potential of going far with the company.

Currently, Bree had the longest running Dominatrix show on the website. Several of her customers could run up a couple of hundred dollars worth of charges in one afternoon, all in hopes of keeping her to themselves for as long as possible. These were the men she tended to focus on when they signed in.

Bree started to become dependent on the amount of money she earned in a single afternoon. Right now she earned more in one week than Tom did in a month working two jobs.

Before today's performance, she poured some oil into her palm and massaged it over her breasts and the rest of her body. The oil gave her skin a shiny appearance, and kept her skin feeling soft.

With *"Closer"* by Nine Inch Nails playing softly in the background, she let her robe drop to the ground as she showed off her goods to the anxiously waiting clients. She felt like such a sex goddess right now. Today she wore a black latex bra and matching thong. After all, it was all about presentation, even if the costume ended up on the floor in minutes.

Her eyes never once looked away from the laptop monitor. She wanted each of her clients to feel as if she were looking directly at their desperate, lonely faces.

She liked to tease the men, especially the new ones. Just by looking at the user names she could tell that she had ten new clients in this session.

"Are you ready to listen to your Mistress?" Looking into the computer monitor she ordered, "You WILL do what I tell you to do. No excuses." To show that she meant business, she let the whip move through the air.

She caught a glimpse of her breasts in the monitor. Her girls look especially good tonight. The oil she massaged on her skin gave it a luster that had the men drooling.

She didn't understand how two mammary glands could be such a motivator. Breasts could control a political leader, disrupt a man's thoughts, and even have a man willingly part with his hard earned money.

Once she removed her bra, she slid her hands down her body, catching them in the elastic of the thong. She inched the thong down her right hip in hopes of obtaining a few requests for private sessions. A few men had requested she perform certain moves in great detail, which meant more money for her. She had become detached from what she did; reminding herself this was just a job, a very well paying job.

Instead of removing her thong she shook her head, commanding the men, "I don't think you deserve any more viewings tonight. At least not now, you haven't shown me you are subservient just yet."

With that single move, the tips poured in. Yes, today may be very profitable.

Chapter 32

When she walked into the room, his blood heated up. His eyes were drawn to the heels she always wore. He wondered if she had a height complex. She couldn't be more than five feet six, but even with the heels she would barely reach his chin.

This woman took pride in her body. She was slim and fit for someone who had two children. Now, the children may be a problem, but one that he would remedy if needed. When the time was right, he wanted her all to himself.

He spent hours watching her, learning all that he could. He managed to access the camera in her phone and was no longer forced to watch her from the confines of her bedroom.

He watched as her head dropped back, and eyes closed as she began her performance. Her body pulsated to the rhythm of *"Anywhere"* by 112 softly playing in the background. This woman knew how to create the perfect setting for her performances. What would it be like to have her pleasing his body day in and day out? She would keep things interesting; there would be no dull moments with her.

As soon as he saw her, he knew he had to have her. He kept himself hidden, waiting for the perfect moment to move in.

His heart was pounding by the time she started to unhook her bra. This was his favorite part of the show. His breath caught as he imagined it was just the two of them, alone in her room. He never met a woman so relaxed and uninhibited, a woman so comfortable dominating a man.

This was his Bree; the sultry woman meant to tempt men with her body. Here, with him, she was not a wife or mother but a temptress. He didn't see her as a stylish urbanite or dutiful daughter.

He shifted in his seat as his manhood began to swell. What he wouldn't give to have her writhing under his body right now.

There would be no sleep for him tonight. Soon he had to satisfy this lust for her, or he would not get any rest. He took a deep breath in and swore that he could smell the exotic aroma of her scent. It would be very soon when they made love.

That was the only thought that kept him sane. She had become his whole world, his every thought. He was no longer satisfied with merely watching her.

Chapter 33

As Bree rolled off her latest customer, he exclaimed, "Damn, woman, you are amazing. That was by far the best sex I have ever had."

Bree lay next to him, gasping for air. Her body convulsed in spasms as she stared at the ceiling. Fireworks were still erupting between her legs. She never expected the sex to be like this, but this man knew how to use his hands. Was it the newness with this man that made it so exciting? The sensations he sent through her body were better than anything she had ever experienced. It was almost a shame to charge him, almost.

Over these last few months she had a number of slaves, but he was the first who made her see stars. She never had a man as obedient as this one. When he confessed that he wanted to be totally subservient, she had her reservations. She feared that he was one of those men who had no idea what he wanted. That was far from the truth with him. She knew better than to ask why the role play, but she had no arguments.

As he sat up, she took her role into overdrive. She pushed his chest down, "Did I say that you could sit up? You still have some time left, and I plan on putting it to good use."

He lay back down as she stared at his body once more. This man was the perfect male specimen; rock hard in all the right places. Even his manhood was perfectly shaped and made for pleasure. His very presence was enough to make a woman wet with desire.

She let her hands move over his body as her mouth brought him back to life. As it sprang forward, she climbed on top of him. She moved faster and faster as her hands moved up and down his body. She felt the muscles in his chiseled torso move under her fingertips. His hands slowly moved up and down her body before finding their way to her breasts. He tweaked her taut nipples in between his fingers.

She pulsated around his manhood as the fireworks built up inside of her once more. She let out a deep moan as the orgasm exploded deep inside of her. Whispering in his ear, "I am not done yet."

She turned around and leaned on his legs, riding him like a bucking bronco. He brought his hands up to her hips and helped her increase the speed. Just as she was getting into the role play, her alarm went off, letting them know that their session was almost up. Today she didn't have time to allow him any extra minutes. She needed to get cleaned up before her children arrived home.

They increased their speed until they were both breathless. With no time to spare, she informed him, "Go shower and leave through the back door."

He nodded in obedience.

As he left, she went into the bathroom to clean up. She had an hour to get the house back in order and finish preparing supper.

She stepped out of the shower and wrapped herself in one of the large terry towels. She made sure her feet were nice and dry before stepping across the cold marble tile. Before dressing, she rubbed her entire body down with a scented lotion that smelled of pure seduction.

Bree slipped on a blue and white chevron sundress and white espadrilles. Before leaving the bedroom, she looked around to make sure that she didn't leave any evidence behind from earlier today. Thanks to the candle she had burning, there was no smell of sex in the air. The last thing she needed was for Tom to come home and find any of her day job left behind.

What started out as just a way to make ends meet had become an addiction. She became addicted to the power she had over these men. It seemed surreal that just a few months ago they were in dire financial troubles, and now, thanks to her, their bills were caught up. It amazed her that Tom still had not asked her how she did it. He had no idea that she managed to build quite a nest egg for herself. It would be a long time before money should ever be a problem for her.

She wondered what her neighbors would think if they found out what went on in this pristine neighborhood. Since most of her neighbors were gone during the day, it allowed her to run her business with very few interruptions.

From the outside, her house and family were picture perfect. Even the inside of her house was immaculate. There was never anything out of place.

Not long after the children came home, so did Tom. As soon as he walked into the kitchen, he smiled over at her, "Supper smells good."

"I cooked your favorite. A nice beef roast, rice and gravy, green beans, and bread pudding for dessert."

Instead of giving her a kiss hello, he walked straight over to the bar and poured himself a whiskey on the rocks. She asked, "Could you please pour me a glass of red wine?"

He walked back into the kitchen with his drink and a nice sized glass of red wine for her. Over supper, Tom informed her, "We were invited to a dinner party at the Savoie's Friday night. Elizabeth asked if you could please bring a dessert."

"A night out sounds nice. It has been a while since they had a dinner party."

Nodding in agreement, he answered, "Elizabeth went back to work. Brad is always complaining that she has no time for him anymore. That is one of the reasons I was so adamant about you not going back to work."

Walking over and giving her husband a kiss, "I will always have time for you, my love."

Kissing her back, he said, "I was hoping that you could wear something nice. If we can afford it, I would like for you to buy something new."

"I believe I can manage something. Did you want something as well?"

"That would be fantastic, but I don't want you to splurge."

Bree planned on keeping her Friday schedule open. She planned to have a complete day of pampering and shopping. She wanted to leave Elizabeth Savoie drooling with envy. Since starting her side job, she managed to get her body in better shape; there wasn't an ounce of fat on her now. The last time she saw Elizabeth; she bragged about one of her job perks was a gym membership and discounts at the stores in the mall. What Elizabeth left out, but Brad made sure to tell Tom, was that she worked long hours for minimum wage. However, without another income, there was a chance they would lose the house. Brad worked for the same company as Tom and his hours were also cut back. Out of all their friends, Bree was the only one not forced into a minimum wage job. She wanted to see their eyes full of envy Friday night.

Come Friday night, Bree made sure Tom wasn't disappointed. Her hair and makeup were perfect. The dress molded her body to perfection, showing off her well defined curves.

While at the Savoies, she played the perfect wife. Her performance was flawless. No one there had an inkling of an idea of the voracious vixen she truly was. Even her husband didn't know of her secret identity. She'd canceled her appointments for today, so right now she had a sexual fire burning so hot she was surprised she wasn't smoking.

Chapter 34

He watched the computer monitor intently, never once letting his eyes stray. He grew impatient as he waited for her to start the show.

She became his whole life, his everything. His world revolved around her and her alone. There had been others over the years, but this one was different. She deserved his love and devotion. She was worthy of his time and attention.

He waited anxiously for her website to come on, his heart started to pound. The frustration of the long wait subsided. Just the sight of her mesmerizing blue eyes, filled with desire for him caused him to reposition himself in front of the computer.

If only he could be right there next to her. He desperately needed to be near her, to smell the very essence of her. Was she wearing the perfume he picked out especially for her? As soon as he smelled it in the department store he knew he had to have it for her. The scent was how he envisioned she would smell. Sultry, seductive and forbidden.

Just knowing something he purchased for her caressed her skin sent a rush of desire through him. He could picture her in his mind, putting the perfume on. Applying it between that delectable cleavage of hers, to all of her hot zones. He picked up the spare bottle he bought, spraying a fine mist around him and immediately hardened.

He watched as she caressed her body with her delicate hands. His breath caught in his throat as the excitement built inside of him. His fists tightened as the urge to reach out and caress her became overwhelming. He wasn't sure how much longer he could hold off before they joined bodies.

It still angered him when other men dared to touch that perfect body of hers, and he had yet to taste her sweetness. Although after a little digging into her life, he fully understood why she did it. It would be so easy to swoop in and save the day. Her husband was a poor excuse of a man. One who did not see that his wife's needs were met, or even brought home a sufficient amount of money to pay the bills.

When they did meet, it would be explosive. The anticipation was part of the excitement for him, though. His body tingled at just the thought of her body under his. He had to urge his body to relax as images of her pleasuring him rushed through his mind. Her soft flesh would create a friction of raging desire against his hard body. She would be on top, riding him feverishly. Her long auburn hair cascading down her shoulders in luscious waves. His hands would trace all of her womanly curves.

For now, he must be content with watching her. She still did not know of his existence, not until the time was perfect.

As she stared into the web camera, he felt her eyes on him. He felt her warmth penetrate his very soul. Her lips turned into a sultry smile, just for him. He stroked himself faster as his all consuming desire for her built.

He watched as the crescendo built in her own pace. They would find their sweet release at the same time. His eyes remained glued to her hand as it moved in and out of her body. His strokes matched her own feverish movements. At the same time, their moans shattered the silence of the room.

Chapter 35

As Tom left for work, he gave Bree a kiss goodbye that was so cold and disconnected. She tried to remember the last time he showed her any passion. Lately, all he thought about was work and their financial situation.

Her mind was already fantasizing about performing in front of the web camera and then her lunch time appointments. It had been three days since she had a sexual release, and she needed some satisfaction.

As she slipped her mask on, she slowly rubbed her fingers along her face. Strange how something as small as a mask gave her such a sexual charge. This mask freed her, liberated her. It allowed her to do things she never dreamed of.

As she clicked on her website and saw all the clients waiting for her, a rush of excitement flowed through her. She tingled with anticipation. Today all she would wear was her mask. No costumes, just her naked body in all its glory. She was anxious to see how well this drove up her numbers. Some men preferred the fantasies, while others preferred to see her naked. Most of her clients missed seeing her these last few days and were anxiously awaiting her. All the power she had over these men brought a smile to her face. If she played this right, she would make up the money she missed out on Friday, plus the money she spent shopping. This was more of a rush than drugs ever were. Even when she was younger she didn't get this kind of a rush from her sexual escapades.

These men saw her as more than just a housewife. They saw her as a desirable, sexy woman. It aroused her to no end.

***

He reached out and caressed the computer monitor. Sighing, he closed his eyes and imagined that she was sitting right here in front of him.

"My beautiful Bree soon you will be mine and mine alone."

How he loved these last few days, getting to know her so well. During those most intimate of times, he felt that anything was possible. Today he planned to slip a note underneath her door.   He was ready to take the next step in this affair of theirs.

Chapter 36

As Bree pulled away from the school, she suddenly stopped the car and slowly looked around in every direction. Lately, she couldn't shake the feeling that someone was lurking in the shadows, watching her every move.

The feeling swept over her body once more. Even though she saw nothing out of the ordinary, goose bumps popped up along her arms and legs. Pure unadulterated terror raced through her body. The feeling came out of nowhere.

She laughed at how silly she was acting. There was no one watching her every move. On the drive home, she paid attention to every car she passed. The feeling of terror continued to grow until she feared it would suffocate her.

Once home, the overwhelming sense that she was being watched remained. In the kitchen, while pouring a glass of water, she looked outside the window. The trees swayed gently in the light breeze. Even safe inside her house an unfamiliar shudder worked its way down her spine. She felt like a mouse caught in a trap, rushing to the back door, she checked to make sure that it was locked.

On trembling legs, she checked the rest of the doors. Taking a deep breath, she tried to steady her nerves. She was shaking from head to toe. It was an illogical fear, but one that she could not stop.

By the time she calmed her nerves, it was time to get ready for her show. She laughed at herself, feeling a little stupid that she allowed her imagination to get the best of her.

Just as her last client left, her cell phone rang. She jumped in fright; she was still shaken from the uneasy feeling from this morning.

"Hi Mom." Her voice still held a slight tremble, one that her mother picked up on immediately

"What's wrong? I can hear the anxiety in your voice. Are you and Tom fighting again? I told you that your dad and I will be glad to help you out."

Groaning to herself, she walked into the kitchen, "It's nothing Mom."

"I know something is wrong. I can hear it in your voice."

"Nothing is wrong. I am rushing to get supper started is all. Time somehow managed to get away from me today."

While listening to her mother go on about the events that took place that day, she opened a jar of spaghetti sauce and began to prepare supper. When her mother again asked her if she was okay, she replied, "I'm fine, Mom. Seriously, nothing is wrong."

There was no convincing her mom that she was fine. Turning the burner on medium heat, she started heating the sauce while taking the meatballs out of the freezer. While she put the water on to boil for the noodles, her mother continued to complain, "I don't understand why you just don't tell Tom how bad your financial situation is."

Sighing, she responded, "Mom, that was a while back. I told you; we are doing okay now. Besides, I don't want him to feel guilty. He works hard enough as it is."

Stirring the sauce with a long wooden handled spoon, she multi-tasked while talking to her mother. "It's just that you both should have worked on a plan together."

Bree regretted ever telling her mom about their financial problems. "Mom, it has all been resolved. We are fine; I promise."

Not wanting to continue listening to the never ending conversation about her marriage, family, and bills she tried to stop it before it could even get started. She still needed to shower before everyone walked in the door.

A thump from the living room made her jump up. Spaghetti sauce splashed out of the pan, sizzling on the burner. Placing the spoon down on the counter, she walked into the entryway and looked around. She saw nothing out of the ordinary. While her mom continued lecturing her over the phone, she pulled the phone away from her ear, listening more intently for noises. Hearing none, she brought the phone back to her ear and said, "Mom, I need to go. The kids will be home soon, and I still have to finish cooking supper."

Another noise, this time from her bedroom, caught her attention. She desperately tried to convince herself that it was nothing.

Checking the living room, it was no great surprise to find no one there. She decided to keep the hall light on, allowing it to illuminate every nook and cranny. Although, the presence of a light would do no good if she did have an intruder at least it made her feel safer.

She found nothing amiss in any of the other rooms, but could not bring herself to look under the bed or even rationalize looking in the closet. Even though nothing seemed out of place, and the only movement came from the ceiling fan, she couldn't shake the feeling that she was being watched.

She told herself that the noises she heard were nothing more than tree limbs hitting the windows. Still, an uneasy feeling clung to her, but nothing was out of place, missing or indicated that anyone was in the house. The doors were locked, and the windows secure.

Letting logic be her guide; she took a deep breath and put the noises out of her mind. Pouring herself a glass of wine, she lowered the heat on the stove and headed back upstairs to take a shower. Upstairs in the bedroom a sensation unfamiliar, but menacing, swept over her. The hair on her arms rose as an overwhelming, irrational fear washed over every sense of her being. Her heart skipped a beat as her breath caught.

She found herself frozen in place by instinct alone. There was no conscious thought to the act and time seemed to stop as if she was merely an observer in her own horror story. She could literally step outside of her body for a moment and watch the scene as it played out in front of her, unable to move or utter a word. She simply stood there and let time drag by. She became certain that danger was near, yet, she couldn't find it inside of her to move. Her senses told her that it emanated from one direction, in her room.

She could not find the courage inside of herself to turn around and run. That was perhaps the most frightening feeling of all. It threatened to suffocate her. As the seconds ticked by the fear became more palpable as her hands started to tremble. The trembling crawled up from her hands to her forearms, radiated down into her chest and then into her legs.

She feared that someone was in there waiting for her. When nothing happened, she shook off her irrational feelings and let out a sigh of relief. In the bathroom, Bree stood under the hot pulsating water washing away any remnants of her day. No sooner than she walked out of the shower she felt a hand cover her mouth. In a menacing whisper, he said, "Don't make a sound and I won't hurt you."

Terror paralyzed her. She feared that she was about to be raped, or worse murdered. She never once thought that a madman would dare enter the confines of her home. She caught a glimpse of him in the mirror. All she saw was a man dressed all in black with a black ski mask over his head.

Panic ripped through her body as her heart beat ferociously in her chest. She could have sworn all of the doors were locked, and wondered how he got in. She prayed that he was gone before her children came home.

She let out a soft whimper as he shoved her in front of him. As soon as she entered the bedroom, she saw the gym bag on the floor. How did she miss that earlier? This was worse than she imagined. He had planned this out. Peeking out from the bag, she saw a roll of duct tape.

Tonight, she would experience a new definition of violence. It would be filled with hatred, rage and jealousy all rolled into one. There would be nothing tender and loving about this experience. She hoped that it came to a quick end.

"Please, take whatever you want, just don't hurt me."

Pushing her down on the bed, the intruder pinned her hands down over her head as his body pressed her into the bed. His erection pressed into her. His touch made her feel dirty and unclean. His raspy voice confirmed her worst fears, "I plan on taking for free what you peddle right here in this house. You are a dirty whore, one who needs to be punished."

Begging, she said, "Please, my children will be home soon."

"Don't play your little games with me. I know what time your children will be home."

While sitting on top of her, he tore off a piece of duct tape and placed it over her mouth. As he bound her wrists and ankles to the bedposts, she struggled against him, kicking with all her might. Her struggles angered him. With the back of his hand, he slapped her hard against her face. Next he started moving his hands up and down her body. "I watched you fuck all those men. Does your husband know what you do while he is at work?"

The thought of someone watching her sent a chill down her spine. How did he know what she did inside of her house? How long had he watched her?

Bree furiously tried to loosen the constraints on her arms and legs, but it was impossible. The bindings were too tight.

"You will give me for free what those men have to pay for, and you know what? There is nothing you can do about it. I know that you won't call the police because they will ask questions. Questions you don't want to answer."

She felt his hot breath on her cheek and cringed at the feel of his lips on her face. She moved from side to side in hopes of bucking him off. As he laid himself between her legs, silent tears fell from her eyes. She forced her eyes closed; not wanting to watch what was about to happen to her. He grabbed her face, "You will watch my every move. I want you to see what I am doing to you."

Please dear Lord, let him finish soon. Bree concentrated on the rapid beat of her heart, staring at the ceiling. She tried to pretend that she was somewhere else, that the man on top of her was someone else.

In sheer desperation, she attempted to remove herself mentally from the reality of this moment. With each thrust, though, she was unable to fully escape into her mind.

She told herself that she had to try harder, that he would be done soon and gone from here. She prayed he did not kill her. She did not want her children to find her like this, murdered in their house.

As if sensing that she was retreating into her own fantasy, he furiously rammed into her. His fingers dug into her hips as he forced her body upward to meet his savage thrusts. As if talking to a lover, he voiced his needs, his desire for her.

Bree, however, lay beneath him silent, unmoving. He gripped her face painfully, "I want you to watch as I make love to you. I want it to be me that you see and not one of your lovers, you dirty whore."

She stared up at him through a mist of tears. She was determined not to cry, desperately trying to keep them from spilling in front of him. She despised him for what he was doing to her. No, despised wasn't the right word; she hated this man.

He looked deeply into her eyes, "I knew I had to have you at first sight. I wanted you more than any of the others."

She never wanted this from any man. No matter how many times he tried to convince her she deserved to be made love to this way, it was not lovemaking.

As he thrust inside of her, she held back a grimace. He smiled down at her as he thrust into her again and again. She choked back the tears as one of his hands gripped her breast hard. She saw the enjoyment in his eyes as he brought her pain.

"You know you love when I make love to you like this. This is what you have always wanted," he whispered in her ear.

He gripped her face and made her look up at him, "You will come to love me. Soon you will beg me to make love to you, cher."

As he continued to move inside of her faster and faster, she could tell he was close to his own release. His hands gripped her hair, forcing her to stare up at him. His breath was hot against her face as his sweat dripped onto her body.

"I want to hear you say you love me," he said as he ripped the tape away from her mouth.

She couldn't make herself say it though. Those three little words made her sick to her stomach. As he tightened his grip on hair, pain seared through Bree's scalp.

She forced out, "I love you," as he continued to grunt.

Kissing her fully on the lips, he said, "I love you too."

She could not believe how sick and twisted this man was. What was even scarier, he truly believed that they loved each other. In his mind, this was a relationship.

As he collapsed on her, "It is our destiny to be together. I will be back soon."

Once finished, he left as quietly as he appeared. She was grateful that he untied her before leaving.

She rushed into the bathroom, letting the hot water beat down on her from the shower. She scrubbed her body hard, until it turned red and tingled. Still, she kept scrubbing until her skin was raw. She dried her tears and did her best to reduce the puffiness around her eyes. The last thing she needed was her children to ask why she was crying. The man who raped her was right in his assumption that she wouldn't call the police. She didn't need them asking questions.

Later that night as she crawled into bed, her limbs were heavy as the day's stress caught up with her. All she wanted to do was fall fast asleep and forget this day ever existed.

As she closed her eyes, the masked man's eyes flashed in her mind. She felt his hands touching her, caressing her body. She heard him breathing in her ear as he forced himself inside of her.

His maniacal laughter radiated around her. Bree bolted upright in bed, her body drenched in sweat. She reached over and curled into Tom's sleeping body.

Chapter 37

As Bree dressed for today's appointment, her mind kept wandering back to the events of yesterday. She considered canceling all of her appointments, but realized that if she did she let that man win. She would not let that happen. She would not give into the fear he instilled in her mind. She would, however, do something that she had not done before - set her alarm as soon as her client was inside. If anyone opened a door or window, she would know instantly. She previously checked the system to confirm that it indeed worked.

That man may have called her a dirty whore, but he was wrong. She was simply a facilitator of needs and wants. She did nothing wrong. She slept well at night and made a lot of money doing what she did. Besides, these men PAID her to do what she did. She made their dreams come true, well technically their fantasies. If they didn't come to her, they would just seek out some other woman to make their sexual fantasies come true.

She didn't love these men. This was simply a business relationship. She gave them what they wanted for a price. She also made sure each and every one of her clients were extremely satisfied. So what if she was also satisfied in the bargain? It was a win-win situation for all involved.

Besides, she must be good at what she did since most of her clients were repeat customers. They also liked the fact that she was discreet. However, recently, she considered jotting down some of her escapades. Of course, changing the

names in order to publish a book. Some of her clients'
fantasies were so absurd that they would never be
repeated, while others were so hot that she was certain
people would pay good money just to read about those
exploits.

Bree looked in the mirror once more to make sure that the
costume the customer sent her was perfect. A chill crawled
up her body when she originally saw it, but on her it did
look seductive. Still, it bothered her that men fantasized
about women in young girl's clothes. Although, it was
better that he lived out his fantasies on an older woman
rather than seeking out the poor, unsuspecting young girls.

No sooner than she showed the man to her bedroom did he
have her pinned up against the wall. He pulled her face to
his, drawing her bottom lip into his mouth, biting the soft
flesh hard enough to draw blood. His tongue delved deep
inside of her mouth as he brought her body close to his.

Bree wrapped her arms around his neck as he kissed her
savagely. His hands slid up and down her body before
finding their way under her skirt. She wrapped her legs
around his hips, pushing herself against his throbbing
erection. His breathing was fast and labored against her
mouth.

With his free hand, he ripped open the blouse. Buttons
flew across the room and the lace bra she wore barely
contained her full breasts. Her rosy nipples were already
hard and begging to be touched. He pushed the top of her
bra down as he greedily took a taut nipple in his mouth. A
wave of pleasure washed over her at the feel of his lips on
her body.

She looked at his face as passion consumed him. He was fervid, feral in the throes of pleasure as a devilish smiled played across his face.

His need was so great that he entered her vigorously, but Bree cried out in pleasure. As his rhythm quickened, so did his breathing. He thrust into her faster and faster, pulling her body to meet each thrust. He only focused on his pleasure. With each frenzied thrust, he became harder and more demanding.

Bree let him possess her, dominate her. This was how he wanted to play out his fantasy; he wanted her to be the submissive. With him still deep inside of her, he laid her on the bed. "Turn around," he demanded.

Bree did as ordered. Once more he thrust deep inside of her, harder each time. He finally collapsed on her back; his breathing strained and ragged.

Chapter 38

Due to the thunderstorm that moved into the area Bree and her family were playing board games by candlelight. The electricity had been out for an hour, and as the thunder resonated through the house once more, there was no telling how long before it was restored.

She still couldn't get over how sitting right here at the table, they looked like the typical all American family. To everyone around her, she was the perfect mother and wife. She woke up every morning and cooked breakfast for her husband and kids. It was only after she sent her husband off to work and the kids off to school that she let her hair down.

While she waited for her turn, her mind wandered back to what happened earlier today. This afternoon was her first request for a ménage à trois. She had a request from two men who wanted to join in for an afternoon session. Truthfully, she figured it was the cost that made them want to share the appointment, but as long as they paid her she didn't care. Besides, it had been an enjoyable experience. She wouldn't turn them down if they asked for a repeat appointment. While this appointment had not been a request for a Dominatrix, something inside of her could not say no to it.

They tangled themselves in each other, and their sole purpose was to give each other pleasure. She showered attention on the men, keeping herself busy with their firm and throbbing parts that ached to be touched. She made sure to tease, worship and dominate each man equally.

As Bree picked up the game, she noticed an envelope on the ground near the front door. For a moment, she just stared at it before bending down to pick it up. When she turned it over her name, Mistress Azaria, was handwritten on the front in black ink. Her heart skipped a beat as she looked to see if any of her family members were watching.

She slipped a finger under the sealed edge to open the envelope. Her breath caught as she stared at the folded piece of paper. Her heart was pounding in her chest. She was almost too afraid to read the letter.

Slowly, she unfolded it. "Mistress Azaria, I just wanted to let you know that I was thinking of you. How I wish it was me worshipping your body right now."

Bree shoved the letter in her pocket as a bolt of fear pierced her body. Time suddenly stopped. Tears threatened to spill as she tried to compose herself. The note left her feeling hollow and empty inside. Who could have sent this?

So far all of her clients had kept their correspondence with her strictly via her private email. Which one of these men would have the audacity to send a love letter straight to her house? Since there was no postage, she knew that it was hand delivered. It infuriated her that someone would come up to her house while her family was home.

Yet, none of her clients acted as if she was anything more than a vessel to play out their fantasies on. None of them pledged their undying love to her. They were each looking for the same thing as her, a release and nothing more.

Then a frightening thought entered her mind. Could she have an admirer who found out where she lived? She tried to be careful of just who she gave her address to. She was selective with her clientele. If any of them gave her the creeps, she quickly turned down their offer to meet. But then again, she never knew what sinister motives lurked behind any of the men she welcomed into her house.

Could this admirer be the same person who was calling her? A chill of fear snaked down her body at that very thought. What if it was the man who raped her? She had just started to relax, but perhaps he was still watching her, waiting for another opportune moment to strike.

As various thoughts entered her mind, Bree knew that was, once again, she could not go to the police. This man knew her hands were tied. Her back was against the wall, and she didn't like it at all. She refused to allow some man to come in and threaten not only her but her family.

This note was nothing more than a coward's attempt to frighten her. She refused to allow some deranged admirer to throw her off balance. As she willed her racing heart to calm down, she convinced herself that the note meant nothing at all.

Chapter 39

Bree rushed through the house this morning, trying to get everyone where they needed to be on time. She slept later than anticipated this morning and regretted staying up so late now. While Tom slept, she emailed several clients back and forth as well as researched a few new positions. Now she was paying for her late night.

With a coffee mug in one hand and keys in the other, she wedged her feet in her shoes as she called out, "Get a move on Gracie and Jonathan! You are going to be late for school."

The aroma of fresh blueberry muffins still filled the kitchen as she scooped up her purse and yanked open the door. The humidity of the day slapped her full force as she walked out to her car. The air was thick and sticky. Thankfully, she would be in the cold air conditioned house for the better part of the day.

She clicked the remote to her Range Rover as coffee sloshed in her cup. If the kids didn't hurry up, she would waste even more time by going inside the school to sign them in. All around her everyone rushed to get to where they were going.

The neighbor right across the street from her rushed to put out her green recycling bin. Her heels clicked angrily against the cement as she cursed her husband yet again about his forgetfulness. To her right, Neil Chaisson juggled his coffee cup and briefcase as he unlocked his Mercedes CLS 550.

As always, everything around her was painfully predictable. Which was how she liked it.

As she opened the car door, she saw the note tucked under her windshield wipers. Her name was written in black on the rich, ivory linen envelope. Tearing open the envelope, she pulled out the card.

> *My Love, you are always on my mind. You are my whole world.*

The unexpected endearment sent a rush of excitement flowing through Bree. Time stopped for her as love swelled deep inside of her heart. She couldn't remember the last time Tom wrote her a love note. Lately, she worried that he was falling out of love with her. She held the note close to her heart and smiled. She planned to wear something especially for him tonight and show him that she loved him even more now than when they were first married.

She traced a thumb over the note as she waited for the children. The note touched her in ways she couldn't explain. It was simple, endearing, heartfelt and so unlike Tom. Was he trying to rekindle the passion?

Once the children were buckled and ready, she backed out of her driveway. On the drive to school, she noticed the For Sale signs adorning the houses in the neighborhood. All around them, their neighbors had felt the impact of the economy. It surprised her that she stayed as busy as she did. Most of these men must tuck away as much money as they could in order to pay for her services.

On her way back home, a nagging fear entered her mind. What if Tom didn't send the note? What if her secret admirer sent the note?

She scolded herself, the note had to be from Tom. She refused to allow her mind to even contemplate that the note came from someone other than him. Besides, this time it was addressed to My Darling Bree and not Mistress Azaria.

When Bree returned home, a long, white flower box lay by her front door. It was wrapped with a thick red ribbon. It had been a long time since Tom had sent her flowers.

As she bent down to pick up the box, she gingerly caressed the box. A shiver of fear ran down Bree's spine as her phone rang. "Hello."

"My dearest Bree, did you receive the flowers yet?"

Gripping the phone, she asked, "What do you want with me? Why are you doing this?"

"Cher, I just wanted to call and tell you that I love you. The flowers are to show you that I am thinking of you and care more for you than your husband ever will. When was the last time he sent you flowers?" A moment of silence had passed before he spoke once again, "Or a love note?"

Taking in a deep breath to calm her jangled nerves, she exclaimed, "Leave me the hell alone!"

Without bothering to open the package, she dropped it along with the note in the outside trash can. Then she went inside and gathered all the trash from the house so that she could bury the package.

Chapter 40

As Brad Savoie weaved his car through the traffic, his mind wandered back to his delectable neighbor. Even though the woman wore a mask on the website, he was fairly certain she was Bree LeFleur.

Even before Elizabeth took the new job, she had lost complete interest in sex. He was never into self gratification, but he had a severe case of blue balls and needed some relief. While he watched the lady in the mask perform, he found his release.

As if sensing what he was doing, she sent him a private message explaining that she did have certain clients she entertained in her home. He considered the tempting offer.

If she was half as good as she was with pleasing herself on the computer, then it was sure to be a mind blowing experience. He could just imagine how sweet her warm body would taste. He could feel those full breasts resting heavy in his hands and her warm folds closing in on his hardened manhood. Just the thought of her body convulsing around him sent a shiver through his body as his pants pulled tightly against the growing bulge. As desire coursed through his body, his manhood jumped to life.

He needed to rekindle the excitement that had once been between him and Elizabeth. When they first met they couldn't keep their hands off of each other, now he was lucky if they had sex once a month and forget about a blow job. He couldn't remember the last time his wife was even interested in sex. After he begged and pleaded for it, she showed as much enthusiasm as a root canal. Their lovemaking had become stagnant. They always made love in the same position, and he initiated it. Elizabeth never took any initiative in their marriage.

It wasn't that he didn't love Elizabeth. He loved her very much, and he still desired her, but the feeling seemed to be unreciprocated lately.

***

At first it surprised Bree to have a man send her a request for blow jobs being part of the services provided that she almost turned him down outright. Then the longer she thought about it, the more she realized that the email probably came from a desperate husband who wasn't getting what he needed from his wife.

She responded back, including the price for her services. An hour later he accepted the price and date. As she penciled him into her calendar, she realized that this week was full. She had been quite busy lately. She almost dreaded spring break this year. There was a chance that missing an entire week could cause some of her regulars to search for another woman. She would hate to lose a client, plus she might lose out on any new customers. Worse, she would miss out on earning money during that time.

Bree found herself anxious to see what her latest client looked like. Most of the desperate husbands that she saw were balding men whose middle was growing as fast as they were losing their hair. When she answered the door, she was shocked to see Brad Savoie at her door. She stared at him dumbfounded for a moment. She needed to get him out of here fast, before her appointment arrived. "Brad, I am sorry, but Tom isn't home."

As Brad made his way inside, he stated, "I kind of figured that. I suspected that it was you I was watching the night of the party. I take it Tom doesn't know about your day job?"

Bree looked at him, surprise clearly showing in her eyes, "You're my next appointment? You saw me on the website?"

"I have watched your little show now for several weeks. I don't guess I have to worry about discretion?"

Bree quickly said, "Your secret will be safe with me. You have to promise not to tell anyone about this. Tom can never find out."

"Ha, if either of our spouses found out I have a feeling that it would be the end of our very lives."

As he followed Bree into her room, he noticed just how beautiful she was. In all honesty, beautiful didn't even do this woman justice. This woman exuded sex from her very pores. The web camera did her no justice whatsoever.

Today she applied a dark makeup around her eyes, giving her a sultry appearance. Her lips were painted cherry red and the bustier that she wore pushed up her voluptuous breasts.

Once in the bedroom, she purred seductively, letting her eyes rest on his groin area, "Well then, honey, I think that we should get down to business. I am anxious to get better acquainted with you."

As Bree pushed him down on the bed, his manhood gave an excited lurch. He wanted her lips on him, hungrily devouring him. As she performed a striptease for him, he greedily took in her taut, rosy nipples, and full breasts. As she moved in closer to him, the musky, female odor of her mingling with her sensual perfume set his senses on overload. As her very essence permeated his nostrils, he was maddened with desire for this woman.

She slowly unzipped his pants and pulled his engorged member into her hands. Electrical shock waves shot through his body as she touched him. He was silky smooth and scalding hot with need. She placed a soft kiss on the tip of his shaft as she stared into his eyes.

Beforehand, he gave detailed instructions in his email of exactly what he wanted. So she began to play out his fantasy. She traced her fingers lightly over the head as she placed protection on him with expert ease. She slowly slid her hand up and down the same path her tongue just took.

After torturing and teasing him several minutes with her tongue, she took his manhood into her mouth. He tangled his hands in her hair, and she allowed him to control her movements.

"Woman, you have a way with your mouth."

Smiling up at him, she said, "But I am not through with you yet. I want to make sure that you get your money's worth."

Gripping his manhood in her hand, she stroked him while she nibbled on his chest. She kept her movements slow and steady as she kissed every inch.

He pulled her up to him, smashing his lips down on hers as their tongues danced seductively with each other. Bree's hands expertly ran up and down his body, teasing all of his most sensitive areas. Flipping her over, he molded her body to his as he ground his pelvis down into her.

"Oh yeah baby," she moaned, snaking her legs on either side of him. He rode her with long, savage strokes as she returned thrust for thrust.

***

Brad found himself consumed by uncontrollable flames of passion. As passion and lust converged, they found their release.

Afterwards, guilt started to plague Brad. Sex had never been like this with Elizabeth. With Bree, he felt a raw power of masculinity.

***

He stared into the computer monitor with a deep scowl on his face. The dirty whore was screwing another man. This man was new, and the slut WAS enjoying it! As he listened in on the conversation, he became disgusted. She didn't even bother with playing the role of a Dominatrix, but that of a common trollop.

What would her husband do if he knew just how dirty she was? Would he be so forgiving? No, he doubted her good husband would appreciate the fact that she spread her legs for these men. Even he didn't know if he could forgive her betrayal this time.

As he continued to watch the couple, he found himself running his hand up and down his erection. He should turn away, but he couldn't. Instead, he imagined that it was him thrusting deep inside of her.

As he watched the man leave, he knew to give her several minutes before making the call.

"Hello."

"Did you enjoy screwing that man? You sure looked like you enjoyed it, you dirty whore."

He envisioned the color drain from the slut's face. She knew that he was watching her, "Where the hell are you hiding, you son of a bitch?"

Laughing as he responded, "I wonder what your husband would think of your extracurricular activities?" Just the thought of these men touching her delectable body burned an acid hole in the middle of his chest. He wanted to hurt her the way he hurt.

***

For a moment, there was nothing but silence as she tried to place the voice. "Would your husband like the fact that you taunt these men with your body for money?"

Bree dropped the phone as desperation set in; this one man could destroy her whole life, her marriage. A dead weight settled deep inside of her. He hung up the phone knowing that he had rattled her cage. Perhaps he scared her enough to where she would stop spreading her legs for these men.

As Bree looked down at the cell phone, she fought off the nausea that worked its way up her throat. She fought back the terror that threatened to shatter her body. Her family, or even her friends, could never find out how she made ends meet. She would not only lose her husband, but the respect of her children.

As she walked into the bathroom, she wondered how the mystery caller knew when someone was at her house. Was he sitting outside of her front door right now watching her every move?

Chapter 41

Elizabeth couldn't believe that she lost her temper with Brad once again. Lately, he had been utterly complacent in his indifference to her feelings. What was worse, she sounded like a whiny, ill-tempered wife.

If only Brad would talk to her instead of pretending nothing was wrong. His façade irked her more than anything and added to the ever growing resentment she felt for him.

As she made her way home, she told herself not to allow thoughts of him ruin her evening. It had been a while since she arrived home at a decent hour. She tried to call Brad to find out if he had any plans, but his phone went straight to voicemail.

As she walked out the door, Candace called to ask her if she wanted to get together for drinks. Rather than go out, Elizabeth asked her best friend if they could fix drinks at the house and talk. Right now, Elizabeth needed someone to listen to her.

With Candace, she could talk about her innermost thoughts and feelings and not be judged. As Elizabeth pulled into the drive, she was surprised to see Brad's BMW there. Walking into the house, she called out, "Honey, I'm home."

Brad walked out of their upstairs bedroom, surprised to see her home so early. As Elizabeth walked up to give him a perfunctory kiss, she could swear that he had just showered. "I tried to call and let you know that I was coming home early, but it went straight to voicemail."

"Oh, I was probably in the shower. I am meeting Andy for a drink tonight, but since you are home I can cancel if you like."

She smiled up at him and said, "If you want. Candace is on her way over if Andy wants to come over for a drink."

***

"I'll call him and see." As Brad called Andy, he knew that he had to do some fast talking. Andy would have no problems covering his back, especially if it involved a chance to talk to Candace. He had the hots for her and was looking for an opportunity to get some time alone with her. This could be his one good chance.

Just seeing Elizabeth had him writhing in guilt. As good as the sex had been with Bree, it could never happen again. The guilt was too much to handle. Instead of being with another woman, he should spend time paying attention to his wife in an attempt to win her love back.

He wanted to sweep her into his arms, and apologize for what he did. As he watched her, he had forgotten just how beautiful she was. Her dark hair framed her delicate face in cascading waves. As usual, she wore only a hint of makeup. Her lips were full and painted a shade of coral that stood out against the deep dark tan of her skin.

As luscious as he found her lips, her eyes were what drew him to her. They were a rich chocolate brown with the faintest of gold flecks in them. He had no desire to see those eyes filled with tears if he would confess his infidelity.

No, instead, he wanted to see her eyes once again filled with love for him, a love that was undeniable.

He would punish himself every day for his sins before he filled his wife's eyes with hatred for him. He refused to break her precious heart. He would spend the rest of his life making up for the wrongs he did.

Chapter 42

As Bree prepared breakfast, Tom called out from the room, "Honey, have you seen my tan golf shirt?"

Sighing, she replied, "It should be hanging in the closet with your other shirts."

Peeking his head down the hall, he asked, "Can you find it for me, please? I am already running behind this morning."

As Bree walked into the massive master bedroom closet, she had to bite her tongue. There, with his other shirts, was the golf shirt that he was looking for. As usual, he probably didn't even bother to look for it.

She arranged it on the bed along with his golf pants, socks, and shoes. She then walked into the bathroom and laid a pair of boxer briefs on the counter for him. From the shower, he told her, "Thanks babe. I don't know what I would do without you."

Rolling her eyes, she asked, "Did you want me to fix you a late lunch?"

"Nah, that's okay. I will grab a bite to eat at the clubhouse with the guys. It will be late by the time I get home."

As Bree walked downstairs, she heard the kids in the kitchen eating their breakfast. Both informed her last night that they had plans for today. Her daughter, Gracie, asked, "Mom, Brandi called and asked if I can spend the night."

"If it is okay with her parents, then it is fine by me."

Her son, Jonathan, said, "Lee's mom said that we can stay over there tonight instead of going to the movies. Is that cool with you?"

"That's fine with me. I will call and see if Lee's mom wants me to bring anything for y'all to snack on."

Smiling, he replied, "Pizza would be great."

Reaching into her purse, she handed him some money, "Why don't you guys just order what you want instead of me trying to get the order right."

Stuffing the money in his pocket, he gave her a kiss on the cheek, "You are the best mom."

Gracie held out her hand, "If you are handing out cash, can I have some too?"

Reaching into her wallet, Bree gave her daughter some money, as well. It had been a while since she had a Saturday all to herself. This was a new experience for her, but one that she planned to enjoy.

After everyone had left, Bree finished loading the dishwasher with the breakfast dishes. As she applied some lotion to her hands, she contemplated what she would do for the day.

Settling in on the couch, she flipped through the television channels. As usual, there were more than one hundred channels and nothing on.

When the telephone rang, she let out a low groan. After their latest fight with debt collectors, she now feared hearing a phone ringing. Thankfully, all of their bills were caught up; actually most were paid in full.

Hitting mute on the remote control, she went to answer the phone. When she saw "Blocked" on the caller id, she considered letting it go to the answering machine. Curious, though, she answered "Hello."

"Hello, my Dearest Bree. Did you get my note?"

A shiver ran through Bree as she asked, "Who is this?"

Bree tried to place the man's voice, but the deep baritone voice didn't sound familiar at all. Perhaps if she could get him to talk a little more she may be able to place it. The only problem was most of her clients did little talking, just moaning and groaning.

"I am the man of your dreams, but you, cher, are still being a dirty little whore."

Bree's blood ran cold as the man talked. This man was some kind of nut job. His voice didn't sound familiar at all. Was he, perhaps, one of her regulars from the website? Could that be why he called her a dirty whore? Yet, he knew where she lived, and worse, he had their private number.

"Have we met?"

He quickly told her, "Soon, we will meet. I thought, perhaps, today since your family is gone."

Rushing to the window, she looked out to see if any strange cars were in front of the house. "Just how in the hell do you know my family is gone," she asked.

"Cher, I know everything about you. I know that you bring men into your house and pleasure them while your husband is at work. You pleasure yourself for men on your website. You have no secrets from me, cher."

"Brad... Brad, is this you?"

Angrily, he yelled, "No! I am not one of the men you please behind your husband's back. I am the lover who longs to worship your body, the one who will whisper sweet nothings in your ear, and the one who will fulfill your every fantasy. When the time is right, I will reveal my identity but until then I want you to know that I am watching you. Enjoy your day alone cher. Soon we will be together."

Before Bree could respond, the caller hung up. Who in the hell was this man? For a moment, she thought perhaps it was Brad since he knew that she was by herself. Yet the voice didn't sound like him. Plus, he was golfing with Tom. He wouldn't take time away from his golf game to call her. Besides, she hadn't even heard from him since their first time together. Bree suspected that the guilt of what they did was getting to him. More than likely, she would never hear from him again. Tom mentioned in passing that Brad informed him his relationship with Elizabeth was back to the way it was when they were first married.

Hitting the mute button once again on the remote, she resumed watching television. However, her mind kept wandering back to the phone call. Just who was the man calling her and sending her love notes? Was it the same man who raped her?

Chapter 43

Lisa Chaisson had lived in this subdivision since it was built ten years ago. Her husband immediately fell in love with their house, but Lisa didn't feel comfortable moving to such an affluent place. But as crime increased in Campton, she was glad that they had purchased a house here. So far nothing had happened, which was why she was surprised to see all the traffic that came and went over at her next door neighbor's house.

If the doctor hadn't ordered her to take it easy, she would still be at work. However, carrying twins caused more of a strain on her body than they previously thought. Thankfully, Shelly was a competent person and Lisa was comfortable leaving the shop in her capable hands.

She owned the local bookstore for about seven years now and recently added a coffee shop to it. It turned out to be one of the best decisions she could have made. It not only brought in an entirely new crowd, but the local book clubs started using her business to conduct their meetings. It was a win-win situation for all of them. The book club members may not shell out a lot of money for books, as most of them used their eReaders, but they spent money on coffee and pastries while they discussed the latest book they were reading. She also kept a current schedule of what each club read. She found that more and more of her patrons would purchase that very book.

It also helped that the shop was centrally located in downtown Campton. Not only was business good, but she caught tidbits of information that went on around town. Which was why she was curious about the traffic at the LeFleur's house. She heard whispers about how the bank was ready to foreclose on their house and that they were past due on most of their bills. At first, Lisa had dismissed the rumors. This town was known to embellish gossip, but now she couldn't help but wonder. The news constantly reported how houses in nice, ordinary neighborhoods were being raided for drugs. There were even reports of houses exploding from meth labs. Thankfully, that hadn't happened in this neighborhood, but with the amount of traffic going in and out she found herself speculating if they indeed were dealing drugs there at the house.

Neil, her husband, told her to turn a blind eye, but when cars started driving by at all hours he began to complain. He kept mumbling something about a decrease in property values if a drug ring was busted here. It aggravated her that now he was worried, but only when it bothered him.

Well, that was okay. Bored out of her mind, she started writing down license plates. If he really wanted to pursue this, then she would give him all the ammunition he needed.

Even if it wasn't drugs, something odd was going on at that house. Several of the cars were frequent visitors. Oddly enough, several came on the same day of the week and at the same time, almost as if for an appointment. Plus, they tended to stay at the house for an hour, and the least amount of time was thirty minutes. Whatever went on over there, it only took place during the day. Other than the stray car Neil noticed, the activity did not take place at night.

Chapter 44

Anger swept through him when he saw Ben Taylor, the man who raped the love of his life. Stepping from the shadows, he informed him, "I've been waiting for you to come home." In a harsh voice, he stated, "I came to teach you a lesson. It is not nice to take things that don't belong to you."

Holding up his hands in defense, Ben Taylor pleaded, "Hey, mon ami, you have the wrong guy. I haven't stolen anything."

Fury blinded his vision for a moment, "You broke into her house and took her body without asking."

"Mon ami, those women are nothing but sluts. Why should I pay for something they give out willingly?"

He clenched his fist tight, reared back and punched him squarely in the jaw. "She didn't want to give it to you willingly, you bastard. I came here to stop you from hurting her ever again."

If only this man could endure a slow and painful death, but he couldn't take the chance of a neighbor hearing his screams.

Ben watched in macabre horror as the killer raised the knife blade to his throat. A chill snaked down his spine. He remained frozen in fear as the knife sliced through his throat. He was dead before he even hit the floor.

He watched as the blood pooled on the floor. He had no pity or second thoughts about what he did. This guy deserved this. He saved the town some money by executing him. He would no longer rape another woman. Ashes to ashes, dust to dust – this man's life cycle was complete.

***

Insomnia had become Bree's pernicious bedfellow who released her from its cruel embrace reluctantly after hours of tireless taunting. Just as she hovered on the cusp of slumber and slipping into sleep's warm embrace; the jarring ring of the telephone snatched her back to consciousness. She looked to see if Tom would answer it, but, of course, he was sound asleep. For a moment, she considered ignoring the ringing telephone, but feared a call this early in the morning meant something happened to one of their parents.

"Hello." There was nothing but silence. She repeated, "Hello."

A chill washed over her body when she heard a voice. It spoke with an unmistakable malice that crackled through the wires. "I did you a favor, cher. I am sorry that I was unable to protect you beforehand, but he will no longer harm you."

With fear in her voice, she asked, "Who is this? Who is there? Hello!"

Instead of waiting for her to answer, the connection went dead. Bree looked down at her phone.

What did the caller mean by the man would no longer harm her? Did someone possibly know about the rape?

She wished she could curl up in Tom's embrace. He could never know about the phone call or the rape, though. He would insist that she call the police, and she could never let that happen.

Chapter 45

No sooner than Lisa walked into her shop that morning did Joshua Guidry walk in. It took all that she had to hold back a groan. "Good Morning, Mr. Guidry."

"Mrs. Chaisson, while you were away your store put this book up for sale!" He slammed down a copy of the newest book that the book club was reading, "This book is the epitome of blasphemy, and you are encouraging the good people of this town to read it!"

Letting out a soft sigh, she explained, "Mr. Guidry, this is a free country and there is such a thing as freedom of speech."

"This... This smut should never have even been allowed to be published. It encourages the vilest of sins."

"Mr. Guidry, this is a work of fiction. It is a novel, which means that it is a made up story. The author did not intend for it to be read like an instruction manual."

Huffing he continued, "It encourages our young people to commit a sin against their God. It encourages young men and women to... to... to fornicate out of wedlock!"

Lisa bit her tongue to keep from speaking her mind. She knew Joshua Guidry long enough to know that there would be no reasoning with him. "Mr. Guidry, I promise you that none of the staff here will encourage our youngest of readers to pick up this book." Opening the book to the contents page, she pointed out, "The author has even written that this book is intended for mature audiences only."

"Well, I will be watching this store closely to make sure that no young children purchase or even look at this book. If you refuse to pull it off the shelves, then I shall ensure that it is not sold to any of the good-natured citizens of Campton."

"Mr. Guidry, while I appreciate your stand, I cannot allow you to stay in my store and harass my customers. If that is your intent, I am putting you on notice that the police will be called."

"Young lady, if I have to stand outside of your door and let every customer entering know that books are sold here which taint young impressionable minds, then so be it."

As Lisa escorted Joshua Guidry out of her store, she warned him, "Mr. Guidry, if you feel that you must do this, please make sure that you do it off of my property, or I shall have you arrested for disturbing the peace."

Without another word, Joshua Guidry huffed away. Unfortunately, she had not heard the last of him and more than likely he and his church group would picket the store in a few hours. Let them picket. While he believed that they were warning the good citizens of the evil books that she sold here, it would actually backfire on him. It would have people flocking to the store to find out just what sort of book would cause such a stir. It may even increase their book sales better than she could ever hope.

As he stormed off Neil stopped by the store, "I came to see if you wanted me to bring you home, but I see you already had some problems this morning."

"Joshua was just informing me how vile the latest book on display is." Suppressing a giggle, she added, "It even encourages young people to fornicate out of wedlock."

Shaking his head, Neil stated, "I warned him that if I have to call the police one more time, I will press charges."

Sipping her Italian Soda, she said, "It won't do any good. I swear that man lives to cause hate and discontent."

Neil nodded his head, "He has to bring drama in all aspects of his life. It's not just us, but other businesses as well."

Lisa agreed, "You may be right. He is so unhappy in his life that he has to make everyone else miserable, as well. If he had a woman in his life, he would probably be a lot more pleasant."

"Good luck with that one. Most women here know what he is like and stay far from him. But with a town as big as Campton surely he can find a woman for him."

Neil shook his head, "Campton may be big, but not big enough. He probably has to go looking for women online."

Lisa reached into her purse and handed Neil a piece of paper. "What is this," he asked.

"I have been keeping a log of the cars that come and go at Tom and Bree LeFleurs' residence. You should look at the list. I believe something is going on there. It may be time for you to make some calls."

Neil looked over the list, surprised by what he saw, "Most of these people seem to have a specific time slot. Are you sure you have the times right? They are there a little too long for just a drug pick up."

Nodding her head, she said, "That's what I thought as well."

Chapter 46

Detective LeDoux heard the buzz of his alarm clock and groaned. He was tempted to hit the snooze button just once. He ran his deeply calloused hands down his unshaven face, trying to wipe away the sleep from his tired body. Letting out a deep sigh, he forced himself to get out of bed. It's five a.m. and if he wanted to get his run in before the heat and humidity was too bad he better get going.

Stumbling to the bathroom, he caught a glimpse of his image in the mirror. Until now he never noticed how much he was aging. He turned forty-two this year. Where had the time gone?

There were a few more gray hairs showing and even the beginnings of crow's feet around his eyes. He always heard that men age gracefully and completely disagreed with that statement. If only he looked as young as he felt.

At eighteen, he enlisted in the Marine Corp. After four years, though, he had enough and was ready to return home. His dad talked him into applying to the police department. With his background, law enforcement seemed to be a natural decision. He moved up in rank quickly, exceeding everyone's expectations and never looked back.

As soon as he stepped outside for his run, the mugginess of the morning hit him full force. It was going to be a hot day. He put on his earphones and turned up the music, needing a distraction from the case.

The run helped to wake him up. By the time he made it back home, he was drenched in sweat. He jumped in a warm shower before getting ready for work.

Once dressed, he took the time to cook him a quick bite to eat. Thankfully, he set the coffee pot before his run. He couldn't start his morning off without his coffee. Before leaving, he unlocked the gun safe and tucked his glock into its holster. As he headed out the door, his phone rang. Early morning phone calls meant a new case loomed on the horizon. Hopefully, their killer had not struck again. "LeDoux."

The dispatcher responded, "Sorry sir, but you have another body. This victim is a male. The neighbors called in to report an odor coming from next door. The vic has been dead for over twenty-four hours."

LeDoux instructed the dispatcher, "Tell Riley to meet me there. Have the responding officer secure the area."

"Yes, sir."

On the drive to the crime scene, LeDoux shrugged off the visions that danced through his mind. He hated dealing with decomposing bodies. He eased his Saxon Griffin onto the interstate before opening up the throttle. His mom called the motorcycle his mid-life crisis purchase. That may be partially true, but he also bought it for the speed. There was nothing like taking this baby for a ride and feeling the way it handled the curves. Whenever he needed to clear his head, he found a long, winding back road to let the horses run free. It was such an exhilarating rush.

Five minutes after LeDoux received the call, he was on the road heading towards downtown Campton. The radio DJ was talking about an oldie but goodies song, when LeDoux realized that the DJ was talking about one of his favorite songs, *Every Rose Has Its Thorn*. Since when did the songs he listened to become known as oldies but goodies? He turned up the radio in his helmet and let the music wash over him.

The morning drive was quiet as very few cars were on the road. If this was their killer, he needed to get into the mind of the assailant. It was highly unusual for a killer to switch victim types, unless the sex of the victim did not matter. There was also a chance that the killer was escalating.

As he parked his car near the crime scene, Riley pulled up behind him. "Mon ami, you ready?"

LeDoux noticed the vultures had arrived. Several members of the media were already reporting live.

He instructed one of the officers working the scene, "Gaudet, make sure you keep this situation under tight control. I don't want anyone from the force talking to the media just yet. The last thing we need is this turning into a circus."

"Yes, sir!"

As they made their way to the crime scene, the forensic technicians were already working. They were busy dusting the entire home for fingerprints as well as searching for any trace evidence the killer may have left behind. A crime scene photographer was taking stills and a video of the actual scene as the coroner arrived.

Riley was already taking notes. He asked Officer Campos, "Do you know who called it in?"

"Yes, sir, the gentleman on the back porch. His name is Henry Cheramie. He and his wife live next door and said that the smell became too bad to ignore."

"Do you know if Mr. Cheramie went into the room?"

"No, sir, he said the smell hit him as soon as he opened the door and called the police right away."

While Officer Campos spoke, Riley continued taking notes.

LeDoux put on his latex gloves and walked over to the body. The victim lay sprawled across the floor, face down in a pool of coagulated blood. A shudder went through him as he looked down at the body; it was already in decomp. "Well, now, I wonder just how he fits into our killer's plans. Could it be that he and our killer crossed paths or were possibly partners?"

Dr. Chauvin instructed her technicians, "I want to make sure his hands are bagged, just in case there is trace evidence."

LeDoux asked Dr. Chauvin, "What do you think?"

The medical examiner looked up, "Well, I suppose, it is better than finding another wealthy woman in a compromising position or having to tell her husband you suspect she was having an affair."

"True, but something tells me the same person did this."

Nodding her head, Dr. Chauvin agreed, "If it isn't the same killer then you have someone who likes the same style of killing. His throat was slashed, but this time with a little more force." "Maybe he was a john to one of the girls? Do you have an idea on the time of death," LeDoux asked Dr. Chauvin.

"Rigor has left the body, so I am saying more than forty-eight hours. I will know more once he is on the table."

Dr. Chauvin couldn't do anything else here and was ready to move the body.   Once at the morgue, she would scour the body for any other trace evidence. LeDoux watched as the body was sealed in a black body bag and placed on the gurney. Once the body was removed, forensics finished searching the apartment for evidence. He hoped the killer left behind some evidence for them to process this time.

A rookie cop called out to Detective LeDoux, "Sir, I ran the man's fingerprints through CODIS, and it appears our victim has been a very bad man."

"Oh yeah?"

Nodding his head, the rookie continued, "Your vic here was wanted in a string of rapes around town. He left his fingerprints, but was never in the system, well that is until now."

Chapter 47

As Bree watched her latest customer leave her phone rang. "Hello."

For a moment, there was only silence.

"Hello!"

"I am glad that your lover left."

The voice was almost a whisper. The hairs on the back of Bree's neck rose. She gripped the phone tighter. Her breath was short and shallow. "Who is this?"

With a snarl on his lips, "How dare you let those other men touch your body! You are a dirty whore. I thought you were worthy of me."

Not wanting to hear anymore, Bree hung up the phone.

He laughed at the fear he heard in her voice. For a moment, he considered calling her back, but then the man he was following turned into his subdivision. He groaned when the car pulled up to the security gate, complete with a guard shack. As a security guard let the car in, he let out a deep sigh. It wouldn't be easy to gain access to the man's house. Cursing under his breath, he found a hiding place to park his car to sit and wait. His only chance to deal with the man was away from his house.

Just when he was ready to give up for the night, the man pulled out of the subdivision. He had started to assume the man would never leave.

He saw the desire Mistress Azaria had in her eyes for this man. He couldn't have her desiring someone more than him. No, he had to eliminate his competition.

He followed the man into the crowded strip club. Disgust filled him as writhing bodies danced everywhere around him. This guy, only a few short hours ago had been with his beloved, and now sought out the pleasure of another woman. Had he no shame? No, his beloved would be better off without this man in her life. He was doing her a great favor getting rid of him for her.

The lights danced all around the room, bouncing off the huge, mirrored disco ball installed over the center of the dance floor. A rainbow of colors showered the patrons and dancers below.

The disco music was loud, enervating. The heavy rhythmic beat pulsated through his body. The air swirled with a haze of blue smoke. The men watched the women with an unquenchable hunger. Writhing, uninhibited women glistened with sweat as men looked their bodies up and down with seductive glances. All around him were men seeking out the fulfillment of their most carnal of desires, groping women with their hands.

His target moved towards a back room, where the S&M crowd liked to gather. Even after seeking out his Mistress Azaria, it appeared he had yet to unleash his complete set of fantasies on her.

Fate worked in mysterious ways. Just when he thought he would be unable to get to this man, he walked toward the bathroom. He quickly followed pursuit after him.

While the man stood at the urinal, he walked up behind him without hesitation. The blade of the knife sliced easily through his throat.

***

By the time LeDoux made it to the crime scene, it appeared as if all hell had broken loose. Two patrol cars blocked off either end of the street. Their flashing red and blue lights danced across the buildings. Crime scene techs and uniformed officers moved about as LeDoux watched the carefully choreographed chaos which accompanied a murder scene.

Riley waved his hand over at his partner, "LeDoux, over here."

LeDoux crossed the street to meet his partner in front of the strip club. A uniformed officer held open the door for them to enter. "It looks like our killer struck again," Riley informed his partner.

"Damn!"

As Riley lead LeDoux to the crime scene, he stated "Only this time it's another man."

"Who found him?"

"Some poor guy who went to drain his lizard." He pointed towards a man sitting at the bar, "I think he forgot all about using the bathroom when he saw the dead body."

"Damn, our guy is brazen killing a man in a busy place like this."

Nodding his head, Riley agreed, "Crime scene techs are working the scene now, but don't hold your breath on any viable clues. This place is a cesspool for contamination."

"No shit. Let's hope the cameras caught something."

Shaking his head, "Don't count on it. The bouncer said tonight was the busiest yet. There was no cover charge, so every Tom, Dick, and Harry was here. According to the bouncer, it was standing room only."

The inside of the club was dark, smelled of beer and urine; not a high class place by any means. LeDoux sauntered over to the bar and signaled for the barmaid. Her body had men begging for more, but her face was another matter. This woman was ridden hard and put away wet more times than he cared to count. She leaned on the counter, her breasts barely contained in the slip of material that was her costume.

In a cigarette abused voice, she asked, "What can I do for you two officers?"

"Did you happen to notice our victim going to the john?"

"I always notice that man. The girls called him a stalker. He was here almost every night. Several girls have complained of his roughness towards them."

"Did you notice anyone going in after him?"

Shaking her head, she answered, "No, it was crazy in here tonight. Normally, I keep tabs on where he is but it was impossible with the constant number of customers wanting drinks."

Chapter 48

LeDoux ran his hands through his hair, glancing at the wall clock in the task room. It was past midnight. After compiling what information they'd obtained so far and updating the task boards, all they had were a lot of theories, but nothing solid to go on.

Riley stood up to stretch his legs, *"Bon ami*, I'm going home. If I don't get some sleep, I will be useless in the morning."

LeDoux also considered going home. Riley was right; if they didn't get any sleep they would be worthless tomorrow. Besides, there wasn't much they could do right now. They were waiting for reports from forensics and the ME. The computer techs were busy going over the victim's computer, but so far there was nothing concrete to use. "We may as well go home and start fresh in the morning."

LeDoux turned off his computer and headed out to his Saxon. His body may need sleep, but his mind was still racing. As he slipped on his helmet, he heard someone call him, "Detective LeDoux, can I have a moment of your time?"

He must be tired if he allowed someone to get the drop on him. He looked around and was startled to find himself looking at the very beautiful Cassandra Evans. She was at least a foot shorter than him. Her deep auburn hair cascaded down her shoulders in a mass of curly waves.

"Detective LeDoux, do you have any updates on the recent murder?"

He should have known the overzealous reporter would try anything to get a lead on a story. "I have no comment for the press at this time."

Before he had a chance to start his motorcycle, she rested her hip on the seat, barring him from taking off unless he shoved her out of the way. To show she meant business, she placed a well-manicured hand on her hip.

"Look, Ms..."

She extended her hand, "Cassandra Evans."

He shook her hand reluctantly, "I know exactly who you are Ms. Evans. I don't have any new information for you. I'm tired; all I want to do is go home and get a couple of hours sleep."

"Detective LeDoux, please, I will only take up a few minutes of your time. I work for the Herald, and I want to give my readers a little more in depth information about the case."

Damn, the lady was persistent. "I have no comment at this time."

"What about your assessment of the case?"

Shaking his head, he said, "You really should be talking to our public relations department. They will give you all the information we are allowed to release at this time."

She refused to back down and continued on, "I already have the press release. Now I want to talk to the detective working the case, to get first hand knowledge."

"Look, lady, that won't be happening. I have no desire to have my ass handed to me on a silver platter after my boss finds out I talked to the press."

"I can keep your name out of it, if you would rather."

"Damn right my name will be kept out of it, because I refuse to talk to you, or anyone else for that matter."

His eyes gravitated to her lower lip as it drooped. She looked so sexy when she pouted. Somehow he missed how perfectly tantalizing her lips looked.

"Look, Ms. Evans, I have nothing against you, really, I just don't talk to journalists or news reporters, ever."

Undaunted by his remarks, she crossed her arms as if to throw a tantrum. Until that moment, her figure somehow went unnoticed by him. Now, he knew he was exhausted. Otherwise, he would have never missed her lovely rack. "Detective, the public has a right to know what is going on. It is your civil duty to serve and protect, am I right? Well, part of your civil duty is to warn people about what is happening in town."

The whole time she spouted off about his duty to the public; all he thought about was kissing those luscious lips of hers. "Again, no comment!"

As he revved the engine, she grabbed his arm. The physical reaction was electric. The heat from her touch sizzled against his body. Her reaction must have been the same; she quickly removed her hand, as if she literally burned her hand just by touching him. Their eyes met as she quietly said, "Detective, I want you to understand that I am just doing my job."

"Ms. Evans, I need to do my job without you harassing me in the middle of the night. I would hate to have one of our fine officers arrest you for interfering with a case."

That statement put a spark in her eyes. "You do remember the First Amendment, don't you Detective? I do believe it is something about freedom of speech."

"I don't need you harping to me about freedom of speech and all that crap. That amendment has caused me more headaches than I care to admit." LeDoux hoped to piss her off, enough where she would storm off and leave him the hell alone. The last thing he needed was to sit out here fighting with an overzealous reporter, especially one that he would rather be kissing. Now was not the time to start a new relationship, especially with a hot little reporter. No, he needed to keep his mind focused on finding this killer and not allow his libido to go into overdrive for this woman.

Instead of storming off, she just stood there glaring at him.

"Look, lady, what is it going to take for you to get the hell out of here?"

Without giving her a chance to answer, he slipped on his helmet, revved the engine, and took off. Leaving, he caught a glimpse of her in his mirror. She just stood there, watching him with her hands on her hips. He fought the urge to turn around, go back and kiss her pouting lips. He needed to stay the hell away from her. Dating a journalist like her would bring him nothing but trouble.

***

The newsroom was alive with the buzzing of tapping keys and running presses, drowning out any conversation. Right now, everyone was busy trying to make their deadlines.

Cassandra sat at her desk, with her white chocolate caramel latte and cheese danish from the coffee shop next door, and prepared to write her story. She was still fuming about the way Detective LeDoux treated her. How she would love to go to the police station and slap that condescending smirk right off his face, or perhaps she would just kiss it off. She shook her head. No, she couldn't think about him in that way, even if he oozed raw, masculine sexuality. Besides, he treated her no worse than you would a pesky mosquito.

Still, her heart skipped a beat when she remembered the way he talked. His accent was pure, unmistakable, Cajun French. She always had a weak spot for Cajun men; they were hot blooded and intensely passionate. It had been a while since she had been with a man and Detective LeDoux could definitely satisfy her hunger. He had bedroom eyes and a wickedly sexy and seductive voice that made her weak in the knees. Even his arrogance turned her on. She swallowed heavily, forcing herself to return to work.

She had to come up with a newsworthy story. She stared at the blank computer screen trying to decide how to begin it. What she really needed was some inside information, an edge over the other journalists and news reporters.

She refused to admit that her father may be right; she didn't have what it took to be a hard core news journalist. Damn it, though, she was more than just a pretty face! She had the guts to get out there and find sources. There had to be a way to coerce information out of Detective LeDoux. How could she get him to open up and talk to her? She thought back to last night and his reaction when she touched him. The look in his eyes confirmed that he had also felt the spark between them. Maybe she could use that to her advantage.

A plan began to form in her head. She could invite him to dinner; tell him she wanted to apologize for the way she acted and get him to drop his guard. Before inviting him to dinner, she needed a little more background information on him. She needed to dig into his past and find out what made him tick. She knew absolutely nothing about him.

Going to the web browser, she typed in his name to see what information popped up. Surprisingly, very little. She hoped for more than the few hits she found. Clicking on one website, she learned that he had been with the force for twenty years. Before joining the police force, he served four years in the US Marines. Being a veteran did explain his attitude though. She dated several military men, and they all had that same structured persona about them.

The next problem to overcome was asking him out to dinner. Currently, he had an obvious dislike for her, or maybe it was her profession. Either way, if she hoped to seduce him she needed him to see her as a woman, not a journalist. For just a moment, she was reluctant to lead Detective LeDoux on.

She hoped LeDoux didn't dig into her past. There were certain aspects of her life she would prefer to remain buried in the past. She was an only child, and while her parents were not bad parents, they were also never there for her. They had their own agenda, and she was an afterthought to them. She sometimes wondered if her dad ever really loved her. Growing up, she suspected that he was embarrassed by her. Her dad was the president of one of the largest shipyards here in Louisiana, and he had wanted a son to follow in his footsteps.

Ever since Cassie could remember, she knew what she wanted to do with her life. When she was little, she walked around with a pen and paper asking people for interviews. By the age of ten, she was writing short stories and begged her parents to submit them for publication. Neither ever took her writing seriously. While in school, she was on the yearbook committee and any other school activity that involved writing. She even joined the drama club, just for the chance to help write the plays. The only person to recognize her love for writing was her English teacher. If not for Mrs. Laura Jameson, she would never have excelled in her writing. Mrs. Jameson always gave her additional assignments and helped her enter contests to further her creative writing abilities. By the time she graduated from high school, she had won numerous writing contests, and several colleges offered her scholarships based solely on her writing skills.

During college, she discovered there were ways for a college girl to earn money. At first she scoffed at the idea, saying that she would never do that. When the bills started piling up, and she refused to turn to her parents for help, she needed an income. The first time she went out on a date it wasn't what she expected at all. She assumed the guy would be a sleaze ball who expected an assortment of kinky things. He had proven her wrong. The man was much older than her, but treated her well. He was just a lonely man who needed companionship more than anything else. The only clients who gave her a hard time were the married men who complained that their wives didn't understand their needs. More often than not, it wasn't that their wives didn't understand their needs; they just couldn't keep their peckers in their pants. Those were the ones who made her skin crawl.

While she dated during college; she never had anyone who beat her or treated her badly. If she had, then she would have quit the business right away. The agency she worked for was an exclusive one that had exorbitant prices, but also paid well. To this day, no one knew about her job, and she planned on keeping it that way. Not too many men were interested in marrying a former escort, especially one who specialized in being a Dominatrix.

Cassie expelled a deep breath and continued to look at the screen. She spent so much time reminiscing, and she was nowhere near finishing her story. Maybe buttering up Detective LeDoux would get her just enough information to make the story juicier. She learned a long time ago that flashing a pair of big eyes and showing a little cleavage went a long way. Although, so far that had not worked with the good detective. She didn't learn squat, and her story lacked the finesse she wanted.

She had been so excited when she heard the report of the dead body come across the police scanner that she bolted out the door. She wanted to be the first one to get the story. Now here it was, a day after the body was found, and she still had no more information than she did yesterday. She needed to make this story happen.

She never heard the editor walk up behind her until he cleared his throat. "So, do you have a story or not?"

She knew sooner or later he would be coming around, but she had hoped it would be later. She had nothing to give him. "I'm still working a few angles."

With barely a nod of his head, he asked, "When do you expect to have something for me to review?"

Cassie told a little white lie to save her some time, "I'm on my way out the door to interview some witnesses. I'll have something for you to look at when I get back."

"Do you think this is a solid lead?"

She muttered, "I sure hope so." Unfortunately, he heard her.

"What!" The next thing she knew, the entire newsroom was blanketed in silence. Everyone immediately stopped what they were doing, more than likely wondering if it was them coming under fire. When they realized who he was hollering at, all eyes focused on her.

She felt her cheeks turn red, "I've got some credible leads that I want to talk to before I finalize the story, that's all. A body was found, but the body was already in decomp. I have it from a reliable source that there are similarities between the recent death and those of the women."

He went on to ask, "Which Detective has lead on the case?"

"A Detective LeDoux."

He chuckled, "Good luck getting anything out of that man. He is a vault when it comes to releasing information. I've had several journalists attempt to gain his trust over the years with no luck. I've been told that he is a tough fellow to crack, but he is a man, and all men have a weakness. You just need to find out what that weakness is."

Cassie inwardly groaned as she took in everything he said. She wondered if she would be able to get Detective LeDoux to accept her invitation to dinner. What would happen if she went there and he decided to have someone throw her out of the police station? That would be thoroughly embarrassing. Perhaps she should wait for him outside and follow him home. He had to crack eventually, right?

Cassandra wondered how far she would actually go to write this story. Would she consider sleeping with him if it helped? She must admit he was a very handsome man, and there was definitely a spark there. She couldn't believe she was even considering it.

Chapter 49

As nine o'clock rolled around, Bree was ready for her day to start. Tom offered to take the kids to school this morning, which surprised all of them. That simple offer gave her an extra half hour to herself, enough time for her to give the house a quick cleaning, change the sheets on the bed and get everything ready for her morning performance. By lunchtime, all of her time slots were filled up. If it didn't mean the possibility of her losing potential new customers, she would stop the website and focus her energy on her private business. She made way more at the house than she would ever make working on the website. However, the website was where she found her clients. She needed to dedicate an hour or so at least each day to that.

***

Henry found himself staring into the woman's eyes as she rode him like a bucking bronco. He wanted to make his money last as long as he could. His heart beat ferociously in his chest as the woman on top of him writhed in pleasure.

He couldn't remember the last time a woman made him feel like this. He missed these sensations flooding through his body right now. The passion this woman had him feeling was all encompassing.

He closed his eyes and concentrated on the escalating waves flowing through his body. She kept bringing him higher and higher as he tried to keep his ultimate release at bay. As he felt her spasm around him, he found his release.

***

He watched her image fill the computer screen. She was so lovely. He moved the camera to where it could zoom in remotely. How he wished it was him in that room with her, moving deep inside of her.

He longed to touch those delectable breasts, look deeply into her eyes. He loved everything about her; the curve of her nose, the fullness of her breasts.

He kept close tabs on her lately; knowing everything that she did. Right now he must wait until she was finally alone. He desperately desired to make some sort of contact with her, needing to hear her voice in his ear.

Just the thought of their future courtship excited him. He could not wait until this woman was completely his. To him, these next few days were nothing more than his mating dance.

It hurt him that she kept betraying him like this. He despised the fact that all these other men enjoyed her body when it should be just him. He was never good at sharing.

Once she was completely his, there would be no other man in her life. He knew it would be hard for her to say goodbye to her husband, but that man must mean nothing to her. It was he whom she loved; he saw it in her eyes. It was only him that she performed for; these other men were nothing more than intruders.

He fell madly in love with her the first time he saw her. When she posed for that camera, he knew that it was him she saw. She tempted him with her sultry body.

When they did finally make love, it would be good. Better than good actually, it would be perfect. Dare he pronounce his love right away or should he wait and let her love for him grow? He needed to hear those three little words come from her mouth. Those three little words would make this all worth it. I love you, three simple words that carry with it so much meaning.

Chapter 50

The day had been extremely long. All LeDoux wanted was to go home and forget about these cases for a brief period of time. It had been a while since their killer struck, but he was still out there waiting for another opportune moment. Perhaps he was stalking his next victim at this very minute.

As soon as LeDoux walked into his house, he went straight to his bar and poured himself a Maker's Mark on the rocks. He needed the fire of the alcohol to spread throughout his body and numb his thoughts. As he slammed back his first drink, the doorbell rang. *Who the hell could that be?*

He opened the door to find the lovely Cassandra Evans standing there. This was *une jolie femme*, a beautiful woman. She wore a tight pair of jeans that showed off her derriere to perfection and a very low cut halter top which left nothing to the imagination. This woman was completely unnerving. He'd never met a woman who affected him this way.

In a sultry voice, she asked, "Detective, aren't you going to ask me in?"

Mon Dieu, this woman was a menace. Against his better judgment, he opened the door for her to step through. "I'm not talking about the case," he warned.

She arched an eyebrow, "Are you going to offer me a drink?"

"What would you like?"

Eyeing his glass, she asked, "What are you drinking?"

He looked over at her, "Maker's Mark on the rocks."

She walked over to him, taking an ice cube out of his glass and seductively used her tongue to play with it. "Mmmm, that sounds good. I'll take what you are having then."

He fixed her a drink and another for himself. "What brings you this way, Ms. Evans?"

"We seem to have gotten off on the wrong foot, Detective. For some reason, you have a very poor opinion of me, and I want to change that."

He let out a deep, hearty chuckle, "It's not just you, Ms. Evans. It's everyone in your profession. You don't care who you step on to get your story. You have no feelings for the victims you write about."

She traced his jaw line and stated, "Detective, I'm not like that. I do care about people. The whole reason I am in this business is because I want to make sure the public hears all sides of the story."

He couldn't believe that the woman who'd haunted his dreams these last few nights was in his home drinking Maker's Mark with him. It was almost as if he conjured her up from his imagination.

"You know you can be one very annoying lady."

She smiled at him, "I guess I have been a little persistent lately, haven't I?"

LeDoux raised his brow in a challenge, "A little? Lady you have been driving me crazy."

She looked directly into his eyes. LeDoux wondered if she knew that she just made a big mistake. He loved her eyes; they were so mesmerizing. He liked her a little more than he cared to admit. He picked up his glass and took a drink.

A large part of him wanted to get to her know her, and not just intimately. Observing her closely, he liked the way she smiled and the spark of interest in her eyes. The only thing he didn't care for was her incessant curious nature. That curiosity of hers would get her into a lot of trouble, if it hadn't already.

Without even thinking of her body movements and the way they affected him, she tucked an unruly curl behind her ear and his groin tightened in response to her innocent gesture. He wondered if she knew the effect she had on him. He shifted uncomfortably. "Why exactly are you here Ms. Evans?"

"I'm here because I want us to get to know each other a little better."

His grin widened in response. "I am afraid that you will find out I am very boring. There isn't anything interesting about me."

She smiled back at him, "Oh, but I disagree. I bet there is a lot that lies beneath that hard surface of yours."

"And just how do you plan on breaking through my hard surface?"

"Simply by getting to know you and letting you learn that I am not a bad person."

His gaze traveled over her body. He ran a hand over his jaw as if pondering his next comment. "You can ask me questions as long as they do not pertain to the case. I came home tonight to forget about work."

She placed her hands on top of his, "I can do that, Detective." This simple movement caused an ache deep inside of him. "I promise not to breathe a word about your work or the case."

Their eyes met and held for several moments. She smiled up at him, "You aren't afraid of me are you Detective? I promise I won't bite... hard that is."

"Lady, there is not a woman out there that I am afraid of."

Rubbing her hands up and down his chest, she said, "Hmmm, I think you protest too much." While she lowered her hand towards his groin, she whispered, "Could it be that you fear you may be unable to handle me in bed?"

LeDoux pulled her into his arms. "Cher, you don't know when to stop do you?"

He bent down and took her lips in his. As soon as they touched, he knew he'd crossed the point of no return. Touching her made him far too aware of her. The moment he touched her silky skin, so tantalizingly soft, he was hooked. One look in her shimmering eyes and all reasoning left him.

She looked up at him, waiting to see what his next move would be. Their gazes were held hostage by the desire flowing between them. A soft moan escaped from her throat. A low, needy answer to the primitive dance they were performing. LeDoux needed no other invitation. He crushed his lips down on hers. He thrust his tongue in her mouth and devoured her. "Ah, cher."

He kissed her again, his hot tongue caressing her mouth. She tasted so good, too good to be true. He wanted her. *Mon Dieu*, she was like a drug. The pull of this woman was too great; she was so very arousing. The feel and smell of her held him a prisoner to a primal hunger he'd never felt before.

***

That sexy voice and smooth Cajun accent of his sent chills down her spine despite the Louisiana heat. She could get lost in his eyes; they were so alluring. He was potent and all male, a very dangerous combination.

She breathed in the scent of him. Considering the way he heated her blood, she bet he was loaded with pheromones. The man was so incredibly sexy. What with his broad chest and strong arms that encased her. There was a sense of raw danger that radiated from him. Surely he felt her heart beating out of control. Desire moved through her like molten lava.

He stole her breath away. She became lost in the sensual storm they created. One of his hands cupped her breast, brushing across her nipples and they hardened in response, begging for his attention. All she thought about was his mouth on her naked skin.

As if reading her thoughts, he brought her shirt over her head and unfastened her bra. His mouth left a trail of hot kisses down her already heated skin, finding his way to her breasts. His lips covered one nipple as his hands massaged the other.

A moan escaped her as she arched her hips to him. His tongue made circles around her nipple as his teeth nipped gently at her sensitive flesh. His touch sent electric currents through her body. She moved her hands down to his waist, pushing at the band of his jeans. She wanted, no needed, to feel him. Her hand brushed against his full erection, causing him to groan.

His mouth and hands left her as he removed the rest of her clothes. He quickly kicked his jeans off his body.

"Are you sure this is what you want," he asked her, his voice hoarse with desire. She nodded, unable to trust her own voice.

Without waiting for her to finish her nod, he carried her off to the bedroom. It felt good to know that she could make him nearly come undone.

Once on the bed, his hands roamed all over her body. She breathed huskily against his skin, "I need you now."

In one swift move he entered her, filling her completely. She cried out, reveling in the feel of him inside her. When he entered her, it awakened nerve endings she forgot she had. She wrapped both legs around him tightly, taking each of his powerful thrusts. "More please. Harder!" She held onto his shoulders as he thrust deep inside her, faster and harder. His muscles corded up thick with every thrust.

He whispered in her ear, "You're so tight. I'm not hurting you, am I?"

She shook her head no. "Faster, faster, faster!"

He breathlessly told her, "I never imagined it would be like this. You're more than I ever expected in a woman."

Her body convulsed around him. The orgasm felt like an inferno going off inside of her. All her muscles clenched simultaneously. He continued thrusting, taking her further and further into sexual bliss. Tremors continuously rolled through her. As good as the first orgasm was - it was nothing compared to what he was doing to her body now. The orgasms kept coming and didn't seem to stop. It was more than she ever expected. In one more powerful thrust, he found his own release. They lay in the bed motionless, waiting for some energy to return to their bodies.

Chapter 51

As Bree cleaned the dinner dishes, an eerie feeling came over her. She slowly turned around and scanned the quiet kitchen. She let out a sigh of relief as she forced her nerves to calm down. She resumed washing the dishes, and looked out the window. Suddenly, an invisible vice gripped tight around her throat, making it impossible to breath.

A masked man stared directly at her through the window. She closed her eyes tightly before slowly opening them, praying that her eyes were playing tricks on her. In the moonlight, she could make out his dark eyes glaring at her.

Instinctively she stepped back as he continued to stand there. As she opened her mouth to scream, she realized her vocal cords paralyzed in fear. She felt the icy hands of terror slowly wrap their grasp around her heart.

Her mind screamed run and find help, but she was frozen in place. As the man smiled, a perfect row of white teeth gleamed back at her. That smile, those teeth reminded her of someone. She closed her eyes and took a deep breath in.

Suddenly, without warning, a hand clamped down on her shoulder. A guttural scream was ripped from her throat. A rush of adrenaline moved through her as she whirled around, "Damn, Bree, it's just me."

Tom's familiar voice filtered through her panic stricken mind as his arms reached out to steady her. "You scared the hell out of me," she said.

"Are you okay? You seemed to be frozen in place when I walked in."

Shaking her head, she replied, "I'm fine. I must have been lost in thought and never heard you come in is all." Giving Tom a quick smile, she looked back outside and breathed a sigh of relief when she didn't see anyone out there. After finishing with the dishes, she decided to join him in the living room.

***

He hurried away from his beloved's house, being careful to blend into the shadows. Once he was at a safe distance he removed his mask, tucking it into his back pocket.

Just the terror he saw in Bree's eyes gave him an instant erection. If only her husband hadn't walked in when he did.

Chapter 52

LeDoux was becoming anxious about the murders still unsolved. He continued to review his notes as he walked over to Riley's desk.

Tapping his pen on the desk, LeDoux asked, "I still say there is a connection between these victims. I keep going back to their pimp, boss, whatever, being the killer."

Riley shook his head, "Mais non, these girls make him a lot of money. I still think it is a jealous client who is the killer."

"But how in the hell did these women contact him? We searched the computers and cell phones, but nothing was there."

"I've been thinking about that. I think our killer takes the laptop or cell phone with him?"

Throwing down his pen LeDoux replied, "Damn, I wish we could catch a break on this case."

He groaned, "I'm going back to the drawing board for a bit."

Once in the conference room, he spread the evidence across the long table, arranging everything by case. He studied each piece of evidence hoping and praying that something he missed would jump out at him.

Riley walked in and asked, "You have been at this for a while now. Anything?"

Slamming his hands on the table, LeDoux said, "No dammit. We have no prints, no foreign hairs, no fibers, nothing. I just don't know where to turn to next. We can't even find any witnesses."

Grinning Riley replied, "Well, I think I have something, mon ami. Come check out what I found."

LeDoux followed Riley to his desk, "Look at this website closely and tell me what you see."

It took LeDoux a moment for the scene in front of him to sink in, "Wait a minute? Is that our crime scene?"

Grinning from ear to ear, "I do believe it is. The lady is wearing a mask, and more than likely a wig, but I believe our latest victim was a virtual Dominatrix."

"Well, it sure in the hell looks like her bedroom doesn't it?"

Nodding, Riley stated, "The only problem, her chat room is no longer active. I found this purely by accident. I kept thinking that she was hiding a secret of some kind." With a shit eating grin, he added, "But it appears that our victim was much more than a webcam girl; she was a Dominatrix."

"I wonder if the other victims were also in the same business." A rush of adrenaline moved through his body, "This could be how our killer finds his victims. Perhaps the women pushed the wrong button while acting out their roles."

"I already have the computer guys looking at the site trying to find out just where the main office may be located. They said not to hold our breath, most of these companies use fake addresses, etc. to keep people like us from finding them.”

“Damn, I hope we can catch a break with this.”

Chapter 53

It took Bree by surprise when she received a request to spend her whole three hour time slot with one man for three thousand dollars, not as a Dominatrix but that of a lover. Did he need that much time to satisfy his whims?

If it hadn't been for the exorbitant amount of money, she would have turned him down, but the amount was too tempting. Besides, she was curious as to what this man looked like.

When she answered the door, though, she was pleasantly surprised. The debonair man standing at her doorstep handed her the envelope with the money and stated, "You can count it all if you like."

Without taking the money out of the envelope, Bree flipped through to see that he paid in crisp one hundred dollar bills. "I must say you are nothing like what I expected."

Smiling, he replied, "I don't have time to spend wining and dining women. Besides, most of the women I date all want one thing, a wedding ring. When I saw your advertisement the other night, I must say, I was drawn to you. After watching your performance, I knew that I had to contact you. But while most of your men want to be dominated by you, I find that a huge turn off."

In a sultry voice, she said, "So I take it you are used to getting what you want and not having a woman dominate you."

"I don't like to wait, and I don't like to share which is the whole reason I booked your entire allotted time. I didn't want your mind on others. I take it from the few hours you have available, you do this to pass the day away."

Laughing, she agreed, "Something like that."

As she took her fill of this sexy man, he stated, "You are definitely in the right profession. Something tells me you know exactly what effect you have on men."

Bree nodded in agreement. She knew that men found her insurmountable charms desirable. While she considered herself a little too top heavy, men loved it.

Having this man desire her, gave Bree a rush like never before. This man, who had enough money and corporate power to get whatever he wanted, desired her. Not only did he desire her, but he was willing to pay a hefty amount to have her. This man, who could have any woman he wanted, wanted her.

When she looked into his eyes, she saw the dark glint of desire for her. With each passing minute, his eyes grew darker. The surrounding air virtually crackled with electricity. His eyes bore into hers as he demanded. "Kiss me."

She wrapped her arms around his neck, kissing him with an intense ferociousness. Tiny electrical charges moved through her body as their lips meet. It shook her to her very core, causing her to gasp in delight. She delved her tongue deep in his mouth, causing him to growl as his arms encircled her.

He tasted of heat and spice. They kissed hungrily as his lips devoured hers. Slowly breaking their kiss, Bree undressed this hunk of a man, being careful not to crease any of his clothes.

The lacy black lingerie she chose for today left nothing to the imagination. Her firm, full breasts threatened to spill from its lacy constraints. Once she undressed him, he ordered her, "Strip for me."

Following his gruff commands, she seductively performed for the man. As he watched her, his eyes grew hooded with desire as she exposed her body to him.

His eyes filled with a raging fire for her, with a huskiness to his voice he informed her, "You are even more beautiful in person. You are one sexy woman."

Her voluptuous breasts bounced as she made her way over to the bed. His eyes were trained on her with obvious lust. Beneath his burning gaze, her nipples hardened and begged for his touch. By the time she reached the bed, his eyes smoldered with need. "You like what you see big boy?"

In a raspy voice, he responded, "Oh yes."

As she pushed him down on the bed, her eyes feasted on the sinewy lines and planes of his body, his chest and spectacularly chiseled abs. This man took great effort in keeping healthy and fit. Her eyes focused on his groin, as her breath caught.

When they kissed this next time, it was as if she triggered an explosion. He pulled her close to his body as their mouths merged.

Once she broke free from his kiss, she moved down greedily. She wanted to devour his whole body, and she had all afternoon to do just that. She stroked him firmly as her mouth hovered over his erection. Compelled by lust, she teased his tip with her tongue, just playfully swiping at it. She made sure to twirl her tongue around him over and over, before taking him slowly inch by inch. She sucked hard, teasing the underside with her tongue. The heat of her mouth caused him to harden even more. A deep sound of pleasure echoed from her throat. She felt him twitch with excitement. This man underneath her body was rock hard and pure muscle. He was not like most of her potbellied, middle-aged clients.

She played with his balls before taking them one by one in her mouth. Without warning, he pulled her off of him and tossed her on the bed as if she weighed nothing at all. As his face disappeared between her thighs, his hands reached up and began fondling her breasts. Her hips moved up and down in delight as he twirled his tongue around her sensitized bud. He sucked hard as his fingers pinched her taut nipples. Electric volts of sweet pleasure shot right to her very core.

Her body was engulfed in searing flames of desire. As one of his hands made its way down her body, she waited in utter anticipation. As his finger slid into her wet folds, her heart pounded ferociously in her chest. The pure bliss of his touch was almost unbearable. The feel of his rippling, hard muscles against her body was earth shattering. The feel of his hard body against her had her wanting more and more.

Sensing that she was close to climaxing, she rolled them over, and slowly brought herself down on his throbbing erection, savoring each delectable moment. Her body parted effortlessly for his hardness. Once buried deep inside of her, she rocked her hips back and forth as the sensations of the friction of his movements ignited the fireworks from deep inside her core.

She made sure to position herself where with every movement he hit her g spot. The next orgasm was hard, fast, and hot. His movements inside of her picked up as her body convulsed around him. He moved with a speed and precision that sent her body into overdrive.

This became primal as unadulterated lust took over their bodies. The man underneath her was pure ecstasy. He had her completely submissive as each powerful thrust had her taking stock in the sheer ferocity of his lovemaking.

Her body throbbed with pleasure from all the attention he gave her. His hands never once left her body. They fondled, kneaded, and caressed. With him deep inside of her, he grabbed hold of her hand, "I want you to feel it as I slide in and out of you."

Gripping the base of his erection, she felt as he glided effortlessly up the length of her wet folds. With one of his hands over hers, his thumb sensuously moved around her tender nub causing her to want even more of him. "You like that, don't you?"

Nodding her head yes, she wasn't sure if she could talk as waves of desire washed over her. Her body responded to his voice, to his commands. She succumbed to the orgasm, writing on top of him. Instead of letting her collapse on him, he held on to her tight, thrusting deep into her as he pushed her toward another climax.

She placed her hands on his chest, running her delicate fingers over his bulging muscles while she rode him relentlessly. Pure satisfaction filled her as she exploded from his expert ministrations. It was so intense that she felt herself growing weak from the fireworks going off deep inside of her.

When she looked into his eyes, the look stole her breath. It was the most intense, lust filled feral look that she ever saw in a man's eyes. Desire coursed through her body as the realization hit her that she was the one who put that look on his face. She would love for Tom to look at her like that. When he rotated his hips, she lost all control.

The orgasm caused her body to tremble uncontrollably. Before her body stopped convulsing around him, she felt his own release deep inside of her body. "That was unbelievable. We have to do this again."

Bree almost told him that she would gladly do this for no charge.

Chapter 54

As Bree slid her key in the lock, she was surprised to find it unlocked. Damn, did one of the kids forget to lock the door when they left this morning? Thankfully she hadn't been gone from the house that long.

Still, the unlocked door jangled her nerves, especially with all the notes and the rape. Shaking off the fear escalating in her body, she pushed the door open. She peeked into the foyer and listened for any strange noises.

All that greeted her was silence. On the floor at the front door was her mail. As she flipped through the stack of mail, the last envelope caught her attention. There was no stamp and once again it was addressed to Mistress Azaria. Her heart began to pound as she opened the note. The scent of Mont Blanc cologne emanated from the note. It reminded her of the cologne Tom wore. The hairs on the back of her neck rose, whoever sent this note had been in her bedroom. He must have seen which cologne Tom wore and was letting her know.

She read the note as goose bumps crawled up her body, "Thinking of you my love." If she hadn't known better, she would believe the note came from Tom. If only that were true, but no, in her heart she knew her secret admirer sent the note.

Bree tossed the card in the trash can, rubbing her hands up and down her arms in an attempt to calm her nerves. Her cell phone rang, breaking the silence of the house. The sound made her jump, and nervous laughter bubbled out of her.

For a moment she was afraid to see who was calling. She let out a sigh of relief when she noticed that it was her dad.

"Hey Dad."

"Hey kiddo. I just wanted to check up on you."

While talking to her dad, she poured herself another cup of coffee. "Everything is going good Dad, really good."

"Your mom and I are just worried about you. We haven't heard much from you lately."

"I've just been busy with the kids is all."

"Well, I know that they have a break coming up, and wondered if they would like to go to the camp with us for a few days."

Bree chewed on her bottom lip as she thought about her dad's proposition. It would allow her to continue working while they were out of school, but the problem would be convincing the kids to go. "I will ask them, but I am sure that they would love to."

"Great, well just let us know."

After Bree had hung up with her dad, she finished off her coffee before heading up to her bedroom.

***

He watched her house from his car as he ate one of the blueberry muffins she made for her family this morning. He was no longer just content watching her from the computer. He took a risk entering her house earlier this morning, but he couldn't resist the temptation. Now that she set the alarm during the day it wasn't as easy to get to her. This morning as he watched the kids leave it gave him an idea, one that he had to try.

When they left, they never bothered to set the alarm. It was easy to pick the lock and slip in the back door. Soon he would make his intentions known. Soon she would want no one but him and then it would be time to move in.

It still amazed him that they had known each other for only a few short months. As he watched one of her clients walk up to the door, rage washed over him like a tidal wave. Anger gripped his chest like a vise.

He loathed the idea of them together. He hated to watch as they made love, but something inside of him couldn't resist watching another man touch her. Once his love for her was revealed, she would give up this job to be with him and him only.

His future was Bree. His sultry Bree. The only woman who moved him beyond just animalistic lust.

Chapter 55

Neil knew that Bree LeFleur was up to something during the day. He was determined to find out just what it was. He made himself comfortable in his hiding spot and watched as the day began to unfold.

Well, well, well what do we have here? He was surprised when he saw the Honorable Samuel T. Lofton get out of the car. Taking several pictures of the man as he walked to the house, Neil's heart began to pound in exhilaration. He had to find a way to get some photos of the two inside. If he did, he wouldn't have to worry about money for a long time.

An hour later he caught a picture as the judge clumsily fastened his pants as he headed back to his car. *The stupid fool could have at least zipped up inside.*

No sooner than one car left did a black SUV glide into its place. *Now I wonder just who could this be?* Exhilaration moved through his body as the next man emerged from the vehicle. This kept getting better and better. *My, my, my Mrs. LeFleur it appears that you have been a very naughty girl.*

Blackmail would be the perfect way to build his little nest egg without worry. After all, no one knew what the future held.

Smiling, he headed back home. "What a wonderful day," he told Lisa as he sat his alligator briefcase on the entrance way table.

Lisa waddled over to give him a kiss, "You are home early. How was your day?"

Feeling indulgent, he walked over to the bar and poured himself a glass of Maker's Mark. "I just had an excellent meeting with a potential client and wanted to write down my notes before I forgot them."

His study was one of his favorite rooms in the house; Lisa did well in decorating this room. She kept the feel masculine. From the rich tan color of the walls, the dark bamboo flooring, to the exquisite hand carved mahogany desk and even to the dark brown leather furniture with brass nail studs running down their fronts.

With pleasure, he sat down at his desk and started up his computer. As he wrote up the letter, he included that if she went to the police, he would be forced to hand over the pictures to her husband and also the police.

Once he finished writing the blackmail letters, he left to drop the letters off in the mail. No sense in waiting to mail these little beauties off.

Chapter 56

The following week her newest client, Eric Stevens, requested the whole afternoon. Once again, he offered her another three thousand dollars. She almost felt guilty about taking his money for such a pleasurable afternoon.

No sooner than they made it to her bedroom, he turned her around and pinned her hard against the door. His erection pressed into her from the front of his slacks.

He tilted her face up as his lips devoured hers. She returned the kiss with the same amount of unbridled passion. He pressed his body into hers, reveling in the feel of her body underneath his. His hands ran up and down her sides, teasing her with his touch.

Bree looked up at him as her head spun in a lust fueled haze. His touch sent electrical charges surging through her body. His kisses were unrelenting.

"Are you ready for me," he asked in a voice full of primal lust.

"Always."

As he ripped off her thong, his finger teased her womanly folds. His thumb sought out her sensitive bud, bringing it to life with his magical touch. As he continued to touch her, the only thing her mind registered was the desire he sent straight to her very core. He knew exactly what her body craved. He knew all the right places to tease and torment with his touch. As he continued to circle her swollen bud, an orgasm exploded from deep inside of her.

As she slumped forward, she buried her face into his neck, breathing in his scent.

***

He sat down at the computer and prepared to watch what had occurred during the day. It felt good to sit back and relax.

His head throbbed as the headache he had suffered from all day became worse. Today had been riddled with more problems than he cared to count. Several clients had demanded his attention, and when he couldn't give it right away they complained to no end.

Sitting in front of the computer, he put today's problems behind him. He was home and here he could be himself and drop the façade he had come to detest.

With a scotch on the rocks in one hand, he hit play on the video. As the image of Bree appeared, his tense muscles relaxed. While watching her perform he pondered if it was time for her husband to find out what she did during the day.

Chapter 57

Tom LeFleur was about to leave for lunch when he noticed that he had a new message waiting in his inbox. He considered waiting to open it, but the title had him curious. "Do you know where your wife is?"

His heart skipped a beat, an irrational fear spread through him. Perhaps someone had kidnapped her for ransom. His overactive imagination ran wild as he opened the email. Nothing could have prepared him for what he saw. His wife was naked in their room, or he assumed that was their bedroom. The image was grainy, but he was certain that was Bree. However, the man in the video was not him. Anger filled him as he watched the man put his hands on her breasts and thrust deep inside of her. His wife's face wasn't contorted with fear, but pleasure.

Damn her beautiful lying face. He wondered how long she had lied to him, betrayed him, and used him. How long had he been blind? Damn, he thought she loved him as much as he loved her. He ground his teeth as he watched the images in front of him. He was such a fool. All those times he made love to her did she think of other men? He couldn't stand the thought of another man teasing and nipping at her luscious body, playing with her nipples, bringing her to ecstasy.

His heart pounded wildly, his breath short as the man's fingers toyed with her. The idea of her betraying him in such a way barely entered his consciousness. As he watched his wife have sex with another man, his heart turned to stone, cold and heavy in his chest. An onslaught of emotions moved through him. Jealousy, sadness, and betrayal ran through him at an alarming rate. This man was touching his wife in ways that only he should. His breath caught in his throat as despair gripped its icy grasp on him. His eyes felt as if they were being ripped from his body as his world came crashing down around him.

He forced himself not to rush home, but to remain at work. He couldn't stand the thought of his wife degrading herself like that. On the way home, he decided not to confront Bree just yet about her infidelity. He would wait until he had the proof he needed and then when he was confident he would confront her. The video was too grainy, and some part deep in the recesses of his mind had him believing the video might have been altered.

***

After her last client had left, Bree showered and changed into a pair of slacks and blouse. She went into the kitchen to start supper.

Tonight's menu would be broiled salmon with a rich hollandaise sauce, roasted asparagus, and a creamy lobster risotto. As she chopped the ingredients for supper, she sipped on a glass of chardonnay. With *"Remind Me"* by Brad Paisley and Carrie Underwood playing in the background, she let the music and cooking help settle her nerves.

Once she had everything prepared and ready to cook, she went over to the computer desk to sort through today's mail. The small stack consisted mainly of bills, but for once she had the money to pay them.

As she sorted through it all, an envelope stood out from the others. A shiver chased down her spine as she recalled the other notes that she had received lately. Taking a large sip of wine, she picked up the envelope with unease.

The letter in front of Bree stunned her. She could barely keep a blank face as she read the words. With a shaky hand, she folded the piece of paper and put it in her pocket. Her fingers tapped the computer desk as she tried to think of just who could be blackmailing her.

Letting out a muffled curse, she forced down the tears. If she refused to pay, there was a chance she would lose everything she worked hard for. Whoever was blackmailing her swore that he had evidence that he would show to her devoted husband. She didn't need for Tom to find out about her day job.

The person who sent this letter was not the same person sending the other notes. Worse, there was no way she could go to the authorities on either matter. Instead, she must deal with it on her own. The last thing she needed were the cops sniffing around here.

Who in the hell could be sending these letters?

Chapter 58

As Tom drove to his meeting, he reminisced about these last few years. When he first met Bree he was raking in the money. The more he worked, the more he earned. There was no such thing as forty-hour work weeks, but when he met Bree he made time for their blossoming relationship.

Once they married, he put even more hours in at work, wanting to maintain a steady flow of money coming in. He didn't want Bree working in the public where she may meet another man who caught her eye. He wanted to be the provider and have a wife who stayed home.

Over the years, Bree would kiss him goodbye when he left for work, grab his credit card and shop for clothes and furniture that she didn't need. As the years progressed, he became married to his job, and she had no problems spending his hard earned money. While the money was rolling in, it never bothered Tom that she constantly shopped. However, as the economy took a nosedive so did their finances.

He still worked as hard as ever, but the money wasn't coming in like it was in the past. He had to work hard just to earn a minuscule amount of money. The only problem was that Bree didn't stop spending money.

He came to accept that she married him for his money and not love. He married her simply because she was gorgeous and young. She also allowed him to do whatever he wanted with her body. There was nothing she wouldn't let him try.

So in all honesty, she was his plaything, and he was her bank account.

It was a happy delusion, this marriage of theirs. He pulled up to the private investigator's office and tapped his pocket to make sure the flash drive was still there. With a firm resolve, he walked into the office.

A muscular man sat at an old battered desk, "Mr. Tom LeFleur?"

Tom took the man's extended hand and looked him over. Tom expected a portly, older man and not this man with a muscular physique. He stood well over six feet tall, tan complexion, thick gray hair and cold as ice blue eyes. "Yes, thank you for agreeing to meet with me. I'll get right to the point. My wife is cheating on me." He handed the private investigator the flash drive, "I want to know if he is the only man or if there are more."

Owen Leger opened a desk drawer and pulled out two shot glasses and a bottle of eighteen year old scotch. He poured the man a shot of the warm amber colored single malt scotch. As he tossed it back, Owen looked at his newest client, "Are you certain that you want to know the answers? Perhaps it is a one time fling."

Sneering with pure hatred for his wife, Tom replied, "I want to know exactly what that bitch does during her days."

***

Owen was surprised to find Tom LeFleur waiting at his office door, "Mr. LeFleur, is there something I can help you with?"

"I was hoping that you had something for me," he stated.

"Well, you were just here two days ago. I did some investigating, but these things take time. I don't want to give you any inaccurate information." He had no desire to tell this man his wife was banging men left and right until the timing was right.

Chapter 59

Detective LeDoux asked the young cop guarding the crime scene, "Who found the body?"

"The wife, sir. She was at her weekly book club meeting and came home to find him dead in the kitchen." Taking a deep breath before continuing, "Sir, the killer almost decapitated this one."

As LeDoux walked through the house, he noticed the fine furnishings throughout. He saw more upscale homes these last few months than he ever thought possible. It appeared no amount of money could protect you from a crazed killer. Even more disturbing, was the fact their killer no longer had a preference to men or women who he killed, but why? What changed his MO? Are these men clients of one woman?

In the living room, he observed several photos of a family consisting of a husband, wife, two young girls, and a boy proudly displayed. In the study, the body lay sprawled across the mahogany desk. He was face down in a pool of coagulated blood that dripped to the floor.

The medical examiner nodded her head to acknowledge the detective's arrival. "Even though excessive force was used with this kill, I am reasonably certain that this was your killer. The execution of the slash across the victim's throat is identical to the other victims."

As LeDoux looked down at the body, he informed Riley, "I'm beginning to think we have a deadly stalker on our hands."

Riley ran his hands through his hair. "It appears someone has become infatuated with a working girl and decided it would be easier to take the men out."

LeDoux nodded his head in agreement, "That's what my gut tells me. That is the only explanation I can come up with why the killer switched victim profiles."

"Yep, our killer wants to be the only man in this woman's life."

"Now the question is, how in the hell do we figure out who these men were seeing? It's not as if they told their wives or anyone."

"We need to check their cell phones and computers. They had to have contact with her somehow."

As LeDoux and Riley were about to leave the victim's house the wife called out to them, "Detectives, I thought perhaps you wanted this list."

LeDoux looked at an extensive list, "What is this, ma'am?"

"This, sir, is a list of people who would like to see my husband dead, including his mistress. He was a real son of a bitch."

Riley stated, "I don't see a woman as having the strength to overpower this man."

"No, we are definitely looking at a man."

***

An icy shiver ran down Bree's spine as she listened to the news. She curled up in bed and stared at the TV screen. She felt like she was floating; her mind played the news story over and over in her mind. She lost another client to murder.

What should she do? She couldn't go to the police, but could one of her other clients have killed him? Or could it have been her secret admirer? Was she next?

Chapter 60

As Tom made his way home tonight, he thought about everything he learned with regards to his precious, adultering wife. These last few weeks he had planned his next move. His fury at her was replaced by a firm resolve. What she did was inexcusable and required punishment.

He would make her pay for being such a whore. She would not get away with her infidelity. He refused to become the laughing stock of this town, if he wasn't already.

As he sped down the interstate, he paid no attention to the storm or wet roads. When he lost control of the car, all he thought about was his cheating wife.

The car careened off the bridge and didn't stop until it landed in the unforgiving waters of the mighty Mississippi River. As the bystanders watched the muddy water swallow the car, one lone driver called 911.

Even though the paramedics and police arrived promptly to the scene of the accident, they knew there was no saving the life of whoever was inside. They had seen it plenty of times; some anxious driver had traveled too fast for the road conditions and lost control. The divers would be sent down to recover the body, but that was all they could do.

The driver and any occupants were dead. As the divers prepared to look for their body, they prayed that all the occupants in the car had at least been wearing their seatbelts. If not, then there was a chance that the body wouldn't be recovered. The victims would have been thrown into a watery grave.

All around the scene of the accident the state troopers, firemen, and paramedics waited in hopes of being able to offer some type of assistance in what they were certain had been a fatal crash.

As the divers came up, one diver pointed his thumb down at the state trooper observing the scene. The only clue to the driver's identity was the license plate attached to the bumper. As the veteran officer looked up the plate number on his vehicle's computer, he cringed. It was registered to a Tom and Bree LeFleur.

Soon he would tell a spouse that their partner was dead. Still, there was a chance that both spouses were in the car, and he might have to inform a babysitter that the LeFleurs would not be returning home.

As he looked over the accident scene once more, he noticed that there were no skid marks. The driver never tried to stop.

As the diver walked up to the state trooper, he nodded his head, "I am sorry, sir, but it looks as if the mighty Mississippi claimed another poor soul. We tried to look for the driver's body, but it appears that the current carried it away."

Nodding his head, he asked, "So it appears to have been just a driver in the car?"

"I can't say for sure. The windshield caved in from the impact, but there appeared to have been a laptop bag on the front seat that fell to the floor."

As Officer Andy Bruni listened to the diver, he wished he had chosen a different career. This was not how he wanted to spend his night, and he knew that whoever answered the door at the LeFleur house would not want to hear what he had to say.

Officer Bruni had lost count of all the family notifications he made over the years. Even though this was the most unpleasant part of the job, it was one that he must do.

As he drove to the victim's house, he noticed that the neighborhood was filled with half million dollar homes. Homes that he would never be able to afford on his salary. He bet that the garages housed foreign cars that cost more than his house.

Before exiting the car, he checked the address again. The last thing he wanted was to knock on the wrong door at this time of the night. He grimaced as the notification came up that the victim was an organ donor. It was too bad that they didn't have a body.

As he made his way to the front door, he realized that money didn't buy you everything in life. No amount of money could stop the grim reaper from coming for you when your time was up. By the time he knocked on the door, it was three in the morning. He knocked four hard, deliberate knocks before ringing the doorbell.

A woman's voice sounded through the door, "Who is there? Tom, is that you? Did you forget your keys?"

Officer Bruni replied, "Ma'am, it's the police."

He stepped back as he heard the locks being turned. "Is there a problem, officer?"

"Ma'am, I am sorry to bother you at this hour, but is your husband home?"

Officer Bruni caught a glimpse of fear dance across her eyes, "No, he hasn't made it home from work yet."

 "Ma'am, are you Bree LeFleur and is your husband Tom LaFleur?"

Her voice quivered as she replied, "Yes. Why? What is the problem?"

"I regret to inform you, ma'am, that your husband was involved in an automobile accident several hours ago."

The woman in front of him grasped the door for support, "What? What happened? Is he okay? What hospital is he in?"

"I am sorry ma'am, but his car was found in the Mississippi River. The divers were unable to recover his body."

Bree let out a wail as she dropped to the floor. Tears fell from her eyes as the sobs wracked her body. A teenage boy walked down the stairs asking, "Mom, what's wrong? I thought I heard you yelling."

As the boy stooped down to be by his mother's side, Officer Bruni handed her his business card, "Ma'am, I am sorry for you and your family's loss. Please call me if you have any questions."

Bree extended a shaking hand and took the card. As her son rubbed his tired eyes, forcing himself to focus on the man standing in the doorway, he asked in a shaky voice, "Mom, what is going on? Why is this man here?"

A teenage girl appeared at the top of the landing in a set of pink satin pajamas. "Again, ma'am, I am sorry for your loss," he stated as he backed away from the door.

As the officer closed the door behind him, Bree hugged her two children as tears poured down her face, "Oh my babies, I am so sorry." Through deep sobs, she informed them, "Your father was in a terrible accident earlier."

Jonathan asked, "Where is he? Can we go see him?"

Cupping his cheek, Bree explained, "I am so sorry honey, but he didn't make it."

***

He watched the house from a few houses down, pleased to see what had transpired so far. If only he could have heard the conversations that took place. He wanted to be directly across from the house, but was afraid that it would arouse suspicion. No, it was better for him to watch at a distance.

He couldn't believe that everything was going as he planned. The night ended in tragedy just as it should. As his cherished Bree and her children cried over the death of their beloved husband and father, he smiled. The death of Tom LeFleur was only the beginning. This was the calm before the storm. Soon all of their lives would be forever changed.

Chapter 61

As Neil made his way back home, he shook his head in disbelief. At the front door, Lisa asked, "What in the world is going on? Did the police finally decide to do a raid?"

"No, they came to notify Bree that Tom had been killed in an automobile accident earlier."

Lisa let out a gasp, "What? Oh no, poor Bree."

"His body has not been found, but witnesses confirmed no one jumped before the car landed in the river."

Lisa never particularly cared for Bree or Tom, but still she would never have wished this on them. The poor kids must be devastated by the death of their father. She rubbed her belly as a shiver of fear moved through her. Life was too short, too precious to be taken for granted. Soon she and Neil would have their own children, and she didn't know what she would ever do if something happened to Neil. She couldn't imagine raising a child, much less twins, without him.

As Neil thought about what all transpired tonight, he wondered what would happen to Bree's little side business now.

She had been consistent with her blackmail payments, but since she no longer had to worry about her husband finding out, he may have to find another way to ensure that she continued making them.

Neil's gambling had gotten a little out of hand lately, and he needed those payments if he wanted to keep Lisa from finding out.

Neil never allowed himself to incur gambling debts, but Tom had not been so lucky. Tom owed the wrong people a LOT of money. Neil heard that these men went through with any plans they decided to implement.

The last time Tom and Neil went out, poor Tom thought he was on a roll at the casino. He hit the craps tables as well as roulette. He had been on such a high that Neil couldn't get him to stop when he lost all of his chips. Instead, Tom borrowed more money to continue playing.

Perhaps Neil should never have taken Tom to the casino in the first place. The man looked so depressed though, that Neil assumed a night on the town would help him relax some. That night the drinks were overflowing as their winning streak increased. The flashing lights of the games lured Tom in and it wasn't long before he had no control over his gambling.

Neil never saw anything like it before. He began to wonder if perhaps Tom did indeed know about his wife's infidelity and was looking for his own release.

***

Owen removed the SD card from his camera and inserted it into the small safe deposit box. He made sure to add the photos, as well. It was a shame that before Tom LeFleur could find out just how naughty his wife was, he met his death.

He reviewed the photos again before placing them in the safe. Several photos showed quite a few prestigious members of society visiting with Mrs. LeFleur. These were men who would stop at nothing to prevent these pictures from being released to the public. If anyone knew he had these photos it could be the end of his career, or his life.

Before closing the safe, he read the front page of the paper one more time. As he perused the article on the death of Mr. LeFleur he wondered if the cops honestly believed it had been an accident. Later on he would make some discreet calls to see how they labeled this case.

Chapter 62

As Bree attempted to put her life back together after Tom's death, she was still reeling from all the changes. It appeared that these last few months they were both keeping secrets, only Tom's were much more devastating than hers. While Bree spread her legs and slept with as many men as she possibly could to keep their house, Tom dug them deeper into debt.

She discovered that there were no life insurance policies on him and worse; he took out a second mortgage on their house and never paid that note, as well. She felt sick to her stomach when she heard about their newest financial dilemmas. She honestly thought that the bills were caught up, but it appeared that Tom accumulated even more behind her back. He had continued to dig them deeper and deeper into a bottomless pit of debt.

Tomorrow would be Tom's wake. She was celebrating his life with a memorial when if he were here in front of her right now she would strangle the bastard. How could he do this to her and the kids? Where did all the money he had borrowed against the house go to? He drained not only all of their savings accounts but their investment accounts, as well. If it wasn't for the money she had in her private account, they would be broke. She had to catch up on the second mortgage, or they would be put out on the streets to live.

At least she had managed to pay off the credit cards and miscellaneous bills that she knew about without Tom's knowledge. She had no doubt that if he had known the credit cards were almost paid off, he would have charged them up once again.

She needed to determine how much money they had to live on. She could slowly start depositing money into their primary account to pay the bills that needed to be paid without drawing any unwanted attention. Tears filled her eyes at the thought of Tom not being around anymore to ask questions about the deposits. Should she have let him know how she was earning money? Then maybe he wouldn't have felt compelled to work so hard. If he had known that their financial situation was no longer grim would he have been home instead of working? Could she have prevented his death? Did her deception cause his death?

She considered selling the house, but didn't want to cause the children more distress in their already turbulent young lives. No, she would keep them afloat. Even if it meant taking on more clients or working more hours on the website. Fortunately Tom's death, gave her the opportunity to work on the website at night, after the kids went to bed. That would bring in some extra cash, and also allow her to spend her days strictly with clients.

Bree felt her heart break as her sullen faced son came into the kitchen. Jonathan hadn't smiled since his dad had passed away. It seemed like it had been months instead of a few short weeks.

"Good morning honey. Did you sleep well?"

Shrugging, he replied, "All right, I guess."

As Bree looked at her son, she still couldn't believe how much he had grown this year. His height overpowered hers by almost a good foot now. His boyish good looks were transforming into that of a handsome young man, almost the spitting image of his dad.

She made the decision that day, after tomorrow, both Jonathan and Gracie would go back to school. It was time things returned to normal, or as close as possible.

As Jonathan fixed himself a plate of scrambled eggs and sausage, Gracie walked into the kitchen, "Mom, do we have to go back to school?"

"Yes, you can't afford to miss too many days." Gracie was still mourning her dad's death, but mourning or not she would have fussed about going to school. Gracie and Jonathan were entirely different people when it came to school. Where Jonathan was studious, Gracie would much rather play hooky. Gracie had definitely hit her teenage years and was making Bree's life miserable. She even reverted to throwing temper tantrums similar to that of a young child. She thought Jonathan had been difficult at this age, but Gracie was ten times worse.

There was no doubt in her mind now that teenage girls were an entirely different breed. However, just because her dad passed away didn't mean that Bree would put up with her mess either.

Up in her room, Bree spread out the bills she found in Tom's office. She needed to understand their actual financial situation better. After she had a breakdown of what they owed, she was flabbergasted. She needed to bring in over ten thousand dollars a month to pay for both mortgages, the car notes, insurance, utilities and other bills. That didn't include groceries, getting her nails done or anything recreational they wanted to do.

Bree had no idea just how in debt they were. Tom only let her see the bills he wanted to. She couldn't believe he kept this much a secret from her. What had he spent all the money on? She had no idea he had these credit cards, much less that they were maxed out.

While she played the diplomatic socialite to all of their friends and Tom's business associates, did any of those people know the financial mess they were in? It appeared that Tom owed several businesses around town money, and those same people stopped by to offer their condolences.

Yet, as she tried to make sense of all the numbers, she honestly had no idea what she was going to do. Once again, she had to rob Peter to pay Paul. She would have to add more clients into her daily routine as well as work longer hours on the website. If that didn't work, then she wasn't sure what to do. She knew for a fact that there was no regular nine to five job that paid as well as what she currently made sleeping with these men.

Perhaps she should consider starting her own business. She brought in a considerable amount of money in those few hours that she worked and if Mike had girls working all day then he must bring in some serious money. Her only downfall was that while she still looked good, she was no longer a young woman. She couldn't compete with the young women, but then again, she didn't need a majority of the business just enough to get the bills paid.

As bad as her life was right now, she was the one who got herself into this mess. After all, Tom gave her exactly what she always dreamed of having, a big house, three car garage, pool, and a flashy vehicle. Yes, he gave her everything that she wanted, but it appeared that this life had left them broke.

If she wanted to consider venturing into this new business, she would need to bring in young women. She would have to be careful about who she brought in. The last thing she needed was to alert the police to what was going on. If she wanted to attract the men with money, her girls would have to be credible and insanely beautiful.

As she tapped her pen on the desk, she started making a mental checklist in her mind of all that she would need to research. She may be able to pull up a lot of information over the internet, but something told her that searching for "how to start a porn website" would not be readily available through the various search engines.

She could start dropping hints to her current clients. In this particular business, referrals were important.

After the kids had gone to sleep, Bree perused the escort websites trying to get some ideas on how they liked to run things.

Chapter 63

Just as the rain began to fall from the heavens, Bree watched as a few mourners poured into the funeral home. When she first heard the news about Tom she was too shocked to react. Then, after the reality set in, she wasn't sure what to do. She couldn't have a funeral without having an actual body to bury. Instead, where a coffin should be was a large picture of Tom.

The sun had yet to make an appearance today. The mist hung heavy in the air. Neither of her children made a sound as they sat in the chairs with solemn looks. Each person who came in stood with their head down, as if fearing to look Bree in the eyes.

As she greeted several mourners, tears silently slid down her cheeks. Today she had her long hair neatly arranged in a tight bun. As she gazed around the growing crowd of mourners, a tall figure appeared in the back of the funeral home. Her heart stopped for a moment as she blinked a few times to clear the moisture from her eyes. For just a moment, the man looked similar to Tom, as impossible as it sounded.

The figure disappeared just as quickly as it appeared. Could it be that Tom's ghost was curious to see who all came to tell him goodbye?

A hopelessness came over her as she thought of what she and the children's lives would be like without Tom. Despite all his faults, he was a damn good father, and he truly loved his children.

Looking up, she saw the priest making his way to the front of the room. Father Matthew Blanchard gladly accepted her request to perform a memorial service. The priest was a tall, muscular man who was dressed in a long, black robe.

Bree grew up Methodist but happily switched religions when Tom asked her. Father Blanchard had performed a lovely memorial, and she would be forever in debt. She could never have pulled this off without his help.

Father Blanchard came up to Bree afterwards, "Once again, I am so sorry for your loss. Your husband will be dearly missed."

Taking his extended hand, she replied, "Thank you for all that you did. I cannot thank you enough for all your help."

A movement in the back of the room caught her attention. A tall, heavyset man was staring at her. The way he looked at her was unsettling.

The way he dressed reminded her of a mobster, which was ridiculous. Why would someone like that even be at Tom's memorial? Yet, he had a domineering facade. Of all the people here, he was the only one whose face could be made of marble.

She glanced over at him, certain he wanted to say something. That was until Father Blanchard commanded her attention once more. "If you ever need anyone to talk to, I am here for you."

***

He couldn't resist going to the dearly departed Tom LeFleur's memorial service. No matter how often he told himself it was wrong, he felt an unknown force pulling him there.

He found himself drawn to Bree LeFleur once again. Her husband's death affected her more than he had anticipated. This was perhaps the best time to make his move, while she was down.

Chapter 64

LeDoux and Riley re-interviewed a few of the witnesses, hoping that they had remembered some miniscule piece of information, but their stories all remained the same. No one heard or saw anything. As with the previous times, no one knew anything.

Once again the two detectives reviewed every bit of information, hoping to find one piece of overlooked evidence. LeDoux asked Riley, "Did you find anything?"

Riley made a guttural noise in the back of his throat, "Even with the men, there are no signs of forced entry. Apparently, all of the victims opened their doors to the killer. It is more than likely they all welcomed him in. If these men were clients of a hooker, or Dominatrix, would they casually open the door to another man?"

"I've been asking myself the same thing. Either these men knew their killer or the killer found a way in without breaking and entering."

"It could be that this killer used these clients to satisfy some sick need of his own."

LeDoux looked over the crime scene photos once again. "These killings are too personal."

Riley nodded his head. "But there is no denying that he enjoys the kills."

Sighing, LeDoux stated, "The one thing we know is we are searching for a brilliant killer who is physically strong enough to overpower another man."

Chapter 65

Officer Bruni looked over the reports of Tom LeFleur's accident once more. This accident had haunted him ever since that night. The more he dug into Tom's background, the more he wondered about the crash. A body was never found, and Officer Bruni suspected that one never would be.

His gut instinct told him that his death was no accident. Tom LeFleur owed the wrong people a lot of money.

Looking over the report once more, he hoped something new jumped out at him. It still bothered him that there were no skid marks and according to the witnesses, the driver never slowed down. It could be something as simple as the fact that the driver was driving too fast for the road conditions. Still, he should have slowed down when he saw that he was headed for the river.

It was a shame about the car too. It probably cost more than he made in a year. He did some checking, and Tom LeFleur left his wife with quite a few hefty bills to pay, including the car he wrecked. As with most of the other bills the couple had accumulated, they owed more than it was worth.

Still, even with the financial disaster Tom LeFleur left Bree in, she seemed to be paying off the bills. He couldn't figure out how she was doing it. At first, Officer Bruni assumed that the accident was a possible life insurance scam, but since Tom had let it lapse that wasn't the case. Still, the bills were getting paid. Even before Tom's death, they had been delinquent on most of their bills. One day they faced foreclosure on their house and repossession of their vehicles, then, suddenly, they were almost caught up. He bet quite a few people would love to know what their secret was. As far as he could tell Bree had not held a job since her marriage. Tom's salary had been recently cut drastically. There was no way they should be making current payments, much less catching up.

Chapter 66

Jonathan wasn't thrilled to be back at school, but it beat being stuck at home. Although his dad was never around much, the house seemed different without him there at all. He could tell that his mom was stressed. He heard her pacing the halls late at night, as if she didn't know what to do with her life.

She didn't know it, but he overheard one of her phone conversations telling someone that Tom left them flat broke. With as much as his dad worked all the time, how could they have no money?

As he left class, he noticed Gracie down the hall. His vision blurred when he saw Gracie press her body up against the senior. Of course, to Jonathan, it didn't matter what grade this boy was in. He didn't want anyone to talk to or to look at her as if she was the hottest thing in this school.

As he made his way to Gracie, he heard her laughing and joking with the guy as his hand caressed her arm. Jonathan grabbed the guy by the shoulder and whirled him around to face him, "You need to keep your hands off my sister."

Jonathan didn't care that this guy was not only older than him, but bigger as well. He refused to stand around and let his baby sister become some guy's latest conquest. Jeremy Chauvin had a reputation for loving them and leaving them. He was only interested in a girl's virginity. He loved to brag in the locker room about whose cherry he popped the previous night. Well, Jonathan would be damned if his sister was next on Jeremy's list.

"Dude, what the hell is your problem? I am just talking to your sister."

Shaking his head, Jonathan felt the steam coming off of his body. He had never been this mad before. "You need to stay the fuck away from my sister. I know what you are after, and you can just look some place else. There is no way in hell I will allow my sister to be your next conquest."

Gracie looked at her brother shocked as Jeremy walked away. "Why did you do that? He was asking me out!"

"You don't need to hang out with guys like him. He only wants you for one thing, and one thing only, to screw you. I can't believe you are naive enough to fall for him and his lines."

Letting out an exasperated sigh, Gracie replied angrily, "They were not just lines. He told me that I was the prettiest girl at this school."

Laughing Jonathan said, "Come on, you can't seriously be falling for his crap. Haven't you heard the rumors around the school about him?"

Gracie stopped and glared at her brother, "I don't listen to rumors. They are just things told by mean spirited people who are jealous."

"Not with him. He has a long list of girls that he screwed just to say he did them. As soon as you spread your legs for him, he will be gone."

Gracie rolled her eyes, "I swear. Why can't you let me have some fun?"

Shaking his head, Jonathan told her, "That is not the kind of fun that you need to have. I don't want my sister being the latest slut around school."

Instead of replying Gracie stormed off toward the bathroom. He didn't care if he hurt her feelings. She needed to be told the truth. If not, she would be another notch on the guy's bed post. He would not sit by and let his sister become known as a slut.

Truthfully, though, he wasn't sure why he even bothered. Gracie did whatever she damn well pleased, and there was nothing he could do about it. But as the man of the house, he felt that he should step in. It was his responsibility to look out for his mom and sister.

***

If the whole school wasn't watching, Gracie would stomp her feet and stick out her tongue to annoy Jonathan. He humiliated her. If only her dad were here, he would understand. Right now, more than ever, she missed him.

He may not have been around much, but whenever she needed to talk to him he was there. If he were still alive, he would tell Jonathan to leave her alone.

Jonathan acted like he was in charge now, and there was no getting along with him. Her mom was so wrapped up in her own life that she didn't even notice Jonathan's new behavior. Gracie didn't understand why Jonathan freaked out when she was only talking to the guy. It's not like she would ever do something with him, no matter how much he asked.

Besides, she wasn't ready to take that final step and lose her virginity. She had too much pride in herself to start sleeping with any boy who asked her. She wanted that moment to be special and, so far, none of the boys made her toes curl or even her heart pound.

Jeremy was cute, but way older than her. Besides, he would be going off to college. She wanted a boyfriend who she could hang out with and not wonder when she would see him again.

Chapter 67

Officer Bruni walked into his captain's office and said, "Sir, I have something that I want to go over with you."

Captain Brian Fontenot extended his hand to the empty chair in front of his desk. Officer Bruni handed him the file before sitting down. "Sir, this is about an automobile accident I worked not long ago. Tom LeFleur's body has never been found."

Captain Fontenot quickly looked over the file and asked, "What about the accident bothers you? Besides a body not being found?"

Letting out a long sigh Officer Bruni said, "A lot about the accident bothers me. I know it was a rain slicked road, high speed vehicle, but the witnesses said the driver never once slowed down. I did a little snooping and this couple was deep in debt, on the verge of bankruptcy. Plus, he owed the wrong people a lot of money."

"So you think it was an insurance scam?"

Shaking his head, Officer Bruni replied, "That's the thing, there was no insurance money. He let his life insurance lapse, but here is the kicker - the wife caught up on most of the delinquent bills, but I can't find any work history for this Bree LeFleur since she married Tom LeFleur."

Captain Fontenot drummed his fingers on his desk, "Hmmm, that is very interesting indeed."

Officer Bruni pointed to the financial information he dug up on the couple. "As you can tell, one day they were in financial ruins and then the next she paid off several of the bills. Now, it looks as if Mrs. LeFleur didn't know about some of the bills her husband accumulated until after his death, but once again, she managed to catch those up as well."

"Well, however, she did it; she managed to keep all of her deposits small enough to keep any unwanted attention off of herself." Running his hand through his hair, he asked, "So just how do you suppose the bills are getting paid? Drugs?"

"It could be drugs, but I have also seen this woman. She is a knockout."

Captain Fontenot asked, "So what are you thinking?"

"It wouldn't hurt to do a little surveillance of her house. She found a way to earn some money and my gut tells me that there is something there."

"I do believe your gut instincts are right. Let's have a detail put on her house for a few days. Perhaps we can find out if there is indeed anything going on."

Chapter 68

Bree had to increase her customer base, or she would have to put the house on the market. The last thing she wanted to do was contact a real estate agent. Unfortunately, between the blackmail payments and all the debt her late husband accumulated, she may not have a choice. The only problem is if she did put the house on the market, she would have to move her business to another location for the time being.

Since Tom's death, she entertained customers during the day and saved her nights for the web business. That brought in some much needed revenue, but the cash reserve she had built up was quickly diminishing.

While some of her clients were interested in only spending a small amount of time with an actual woman, others were interested in sex. She must admit, sometimes the sex was pure heaven. This may be a business, but she received a lot of pleasure from it.

If you actually stopped and thought about it, all the women were prostitutes, even though they would argue that very act. Sex, and even companionship, were simply a bartering system. For centuries, women have exchanged sex for some type of compensation.

As a teenager, you gave your date a kiss for bringing you home. The nicer the date could lead to second base, or even third. A series of dates meant that the guy was getting laid.

Since the beginning of time, women have known that sex was power. It was a true motivator where man was concerned. It had been used as currency over and over again in one way or the other. Currently, she traded sex for cash instead of a dinner date.

Bree read over the instructions before she prepared for her client's arrival. When the client sent her the specific instructions and outfit, her gut instinct was to tell him no. Until she saw just how much he was offering her for the two hour time slot.

He gave her precise instructions. If she disobeyed any of his instructions there would be a punishment.

Part of her wanted to forget one of his instructions, but if it meant he would withhold some of the money that was something she couldn't afford.

A noise from downstairs broke her train of thought. In a few short minutes, her client's fantasy would be played out. Her heart skipped a beat as she heard him enter the room. If only she could take off the blindfold, or at least adjust it to where she could see him.

It took all of her self-control not to jump when his fingers caressed her ankle before moving up her leg. Anticipation washed over her as his hand moved seductively up her thigh. Instead of lingering on her most feminine of parts his hands kept moving up her body. It was the slightest of touches, but enough to drive her wild with desire.

Just the feeling of his playful fingers moving over her body lit a fire deep inside of her. She had been touched by him, and others, before, but being blindfolded was a massive turn on right now. She had to bite back a moan as his fingers teased her breasts.

This whole experience was more erotic and tantalizing than she ever imagined. As he gave her breast a firm squeeze, the sensation was pleasurable laced with a hint of pain. Until she started in this business she never considered mixing pain with pleasure. Now it was something she couldn't do without.

As he unsnapped the front closure of the bra, she allowed her body to enjoy his touch. His slow movements drove her wild with desire. He straddled her with a leg on either side of her hips. She ached for attention as he caressed her thighs once more.

As he continued to tease her, the anticipation built as pleasurable sensations moved across her body. If only she could reach out and touch him like he was touching her right now. As if reading her mind, he took her hand and guided it to his erection.

Bree didn't need further instruction; she teased him with the same slow deliberation he used on her. Just from her mere touch, she felt him become harder. She gripped him a little tighter as she increased her stroking, making sure to keep the tempo nice and steady.

As she continued to stroke him, he shifted his attention to her breasts. The biting and sucking became almost too much for her. Without warning, he grabbed her hands and forced both arms up above her head as he kissed her forcibly. The kiss quickly became feverish as his tongue delved deep into her mouth.

In one swift movement, he ripped the G-string off of her body. His touch on her lower body sent electrical pulses through her.

When his moist, hot tongue delved deep into her, she almost lost all control. Every part of her body was hot with desire as his tongue continued to explore her. Her blood turned to molten lava as he teased her. His teasing was almost unbearable as she waited for his next move.

As his fingers and tongue worked their magic on her, she felt as if she was about to burst. It wasn't long before tidal waves of orgasmic pleasure coursed through her body. Before she had a chance to come down from the tidal wave moving through her body, he entered her with incredible force.

As he increased the speed of his movements and drove deeper inside of her, she felt herself losing control once more. Her nails dug deep into his back as she rode the waves of pleasure coursing through her body. The vigor of his thrusts and the intensity of his animalistic grunts turned her on even more. She totally abandoned herself to the raw, primal sensations building up inside of her. Every part of her body came alive with desire. Every muscle in her body quivered from his touch.

As she lay on the bed, fully sated from his lovemaking, she listened as he left. She wondered why a man like him even came to her. He was handsome enough to have any woman he wanted, and it was evident he had money. Could it be that he was married, and his wife refused to give into his wildest fantasies? If that were the case, then she had no idea what she was missing.

Chapter 69

Things were going better than he could have planned. He couldn't have mapped out the details any better than they were going right now. He was closer to spending the rest of his life with the woman of his dreams.

Thankfully, her husband saved him one step by dying. Now to get rid of the kids and convince her she didn't need to work as a whore any longer. She had been the only woman he forgave for this betrayal.

He wanted to build a new life from the ground up with her. He could barely wait to spend each and every day with her.

He knew he would make her happy. She would never be given a chance to find fault with anything he did. He would jump through hoops to make sure she stayed happy.

He turned on the computer, waiting for her nightly show to start. With her husband deceased, she stopped performing during the day and moved her shows strictly to the night. At first he had been upset, but now he found it satisfying to watch her as he drifted off to sleep. If only she would stop meeting with these men during the day.

***

With one eye on the road, Bree searched through her purse to find her cell phone. "Hello?"

The raspy voice hissed, "He's gone. Soon you will be mine."

"Excuse me?"

Instead of replying, the phone went dead. A shiver of fear ran down her spine. It appeared that her stalker kept a close eye on all that went on in her life.

She looked to see if Caller ID happened to pick up the number he called from. She grimaced when she saw that it failed, *Unknown Caller*. Of course, he was smart enough to block his number.

She refused to allow this guy to ruin her day. She had several clients lined up and needed to get back home to prepare.

Just thinking about the voice on the other end of the line, sent goose bumps up and down her body. There was a familiarity to the voice, but one she couldn't quite place. She glanced in her rear-view mirror and felt her heart catch in her throat. A dark colored sedan was following her; she was certain of it. She noticed that same car when she left the school earlier.

Your mind is just in overdrive. No one was following you. Still, her heart pounded inside of her chest as her palms began to sweat. *You're being silly. He's called you before.*

She glanced in the rear-view and noticed that the sedan kept a safe distance from her. Perhaps the driver was going the same way as her. Besides, it was not like he would pull her over to the side of the road right now to kill her. It was broad daylight, and there were too many witnesses.

Still, she stepped on the accelerator and switched lanes. When the car followed her every movement, she started to panic. She considered calling 911, but that was the last thing she needed to do right now.

Get a grip, she told herself. *The guy was more than likely in a hurry to get to work. You are paranoid because of the phone call.*

She forced herself to calm down, and checked her rear view mirror before turning down the street right before her house. She may as well take the long way home to ensure the car wasn't following her.

When it didn't bother to turn down the same road as her, she almost laughed at her own silliness. She completely overreacted. She took in a deep breath and made her way home.

***

A tingle of exhilaration swept through him, causing his groin to tighten. Just hearing her voice was enough to send his blood pumping.

He looked over at the clock. Soon she would be home, and he could catch a glimpse of her. With the husband now gone, it was time to dispose of the children so he could have her all to himself. He couldn't stand to wait any longer. He despised her sharing her body with all of these other men.

Chapter 70

Officer Bruni walked into Captain Fontenot's office, "You should see that place. All afternoon it looked more like a bed and breakfast or hotel rather than a home."

"So you are thinking what? She runs a brothel in her house?"

Nodding his head, he agreed, "That is exactly what I think." Taking in a deep breath, he said, "But, sir, some of the men whom we saw coming in and out of there are some very prestigious members of society."

As soon as Officer Bruni saw some of the men's faces going in and out of Bree LeFleur's, he knew he'd stumbled onto something big. Office Bruni looked over at Captain Fontenot, "There is something else. While performing surveillance on the house, we had the distinct impression someone else was also watching."

"Did you ever see anyone besides you?"

Shaking his head, Office Bruni responded, "No, it was always just a feeling."

"You don't think it could be the FBI do you?"

"No. We would have noticed one of their surveillance vehicles. I suspect the husband faked his death and is now watching his wife's every move."

"Unfortunately, faking your death isn't a crime. He will have a bunch of questions to answer, but that is more than likely all that will happen. There was no life insurance to claim, and none of the loans stipulated the debt would be paid off in the event of his death. No, he made sure to stick his wife with a bunch of bills that she couldn't afford."

"And I believe we discovered just how she earns her money to pay those bills."

Captain Fontenot nodded his head in agreement, "Now, we need to decide what the best way to proceed is."

Chapter 71

As Bree prepared for tonight's show, she pulled out her hidden safe. She was finally replenishing her nest egg of money. Damn Tom and all the problems he caused her lately. If he hadn't let his life insurance lapse, or accumulated the extra debt, she wouldn't need to spread her legs as much as she had. She couldn't complain about the money. She made more than any other woman, even some men, she knew. Soon, she would have enough money saved to purchase another car as well as take her and the kids on a luxury vacation.

She didn't feel guilty about having sex with these men, nor did she feel sorry for the wives. If they were giving it to their husbands, they wouldn't be stepping out, spending all of their money on her. She learned the hard way that, in this world, you have to take what you can get.

She sprayed her body with the body glitter and applied her favorite perfume. She double checked herself in the mirror once more to confirm that the outfit was as sexy as it looked in the store. The men would beg for more by the time she was done tonight. If all went well, she would convince a few more men to seek her out in person.

She turned on the computer, started playing *"S&M"* by Rihanna and began her performance. She let the men's requests dictate the way she acted. Halfway through she slid her hands up and down her body, along her crotch and spread her legs nice and wide. Soon, the right side of the monitor became active with comments from men requesting certain moves. She had them right where she wanted them now.

She pouted, bit her lip seductively, and gave the men orders while she pleasured herself in front of them. She imagined the excited look in each man's eyes. She wondered which ones were hiding what they watched from their wives, which ones were all alone, but wishing they were with her and which ones were spending their last dollar to catch a glimpse of her ass.

With each move she made, each article of clothing she removed, the men became harder and she became richer. It was all in the deliverance of the performance. She made sure to get the men's blood pumping and let them believe that she was wet for them.

She slowly moved her hand down her body once more. She imagined the anticipation in their eyes as her fingers separated her lips. She circled the swollen nub and moved it back and forth, side to side for the camera. She tickled it, bit her lip seductively and felt a climax building. As she slipped a finger inside, she was wet and throbbing. She moved her finger in and out of her faster as her thumb rubbed her swollen nub. She found the g-spot and made sure to rub it. She exploded in satisfaction as she slumped against the bed.   With that single performance, she watched her bank account grow.

Chapter 72

Ever since Harold Jackson decided to run for Senate, he found himself in the public's eye constantly. In a few days, he would begin his official re-election campaign, but right now he needed to relieve some stress. He depended on this woman's animosity. From what he learned, she was exceptionally good at dominating a man and keeping her mouth shut.

He stood a good chance of winning, if he kept his secrets well hidden. In the public's eye, he stood for the values that most Louisianans supported whole-heartedly. His list of backers was staggering. It also didn't hurt that the women found him a handsome devil, all broad shouldered and brooding dark looks.

Mon Dieu, as soon as she opened the door, he knew he had made the right decision. The male in him couldn't deny that she was a knock-out. *Si belle.* He may be playing with fire by letting this woman in his life.

As he followed her inside, he watched her every movement. Her shapely legs went on for miles and miles, leading to other hidden delights. He wanted those sensuous legs wrapped around him, her silky hair falling across her shoulders. *Le bon Dieu m'ait la main.* God help him. She was a hard woman to resist.

He hoped the rumors around town were true. He couldn't wait to turn to putty in her hands, waiting to be molded. Ever since he'd entered politics, he kept his tempestuous love affairs out of the public eye. If his affair with this woman were to be discovered, it could be detrimental to his career.

He spent too much time and money on his career to let anything get in his way. *Mais non*, he would not allow some little affair to mess up his dreams of becoming Governor of Louisiana within a few years, and eventually President of the United States. However, he wanted to find out what interesting talents this woman had.

He had been so busy planning his campaign that he had not taken care of his sexual needs. Being this close to such an attractive and obviously willing woman reminded him of the need to remedy this situation. He was grateful that his friend gave him her number. Hours in the company of this woman, whose only goal was to satisfy his sexual needs, was just what he needed. He was anxious to see if his friend had not embellished on how talented her mouth really was.

***

As soon as Bree opened the door, she knew instantly who this man was. Damn, but the man was better looking in person. The suit he wore fit him to perfection; it emphasized his broad shoulders, trim waist, lean hips and powerful thighs. If he should ever decide to marry, the market would be missing one prime piece of real estate.

As she welcomed him inside, she felt the heat emanating from his body. She caught a whiff of his cologne, and her pulse quickened. Every pore in her body tingled, thirsty for his touch. Her libido had gone into overdrive today. Just the sound of his voice sent shivers down her spine.

Smiling, she informed him, "You are right on time."

"I have been guaranteed that you will be discreet about my visit. Running for office keeps me in the eye of the public. However, I do not think that my constituents would approve of my peculiar fantasies."

Running a hand up his arm, she replied, "I promise you that I will be very discreet. Trust me, the last thing I want is anyone knowing what goes on behind closed doors here."

She looked at her new client with thinly veiled interest. His lips curled into a roguish smile that warmed her to her core. It should be illegal for one man to be this damn sexy. She noticed his high cheekbones and the strength of his jaw. He looked utterly sensual and provocative. She became anxious to get him in the room and kiss those luscious lips. She caught him observing her body. His gaze dropped to the opening of her latex dress and settled on the revealing cleavage. She started to wonder if he wanted her as bad as she wanted him.

Once they were in her room, she began to play her favorite part, the Dominatrix. This was the most powerful aphrodisiac she ever encountered.

She wanted to kiss every square inch of that well defined body of his, devouring every inch of him. He reminded her of an Adonis. She couldn't wait to play her games with him.

"Undress for me slave."

"As you wish, Mistress."

After he had undressed she ordered him, "Get on the bed, slave."

Pulling out the fur lined cuffs, she secured him to the headboard as well as the footboard. She placed the black scarf around his eyes, making sure the knot was secured. She was getting ready to give him one hell of a wild ride. Her body burned with need for him.

But first, she wanted to tease him before they succumbed to this tortuous temptation. She let her hands wander over his body with black silk gloves. Using her mouth, she put on a condom. She heard a low moan escape from him.

She felt his erection brush up against her. Her lips travelled up and down his body. She reached into her bag and pulled out an assortment of her toys. It was time for her to have some fun. When she could no longer control her lust, she mounted him and rode him until he found his release.

***

Officer Bruni couldn't believe his eyes when he saw Senator Harold Jackson knock on the door they were watching. "Well, I don't think she is dealing drugs at this residence. "

His partner laughed as he shook his head, "Mais non, I think our woman is peddling something much more in demand than drugs."

Bruni nodded his head, "Mon Dieu, I am surprised she can still walk straight after the number of men who go in and out of her residence."

Once back at the station he knocked on Captain Fontenot's office door. "Sir, do you have a minute?"

Waving his hand, the Captain said, "Come on in. By the look on your face, you have something big to tell me."

Making himself comfortable in the chair, Bruni started, "Well, we confirmed what goes on at the LeFleur residence."

"Oh yeah, something big?"

"During our stake out today we saw Senator Jackson walk into her residence. It appears the lady runs a well visited brothel sir."

Letting out a loud whistle, the Captain replied, "We sure in the hell need to keep this quiet."

"*Mon Dieu*, I'm still reeling from this latest discovery."

Captain Fontenot ran his hands through his hair as he contemplated their next move, "I need to talk to the District Attorney first of all. When this goes down the shit will hit the fan. If Jackson is a client, then I am certain that there are other prestigious members of society she sees as well."

"Yes, sir. This is the kind of case that could end a man's career."

Captain Fontenot looked Officer Bruni in the eyes, "Mais non son, this is the type of case that could get someone killed." Sighing, he added, "There is no way we can let any of this leak to the media. This is the stuff tabloid dreams are made of. We need to try to keep this away from the media for as long as possible. Especially until we know how we want to handle this matter."

Chapter 73

Cassandra lay in her bed, staring up at the ceiling. She watched as the ceiling fan blades spun round and round.

For the last three hours, she did nothing but toss and turn. Sleep eluded her tonight. If she didn't get to sleep soon, she would be utterly useless in the morning.

There was a story here. If only she could figure out a way to approach the possibility that a serial killer was focused on high priced escorts, or more importantly those who are Dominatrixes. She suspected that some of the women had worked for Amber at one time or another.

She wondered what Derrick would do if she showed up on his doorstep right now. Would he ravage her body? She still remembered the way he smelled, entirely masculine and sexy. She rolled over to her side and clutched the pillow tight against her. It had been a while since she felt this alive from a man. She seldom let any man get close to her heart; they just couldn't be trusted. Every man she met reconfirmed that they were unfaithful and unable to keep promises. It must be in a man's DNA. She didn't need a man for money; she had enough of that, but she wanted to be loved just once.

She glanced around the room at everything money bought her so far. So far no one had ever wondered how someone her age could afford to live the way she did. Most people just assumed her parents paid her way in life. Even her parents never questioned her extravagant spending. Maybe they assumed she was in debt up to her ears. How wrong their assumptions would be, everything was paid for lock, stock, and barrel. Over the years, she managed to build up quite a nice sized nest egg. What would the good detective say if he found out just how she earned her money in the past? Would he look at her with disgust in his eyes? After all, when Bennett Soileau found out what she did, he dropped her like a hot potato.

Still, she couldn't seem to get the handsome detective out of her mind. Ever since she pushed her way into his house the other night, she was reminded of just how lonely her bed was lately.

She tossed back to her side. She was so pathetic. The man didn't even like her and all she thought about was having sex with him. He was not the kind of man she needed in her life. The man could be rude, arrogant and downright wretched.

Kicking back the covers she gave up on sleep and headed to her computer. She decided to research women who were murdered here recently, especially with their throats slit.

As she went over the recent killings, she noticed a definite pattern. It appeared to be someone went from killing escorts to their clients. Could it be that a client became delusional for his paid Dominatrix and was killing off the rest of her clients so he could have her for himself?

But how did she prove she was on to something? Surely if there was a pattern here, the cops would have picked up on it. These murders also gave her another story idea. She began writing since sleep was eluding her tonight. Three hours later she had her story complete and sent it off to the editor for review.

Chapter 74

Harold Jackson walked into his office with a smile on his face. From his custom made navy blue, pinstriped suit, the spun cotton dress shirt, maroon silk tie and black leather shoes his presence screamed politician. He stood an imposing six foot three, deeply tanned skin with wavy auburn hair. His looks made any woman swoon.

As he made his way to his office, he acknowledged several friends and rivals. What would they think if they knew what went on in his mind? The first thing he planned on doing this morning was making another appointment with the luscious woman he recently met. The couple of grand she charged for her fee was well worth it. He had yet to meet anyone who enjoyed the same perverse interests as he.

He glanced at his Submariner Rolex and saw it was eight a.m. on the dot. Surely it couldn't be too early in the morning to call her now. Just thinking about her caused heat to build in his groin. His mouth watered in anticipation of meeting her again. Unconsciously, he licked his lips. He couldn't wait to get his hands on that sweet ass of hers again.

As he walked past his secretary's desk, Kim called out, "Sir, you had a letter dropped off first thing this morning."

Looking at her, he wondered why she was bothering him with such trivial things, "Just put it with the rest of the mail. I will take a look at it later."

Kim jumped up from her desk, letter in hand. Stuttering she replied, "Well, um, sir. You see the messenger stated the letter was only to be opened by you."

Harold looked at the letter addressed to him, marked "Personal and Confidential". He tucked it in his inside suit pocket and walked into his office.

Once seated, he loosened his tie and stared at the envelope. Tiny beads of perspiration formed on his forehead. *Who in the hell would send him a personal and confidential letter? Why here?*

His eyes darted around the room as if fearing someone lurked in the shadows. Shaking his head, he told himself that he was being ridiculous. Besides, there was probably nothing clandestine in this letter.

He slipped a thumb under the envelope's flap and opened the letter in one swift move. He stared at the letter in complete disbelief.

> *Dear Senator Jackson,*
>
> *I wonder if your constituents would vote for you if they knew just what you like to do in your spare time. This is not a request, but a demand. You will deposit five thousand dollars cash into the account mentioned below on the twelfth of every month. If not, the enclosed photographs will be released to the public.*

Harold crumpled the enclosed photos and saw red. *Just who in the hell sent this letter? How did someone find out about his appointment at Bree LeFleurs? Was she* trying to screw him in more ways than one? No, she had just as much to lose as he did. She wouldn't want her business getting out to the public either. But who? Who would know that he had been at her house? He was so careful, making sure that the street was empty, and no one was following him.

With hands shaking, he walked over to his office bar and poured himself a scotch. He downed the drink without bothering to appreciate the liquor's rich taste or aroma. He could not go to the authorities with regards to the blackmail letter. Should he approach Bree to find out if she were being blackmailed as well? *No, that was something he shouldn't do. If she wasn't being blackmailed, then there was a chance she would become too frightened and refuse to see him.* He had no intentions of ending their relationship right now. He finally met someone who fully satisfied him and if it meant paying a little extra for that luxury, so be it.

He knew one man he could call to get to the bottom of this and keep his mouth shut.

***

Owen Leger welcomed the cold air of the building. It was only nine o'clock in the morning, and the humidity was already clinging to the city. It was going to be a scorcher of a day.

He often wondered how different his life would be if his grandfather had immigrated to a northern state, instead of Louisiana. However, his grandfather wanted to follow the rest of the French immigrants and came directly to Louisiana.

After twenty-five years with the FBI, Owen decided he had enough of investigating the most heinous of crimes. He could go the rest of his life without ever investigating another murder.

No one in the FBI wanted to see him go. He always attacked his work like a dog after a bone. He, however, couldn't take any more of all the political bullshit that came along with the job. Instead, he retired and became a private investigator.

With his pension and investments, he really didn't need the work, but he wanted to keep his mind sharp. He could also pick and choose which cases he worked.

He kept his overhead low by being the only employee in his private investigating firm. Just as he walked into his office, the phone rang. "Leger."

Howard didn't even bother with introductions, "I got big problems, bon ami."

Owen propped his feet up on his desk and leaned back in his chair, "What kind of problems?"

"Serious problems that I don't need the public getting wind of."

Owen had to bite back a retort. "Did you want to discuss this over the phone?" Owen was certain he didn't want to know what his problem involved. From his experience, those who hold a high office tend to have problems that most individuals could never imagine. Then, there were also times where the individuals worried over nothing.

"I'm being blackmailed."

Owen let out a soft curse, "And you want me to find out by whom?"

"Yes, but this needs to be kept very confidential. I'm not sure if the woman is involved or not. If she isn't, then I don't want to bring her in this at all."

Owen asked, "And I take it this isn't something you want the cops getting wind of?"

"No, I don't want the authorities involved."

"I'm going to need to see the blackmail letter."

Howard sighed, "I know. This cannot be made public. I will drop it by your office at lunch."

"Let's meet at Porter's for steaks instead. It would be better if it appeared as if we were just meeting for lunch instead of drawing attention to your coming here."

"I can get away at one o'clock this afternoon."

***

Once back in his office Owen pulled out the letter and pictures that Howard Jackson gave him. As soon as he saw the pictures his old FBI investigative skills went off. Now he knew exactly why Harold Jackson didn't want any of this getting out.

The man was a political machine who was on his way up. He was not only politically connected, but he was adored by the elite and working class of Louisiana. A moderate Democrat, he preached fiscal responsibility and believed in feeding the people without the state footing the bill. He painstakingly juggled his political issues so every constituent, rich or poor, felt that they got their fair share. He made sure his political platform had something for everyone. There were rumors that he saw himself eventually running for the President of the United States.

My, my, my, could it be that Mrs. LeFleur was blackmailing her clients now? Perhaps it was time to see what all the seductive Bree LeFleur had been up to since her husband's untimely death.

Chapter 75

Cassandra Evans could not get Detective LeDoux off of her mind tonight. No matter how hard she tried, he seemed to be there. If she had any hope of convincing him that she didn't always put the story first, she needed to tell him about the one that would be running soon. She had to inform him that it would be a short series instead of just one story. Her editor loved the piece so much, especially the aspects that went on behind the scenes, he wanted to turn it into something more. Most of the escorts refused to talk to her since animosity was crucial in their career. However, she knew a few that may give her a story as long as she left out any names. She also planned on talking to some of the girls working the streets, asking about their lives. Perhaps if people knew why they turned tricks, they would be treated with a little more respect. While some were looking for a way to earn some quick cash to get high, others were forced to work the streets to survive. Some found the possibility of living at home too dangerous to stay.

Grabbing her purse and car keys, she hurried to the station to see if he was still there. Just the thought of being in his presence made her heart race. As she went to open her car door, she realized her hands were actually shaking. She was acting like a teenager with a silly crush.

Cassandra's Mercedes SLK 320 zipped down the interstate. The air conditioner was turned up to make the car's interior much more bearable than the mugginess of the air outside. If it weren't for the fact that she was going to try to seduce a man, she would have considered dropping the top. There was just no way to make windblown hair sexy though. She checked her reflection in the rearview mirror to make sure that she was presentable before going to find Detective LeDoux. Satisfied that her lipstick still looked good, she tucked a strand of hair behind her left ear and stepped out into the night air.

When she arrived, Detective LeDoux was already pulling out of the parking lot. *Damn it!* She had to push the accelerator to keep up with him. He apparently had a heavier foot than her when it came to driving, and here she always thought cops would follow the rules of the road.

Cassandra ended up following him back to his house. She parked behind his motorcycle and walked up to him. Every time she saw him she couldn't help but remember how good he looked naked. The very thought made her mouth dry. It should be illegal for a man to be so damn good looking.

"Was there something you wanted Ms. Evans?" His deep voice completely unnerved her.

She bit back the remark that immediately came to mind, *you.* Clearing her throat, she tried to remember what she planned on saying. Her mind was a complete blank. "I just wanted to touch base with you on a story I would be publishing soon."

"You could have stopped by the station tomorrow instead of chasing me down at my house."

"I hoped to talk to you tonight. When I saw you leaving, my mind must have been on autopilot."

"Mm-hmm and you decided it would be best to come to my house instead of asking me in the morning?"

She followed him inside, keeping up the conversation, fearing he may send her home at any minute. "I didn't think you would mind, but if you would rather I catch you in the morning I can."

He walked over to the bar and poured them a drink. Maybe this wasn't a good idea. Cassandra's libido seemed to have moved into overdrive.

Showing her the bottle of Maker's Mark he asked, "Would you prefer something else?"

"That is fine." Maybe the fiery liquid would help take her mind off the fire that was already building up inside of her.

LeDoux took a sip of his drink and asked, "Now, Ms. Matthews, do you want to tell me the real reason you followed me home tonight?"

Cassandra took a gulp of her drink, hoping to settle her nerves, "Like I said, I wanted to talk about the story that is going to run."

As he took another sip of his drink, she knew she was playing with fire but couldn't stop herself. She smiled when he asked, "Are you sure you didn't have an ulterior motive?"

"Perhaps, I did just want to see you."

"And now that you have seen me?" He challenged.

She met his gaze. Getting involved with him could only spell trouble, and that was one thing she didn't need. *Talk about sleeping with the enemy.* Running her hand up and down his chest in slow, deliberate movements, "Do you honestly believe I am such a bad person? Is there nothing I can do to change your mind?"

"Lady, stick around here too much longer and you will find out exactly what I think of you."

Catering to his male ego, she asked, "Do I want to know?"

In a husky voice, he offered a challenge, "I don't know. You are talking to a man, not a little boy. I'm not someone who starts something I can't finish. I make sure the job is done, and done right."

She put a hand on each shoulder and looked up at him. "And who says I'm a tease?"

She watched as he clenched and unclenched his fists to settle his nerves. She reached up and touched his jaw, reveling in the way his five o'clock shadow felt against her smooth skin.

In one quick movement, he had his arms wrapped around her small figure. The instant contact caused her to lose her breath. Her pulse thundered in her ears, silencing the rest of the world. Desire spread through her like wildfire.

She tilted her head up to meet his mouth, anticipating the kiss. She was ready to lose herself in this sweet surrender.

His lips teased hers at first, barely touching her lips. In the next instant, his mouth devoured hers.

"Do you want to know?" He whispered in her ear.

"Know what?"

His tongue teased her lips before responding, "How I feel about you?"

 "Mmm." Cassandra's legs were like Jell-O. She could barely stand on her own two feet as he kissed his way down her neck. His hot lips captured her mouth once more. Her hands travelled up his body, resting on his chest. She felt the thundering beat of his heart. She quickly began to unbutton his shirt, needing to feel his bare skin against her palms.

His touch rendered her completely thoughtless. His tongue traced the outline of her mouth, sending shockwaves of electricity throughout her body. She kissed him back, enjoying his response. His hands grasped each side of her face and held her close, deepening the kiss.

She felt his erection pressing against her abdomen. She moved her hands under his shirt, pushing it off his shoulders. As his hands traveled to her voluptuous breasts, massaging and teasing her, she couldn't remember the last time she wanted someone as much as she wanted him.

Chapter 76

He watched the computer with a storm of anger raging in his belly. His fists clenched with the need to punch something, or someone.

What's the matter with her? He sent her the notes proclaiming his love. He even killed for her. Why couldn't she see that he was all she needed?

The image of her wrapping those glorious legs of hers around another man made him sick. This man, or should he say boy, couldn't be more than twenty-four or twenty-five. He wasn't old enough to know how to please a woman.

He swallowed the taste of bile at the back of his throat. He just didn't understand why she wanted to be with these men. They didn't know what she wanted.

Why must these women be so difficult? All he wanted was to love them. He wanted to be their whole life, protect them, and care for their every need.

He thought he finally met the woman he wanted to share his life with, but so far she had shown no interest in him.

Was it because he was too normal? Was he to all American male for her? Did she want the bad boy image?

How could he get her to pay him some attention? If only she saw him for one visit, he could prove to her that he was the only man she needed.

Chapter 77

As Cassandra Evans walked up to the door, she wondered if she should pursue this story. She knew firsthand what some of these people were like, and they would NOT want a story like this being made public. However, she was a journalist first, and the idea of a headline story pushed her forward. Besides, her curiosity had gotten her into more trouble than she cared to admit, and she always came out just fine.

Pulling her Mercedes along the curb, she stared at the house she was about to enter. Very few people know what business actually went on inside of the place. She had called to ask if she could come by beforehand. This was one place that you never stopped by without an appointment.

Brady was the best boss she ever had and would never steer her wrong. Cassandra opened her car door and made her way up the walkway. Once at the door, she grasped the Venetian bronze knocker and rapped it twice against the plate.

A very muscular bodyguard answered the door. "I have an appointment. Cassandra Evans."

"She's expecting you. Come this way."

Amber stepped into the hallway, "Let's go outside to talk shall we?"

***

Cassandra sat on her back porch watching the wind blow through the trees. The sunset was gorgeous tonight. Bright orange hues and fiery reds flickered over the horizon as the blue sky faded into the night. Lightning bugs came out to play as the day faded away.

The leaves on the maple and sycamore trees had begun to turn lovely shades of red and yellow. Some of the vegetation was still green, blending the colors beautifully. She loved this time of the year; fall could be completely breathtaking. She wished it wouldn't be so late getting here this year. The temperature was just starting to drop by a few degrees, but it was a welcome change.

The peaceful night was welcome after the day she had. She talked to so many young girls who sold their bodies today, all with one sad story after another. It was almost too much to bear.

She breathed in the cool fall air. This was such a respite from the undulating heat that plagued them every summer. A car door pierced the quiet of the night. She went back inside to see who was here. She opened the door to let Detective LeDoux inside. "I'm not disturbing you, am I? I thought you might enjoy some company."

She kissed him and said, "You can never disturb me. I was sitting out back enjoying this nice weather."

"I thought about calling, but decided to surprise you instead."

Cassandra noticed that he was carrying several bags of what looked to be groceries. "What's in the bags?"

He let out a chuckle, "I wanted to show you that I don't think you are a bad person by cooking you supper."

Cassandra led him into the kitchen. "You don't have to do that. Besides, I didn't know men knew how to cook."

He let out a laugh, "Oh, we know how to cook, both in and OUT of the kitchen."

After he put the groceries down, he pulled her into his arms for a kiss. She asked, "By the looks of all these bags, you must be hungry?"

"More than you will ever know, but first I plan on feeding you."

She peeked inside the bag, "Did you bring anything for dessert?"

Kissing her once more, he answered, "I already have my dessert planned out."

With a sultry glance, she replied, "We can always have dessert first, you know?"

"*Mon Dieu* woman, I came here to impress you with my cooking skills and that's just what I plan on doing." He playfully swatted her away as he made himself at home in her kitchen. He turned on the radio and found a local jazz station.

Staying out of his way while he cooked, she sat at the bar and watched him. Her mouth was already watering at the delightful aromas that were so foreign to her kitchen.

"What's on the menu tonight Chef LeDoux?"

"One of my specialties, shrimp etouffee."

 "Mmmm, one of my favorite dishes."

This was so nice and homey, something she always dreamed of, but never had. Even growing up, her family never gathered for meals at the house, most of the time their meals were eaten in restaurants. She could get used to him puttering around in her kitchen.

After supper, they took their coffee to the back porch to enjoy the cool night air. She looked over at him, "Supper was really good. I'm impressed."

Kissing her deeply, he replied, "It was my pleasure."

The deep, passionate kiss continued as he slowly unbuttoned her blouse. She let it drop to the ground. As he went to unfasten her bra, he looked deep into her eyes and smiled. Her bra joined her blouse. His gaze slowly lowered to her breasts. He could play with them all night and never get bored.

He leaned down to fondle, kiss, and suckle her breasts. Desire coursed through her veins, turning her insides to molten fire. She wondered if it would be like this every time. Picking her up, he carried her off to the bedroom. He gently laid her on the bed and started exploring every inch of her body. He stopped at her nipples and gave them a gentle squeeze, sending electrical currents throughout her body. His hand moved down her body, finding its way to her very essence. He began massaging her there. She spread her legs further apart for him. She was swollen and wet with desire. He moved his fingers in and out of her, nearly sending her over the edge. She moved against his fingers, unsure how much more she could take before needing him inside of her.

He trailed wet, hot kisses down her body. He lifted her lower body in the air, proceeding to kiss and tease her. She felt his hot tongue slip inside her and let out a soft moan. She couldn't take much more of this sweet torment. The deeper he thrust with his tongue, the more she arched against him. He used his thumb to massage her, sending her over the edge.

Looking down at him, she said, "It's my turn now."

Using her teeth, she pulled down his boxers. She took his engorged erection into her warm, moist mouth, teasing the head with her tongue in circular motions. She felt him take a finger and slip inside of her. For a moment, she lost her rhythm. For every move she made with her tongue and mouth, he responded with his fingers. She moved up and down on him in a twisting motion. Taking a free hand, she slowly massaged his balls. She heard a low moan escape him; he was becoming more excited.

He pulled her on top of him and helped glide him into her. As she took him deeper inside of her, wonderful sensations coursed through her body. She placed her hands on his chest and met each thrust with as much vigor as he gave her.

He unleashed a passion inside of her that she never knew existed. All of a sudden she was catapulted into a string of orgasms that took her breath away. Each orgasm was stronger and harder than the last. She didn't know if she'd ever felt such a powerful explosion inside of her. It was completely mind blowing. By now they were both thoroughly sated, curling up in each other's arms to fall asleep.

Chapter 78

It was only six in the morning, but LeDoux found himself unable to sleep. Before making his way to his desk, he poured himself a cup of coffee. He planned on reviewing all the information on the homicides again.

He spread the case files out on the conference table, and looked at the dry erase board where the morgue photos of the victims were on display.

As he went over the witness statements, lab evidence, and crime scene photos his mind kept returning to the fact that there had to be one common denominator.

He closed one of the folders he was studying and tossed it on the table. These victims were all over the place. Surely the killer had to screw up. So far the only signature they had found was the way he slit the throats. He believed that the killer was also taking the victims' computers and/or cell phones, but he couldn't prove it.

He was reasonably certain that this killer had become fixated on one woman in particular and started killing his competition. Before then, LeDoux felt that he killed women who somehow disappointed him. If only LeDoux could figure out why he switched from killing women to one particular woman's customers.

This killer staked out the place well ahead of time to discover if there was a security system. He also checked to ensure that there were no cameras to capture his face on film.

The neighbors all confirmed that they noticed numerous vehicles in and out of the women's houses, but other than that nothing out of the ordinary was noted.

They were dealing with a clever man who was physically strong. It would take a man with a lot of strength to kill these men. He didn't see a woman having the strength to subdue them, Dominatrix or not.

Chapter 79

Frank Marcel pushed himself in the front door of Bree LeFleur's house. He ordered Freddy, "Don't let anyone enter the premises."

"Yes, sir."

Frank Marcel grabbed a hold of Bree LeFleur and glared at her, "You know why I'm here don't you?"

Bree shook her head, trying to figure out just why this man was here, "No sir, I don't."

"Your husband died owing me money. A lot of money. I've waited long enough for payment. I have decided today is the day that I will get it."

Bree groaned inwardly, "How much did he owe you?"

"Oh, I am going to get paid, but it will be in a very different way. I don't want your money."

Before making another move, he simply stood there looking at her. He took in the beauty of her large breasts. "I have money, sir. I can pay you what he owed you."

He chuckled softly as he brushed his fingers deliberately down her body. Even though his touch was unwanted, it still aroused her. As he touched her again, she tried to free herself from his grasp.

Laughing, he taunted, "Oh no, my sweet. It is your turn to be tortured."

Once in her bedroom, he threw her towards the bed, "Undress. I want to see that lovely body of yours." Leering at her, he added, "Do you want to know just how I should punish you for your husband's deceit?"

"Please, you don't have to do this."

Laughing, he said, "I have thought about this long and hard since I found out what you did. I came up with a number of ideas and an entire arsenal of implements to use on you. Your torture will be thorough and sexual, but it will be exquisitely painful."

This is not what she wanted. She didn't deserve any of this. Why was this man so determined to humiliate and hurt her instead of letting her pay for her dead husband's debts?

She stiffened as he made his way towards her. She froze when she saw the whip in his hand. "Undress slave!"

She slowly undressed, trying to delay whatever he planned. Apparently tired of waiting, she felt the sting of the whip across her bottom. She howled in pain as he lashed at her once more. By the time she finished undressing, there was a mass of angry red welts on her cheeks.

 "That was for taking your sweet time. You should know that I don't play the same games as you, slave."

Once she was naked, he lashed at her once more with the whip. This time the tip of the whip hit her directly across her nipple. Agony seared throughout her body. She could tell that he loved every cruel, sadistic moment of this.

As he lashed the whip at her body again, he praised himself, "I love tormenting your body. Yes, we may have to make this a weekly appointment." He looked down at her, "Just in case you have second thoughts about any of this, I have filmed everything."

Chapter 80

Cassandra tapped her pen on the desk as she stared down at her notes. What she just learned was beyond huge. Now, if she could find a way to talk to Frank Marcel that would be a career breaker for her. There were rumors for years that he was involved with the Mafia, but never any real proof. If her sources were correct, he ran one of the largest prostitution rings in Louisiana, with the help of Mike Johansen.

She had no desire in turning over either man's name to the cops, but if she could only talk to them and find out just what they knew about this killer. Her gut instinct told her that they were also looking for this murderer.

She stood up from her desk, stretched her back and headed to the kitchen. As she poured yet another cup of coffee, a plan began to take form. She picked up the phone and called Amber, "I believe I just found out who your direct competition is. Mike Johansen is in bed with Frank Marcel."

Amber knew about Frank, but Mike was somewhat of a surprise to her. "Well, doesn't that beat all? Why would Mike Johansen be involved in my line of business?"

"I've been hearing rumors for years that Johansen had dealings with the Mafia. I did a little digging, and it appears that he has a very profitable webcam business using good looking women."

"And let me guess, he uses some of the women for his Dominatrix business."

Cassandra answered, "That is what my sources say."

"So what are you planning?"

Cassandra let out a sigh, "Well, I am hoping that Mr. Marcel will let me interview him for a piece."

"I don't see him talking openly about his involvement in prostitution."

"No, but if I cater to his ego and talk about his philanthropy maybe that will get my foot in the door. I will have to bring up the escort business off the record and out of earshot from any of the others that may be standing nearby."

Amber let out a sigh, "You know, that could be dangerous too. He may not like the fact that you are even questioning him about his side business. I know from a personal standpoint, I wouldn't like it."

After she had hung up with Amber, she decided to go back to the drawing board. Amber was right in that Frank Marcel might kick her ass out the door if she brought up his possible involvement in anything illegal.

Now with Mike Johansen, there may be a way to talk to him. As a bail bondsman, he more than likely saw his share of prostitutes come through the door. That would give him inside knowledge. She could ask him a couple of what if questions before talking about the escort business and asking if any of these girls walked in his door. She knew for a fact that an arrest was the kiss of death for high priced escorts but especially a Dominatrix. Once they had a record, they were forced out of business or moved to straight out prostitution.

Chapter 81

He watched the house in silence, anxious to make his move. They say that revenge is a dish best served cold, but he disagreed with that statement. Revenge was something that burned deep in your soul. It stayed there, growing stronger with each passing minute. It kept building and building until it was all that you thought about.

She was his whole world. She started out as a fantasy, then to an obsession, and now the love of his life. He needed her to love him more than anything. He wanted her to think of no one else, be with no one else. Soon, he would make his move, longing for her filled his very being.

As he made his way back to his new home, a smile formed across his face. Once there he poured himself a seven and seven. Swirling the drink in the glass, he thought back to everything he had done lately. There had been so many pawns in play as he advanced his own agenda.

He wondered if anyone had even discovered he had siphoned money from various business clients for years now. He was skilled at hiding his actions, though, and doubted anyone was ever the wiser about his actions.

Chapter 82

Knocking on the door, Captain Fontenot took a step back as a muscular man opened the door. A feminine voice called from behind him, "I can handle this Jimmy."

He walked in and took Amber Brady's extended hand. "Thank you for agreeing to meet with me."

"I figured for you to call and ask if I could meet, it was important. Especially with the murders going on right now." Looking at her friend, she said, "Please don't tell me one of mine was killed."

Shaking his head, he answered, "No, nothing like that. I had a few things I needed to talk to you about."

As he followed Amber down the hall, he commented on the artwork hanging in the house, "I never noticed the paintings before. Are they new?" He couldn't resist moving closer to one of the pieces.

Making a sweeping gesture, she replied, "I did the paintings and decided it was time to show them off. The piece you are admiring was from one of my moodier periods. If you notice the brush strokes, you can tell that I was mad as hell when I painted this." Amber pointed to the painting and said, "You can tell that there was an urgency to the brush strokes, almost frantic, as well as a few slashes now and then. I can't help it, but my mood tends to come out in my painting."

He could tell from the way she talked about her pieces that the artwork meant a lot to her. "They are very good."

Amber found herself blushing at the endearing compliment, "Thank you."

"I'm serious, they are magnificent. You should have them in a gallery."

"Once, long ago, I had a few in a gallery. The owner liked the direction that I was going and told me to bring in a few more of my pieces for the show."

Finding himself drawn to her every word he asked, "Well don't leave me hanging. What happened?"

"Basically, I ran out of money. Back then I barely made ends meet. Paints and canvas were very expensive."

Showing him into her office, she said, "Make yourself comfortable." Once they were settled, she let out a long sigh. "I guess since you know about my business, there isn't any need to hide anything. Art has always been my passion. Unfortunately, my parents didn't understand that. My dad wanted me to earn an MBA and take over the family business. In truth, he wanted a son, but he got me."

Captain Fontenot watched her facial expressions as she told her story. "It all boiled down to the fact that my parents didn't want me to study art. They informed me that if I decided to pursue a degree in art they would cut me off."

As Amber talked about her past, he could tell she still found it difficult to talk about. "In the beginning I worked any job I could get to pay for a rat hole of an apartment and school. I worked two jobs and barely made ends meet. One of the girls at school handed me a card, telling me if I really wanted to make some money give the lady a call." She looked into his eyes to see if he had a complete look of disdain for her by now before continuing, "That night when I arrived home my landlord told me he was increasing my rent. There was just no way I could afford another rent hike. I never hesitated in calling the woman."

"And I take it that woman was a Madam?"

Nodding her head, she said, "Yes, my new career took off from there."

Captain Fontenot took a long sip of the scotch Amber fixed for him, never once letting his eyes leave her beautiful face. "We have known each other for what ten years now? I never knew this about you, or even how you got into this business."

Amber cringed at the thought of how they met. "Ten years sounds about right. I was still a newbie in this business."

"The business is what I came to talk to you about."

***

Amber looked at him with veiled eyes, wondering when he would bring up the reason for his visit. At first, she feared one of her girls was busted, or worse killed. He swirled the amber liquid in his glass for a moment before answering.

Amber watched him intently. If she were ever looking for a man to marry, it would be someone like Brian Fontenot. Even for a man in his early fifties he was very good looking.

She could tell that the job was starting to wear on him though. There were subtle signs of sleepless nights on his face. She knew better than to ask how his marriage was. Besides, men and women tend to read their marriages differently, which could be why so many married men sought out her girls. They would rather have instant gratification from a stranger rather than actually talking to their wives about what was troubling them. Then again, if they did that, she may have to find a new line of work.

"I wanted to let you know that a bust will go down soon. Someone hasn't been able to keep their business arrangements quiet."

Shaking her head, she said, "Well then I know it isn't me. Please don't tell me that it was one of my girls who ventured out on their own."

Shrugging his shoulders, he replied, "That I am unsure of."

"If you give me her name, I can tell you instantly."

"You know that I can't do that. I just wanted to warn you that a bust was going down. When the media gets wind of this, it will be a whirlwind of publicity."

"Maybe, but it is not any kind of publicity I want. Publicity could mean death to my business."

He looked down at his friend, he said, "And you won't mention anything about the bust."

"No one will hear it from me. Besides, if you are getting ready to take out some of my competition, I have no plans to give her a heads up. I already have enough on my plate."

"I take it business is good."

Shaking her head, she explained, "Not as much as it once was. With the recession, fewer men can afford the charges and then with the webcam porn services starting up most men would rather be safe than sorry. Plus their dollar can go a lot further with those services. So it appears my newest competition is bored suburban wives."

Captain Fontenot gave her a confused look, "I'm sorry, newest competition?"

"I have noticed a trend lately, housewives who are either bored or looking to make some money from the comforts of their home. Either way they are hitting my pocketbooks hard because they come in charging far less than any of the professional services."

Amber started clicking on the computer at her desk, pulling up various websites. She turned the monitor to face him, "You may want to start checking out a few of these webcam companies. Most of the suburban wives start out here, but progress into more adventurous activities."

"Do you think some of the victims were involved in online porn?"

"I'm not sure, but it's a huge business right now. These companies have hit a huge market. Not only are most of the sites legal, but men can watch these women from the comfort of their homes."

"So you think these are huge money making sites?"

Laughing, she said, "You have no idea, and if the person working the site does it right, he can run up the customer's credit card bills without their knowledge."

"But how are webcam girls so much more popular than an actual live person you can touch and feel?"

Amber shook her head, "It isn't always about sex. Most webcams girls offer some of the same services I offer. Between these online sites and the serial killer, I have turned to dating once again. Some of the girls quit because of the recent deaths. A few of my best girls were scared straight."

"Do you know something about these murders?"

"No, but I do know that the girls are scared. I wasn't even sure if you knew some of these girls were in the trade." Looking him directly in the eye, she added, "Frank Marcel has a reward out for information on this killer."

He looked at her surprised, "Frank Marcel is involved in this trade."

"Ha, that's an understatement. When it comes to escorts, call girls, prostitution, basically anything involving sex, you can bet Frank Marcel has his hands in it someway, somehow. That is one man who guards his girls and business like a junkyard dog. If you do venture into this business, he will try to get a piece of the pie."

"What about you? Did he try to get a piece of your business?"

"He damn well tried, but by the time I took over I was well versed in just what he was like. The Madam who I bought from wasn't afraid of him and in turn taught me how to handle him. Now, that isn't saying that I never have trouble. He is good at throwing fits and making threats, which he has no problems making good on. I heard that his prostitution business had started to grow stagnate until he brought in a new partner not long ago."

He looked at her with interest, "Do you think some of these women worked for him, and this was his way of collecting money owed to him?"

Laughing, she explained, "No, he would send Freddy in first to scare the hell out of them. I have no doubt that his method of killing would be a lot simpler."

"Oh yeah?"

"Freddy, who is well over six feet five inches and weighs two hundred forty pounds, who does all of his collection work. This man has biceps the size of your waist. Word on the street is this man has no patience. He attacks without warning, striking with as much force as a freight train. Freddy could easily snap these girls' necks. There is no way he would bother getting blood on his clothes. He may shoot them, but there is no way he would bother getting his hands dirty by slitting their throats. Besides, Frank prefers to use strong arm tactics first."

"So I take it Frank Marcel has threatened you or your girls before?"

Amber unlocked a bottom drawer and pulled out a picture. Handing it to him, she explained, "Let's just say that I have my own insurance where Mr. Marcel is concerned."

He studied the picture, his eyes settling on a very young Amber Brady a little longer than he liked, before handing it back. "I take it Mr. Marcel doesn't want that picture getting out."

"That picture is mild compared to some of the others I have. I may have been young when I started in this business, but my dad didn't raise a fool. I was unsure of this whole business when I began and wanted a way to protect myself in case I was ever recognized. From the very beginning, I had a nanny camera in the room."

"I always thought you were in the escort business."

Nodding her head, she confirmed, "That was pretty much just a cover for my true profession. I am a Dominatrix, as are most of my girls."

Running his hand over his chin, he asked, "That is a word that I am not too familiar with, I guess. Is that a big business here?"

"It is more open lately. There are quite a few men, and some women, who pay a Dominatrix to discipline them."

"And I take it you have quite a few clients?"

"Oh, you would be surprised. I have about half a dozen girls working for me, and they each have about seven or eight clients. Most of the people who seek out my services are looking for Dominance and submission. . Now some of these companies have started offering Dominatrix services online.”

“Wait a minute, online? Then some of the men seeking out the services of a Dominatrix aren’t even interested in sex?”

“Yes, most of the men just want a woman to dominate them. Most who seek out my services are prominent men who have to be in control of their life at all times. Now and then they want a chance for someone else to take control. They want to be the submissive person.”

“And what do you get out of this arrangement?”

“The power. It is intoxicating to have control over what others see as a very powerful man.”

“And so this isn’t about sex?”

“No, this isn’t about sex which is why some of the online companies are making a success of it. Most of the men who seek out the services of a dominatrix are looking for someone to fulfill a certain fantasy they have.”

“And just how well does fulfilling these fantasies pay for you?”

“It is hard to differentiate what I make between the escort services and my dominatrix services since they are all together, but last year alone I brought in 1.5 million dollars.”

He looked at her in complete surprise. “Wait a minute, didn’t you say this was a slow year right now?”

“Yes.”

"You mentioned that Frank Marcel was putting up a reward for this serial killer. Just how much money are we talking about?"

Without batting an eye, she answered, "I put up one hundred fifty thousand dollars to get this guy off the streets. I know some people may look at these women as merely whores, but that is not true. They are mothers, daughters, women with families and lives of their own. They may sell their bodies, but for some of these women it is the only way they know how to earn any money."

"Trust me none of my men are judging these women. You need to realize, however, in our line of work we have seen some heinous crimes. Most of the time killers prey on these women because they know that cops will not care about their deaths."

"Which is why I paid Frank Marcel reward money. I know he wants whoever is doing this stopped." Looking into his eyes before continuing, she said, "I am against killing another human being as much as the next person, but this man has to be stopped. I knew some of these girls who were murdered personally."

Running a hand through his hair, he said, "I'm sorry, I had no idea. Hell, I shouldn't be surprised. Most of the women made sure to keep their business well hidden."

Amber nodded her head, "Well a good Dominatrix makes sure to keep her clients and secret well hidden. It's not as if we go around town wearing our outfits for all to see."

"I know you said that this business isn't all about sex, but these women were found in very compromising positions?"

Amber let out a long sigh, "Well, for most Dominatrixes it is not about sex. Most of the times I don't even have sex with the clients. Several Dominatrixes make it known right away that they do NOT have sex with their clients. However, that is not the case with all of them out there. Some see it as a way to heighten their sexual pleasure."

"What is the main principle behind being a Dominatrix?"

"It's about control and discipline."

"Discipline?"

"Some of these men need someone to give them a little discipline to help them stay focused in their work."

Scratching his head as he thought about what she said, he asked, "And what about the clients that aren't looking for discipline?"

"Some of these men are looking for fantasies to be fulfilled, which are the ones who probably seek out the bored housewives playing Dominatrix."

"These murders, some of the women were tied up. What are your feelings towards that?"

"For some of the women, handcuffs and restraints are their standard. They use them to keep their clients under control. It is easier to discipline a man who is restrained, but a good Dominatrix doesn't have to rely on chains and handcuffs. She can control a man with just her commands.

However, she would never let the client use them on her unless she agreed to be the submissive."

"We did find several, um, toys in suitcases."

"Toys are the norm. Some clients are too afraid to ask for what they want, but they will buy something that they want to use. Actually, a few clients have their own toys that they bring with them." Looking him directly in the eyes, she added, "There is a chance your killer became upset when his Dominatrix refused to turn submissive."

"I take it you have a few clients that don't like to remain submissive?"

"There have been a few clients who did not take to the submissive role. A good Dominatrix knows how to control those specific clients, but a newcomer may not know just what to do. In this business, you also have a few clients who become infatuated with you as well, and see the relationship as a romantic one."

***

Once in the car Captain Fontenot made a call. "Detective, I believe I may have an angle on these murders. We need to see if we can find out if any of the toys you discovered in the homes actually belonged to the girls. The killer may have brought his own set of toys with him."

He had turned a blind eye to the businesses that worked here in the city, but with this involving a murder investigation, he could not let that happen any longer. He just wished the other owners of escort businesses were as low maintenance as Amber. He had never once looked at her with disgust even though she spread her legs for half the men in this city, or at one time did. He was rather impressed with her mind. He could see her going far in a legitimate business. Although she would never make the kind of money she must earn now.

***

As Detective LeDoux listened to Captain Fontenot, he could kick himself in the ass for not considering the possibility the toys belonged to anyone other than the women. The crime scenes played in his mind once more. The cases had him stumped. Hell, most of these women you would never have even suspected were escorts, much less a Dominatrix. He suspected that the murdered men were clients, but how to connect all the dots? Could the killer be a jealous husband, or worse, another client who didn't like to share?

Chapter 83

As LeDoux turned down the road to Cassandra's house, two patrol cars came barreling past him with sirens blaring. Before he could remove his helmet, Riley was standing at his side, "What is going on, bon ami?"

Riley placed a hand on LeDoux's shoulder, "Another body has been found. Mon Dieu, I'm so sorry."

Without waiting to hear any more, LeDoux headed for the front door. Riley firmly grasped his arm, attempting to stop him. "Let the men work the scene. You are too close to this."

Anger moved through his body as he tried to comprehend what was said to him. "Mais non, I am working this case."

He started barking out orders to one of the young officers, "No one comes in or out of this crime scene without checking in with me first, understood?"

Nodding his head fervently, "Yes, sir!"

Glaring at Riley, he asked, "Who called it in?"

"A delivery driver. He went to deliver a package, noticed the front door open and saw the body."

At the front door, Dr. Chauvin met the two detectives. She held out her hand and ordered, "I don't want you in here LeDoux."

With a scowl on his face, he said, "I appreciate the warning, but with all due respect, get the hell out of my way."

Riley stood in front of his partner. "Bon ami, you need to listen to us. This is not how you want to remember her. Let us work this case for you."

Pushing his way through his friends, he walked into the house. The smell of blood permeated the air. The sight in front of him was almost too much to bear. Blood that just hours earlier surged through Cassandra's body was sprayed across the room. The gash in her throat was in stark contrast to the white shirt she wore.

Trying to keep any emotion out of his voice, he asked, "Has the house been secured?"

Captain Fontenot commanded, "LeDoux, I want you out of here."

As one of the young officers attempted to escort LeDoux off the scene, he easily shook him off, "Captain, I need to work this."

The lost look in his eyes, combined with the emotions moving across his face, Captain Fontenot merely nodded his head, "What have we got?"

Dr. Chauvin cleared her throat, "This is a copy cat killer."

LeDoux looked at Dr. Chauvin in surprise, "Are you certain?"

"Yes, there are clear hesitation marks on the body as well as the very simple fact that a serrated blade was used to kill the victim. This killer was very sloppy, not near as in control as your killer."

***

It was midnight by the time Riley and LeDoux made it back to the station. At his desk, LeDoux stared blindly into a cup of cold, day old coffee. Closing his eyes, he watched the day's events replay on the back of his eyelids. The sight of Cassandra's body kept playing in a relentless loop.

Riley set a fresh cup of coffee in front of him and said, "Dr. Chauvin said that she would have the autopsy report on Cassandra soon. She wouldn't go home until she was done."

Sighing Riley asked, "Is there anything I can do for you bon ami?"

Taking a sip of the scalding coffee as he fought the tears threatening to spill LeDoux replied, "No. I just don't understand why someone went after her."

Amber Brady cleared her throat as she looked down at the detective, "I think I can answer that for you."

Captain Fontenot looked at all of them, "Before we continue this conversation, Amber, I think we need to head into my office."

Once they were seated in his office, Captain Fontenot nodded his head to Amber, "Why don't you start from the beginning?"

As Amber wiped away the tears, she said, "Cassie and I have been friends for a very long time. Detective LeDoux, I don't know if Cassie told you or not, but she used to work for me. Even after she left my company, we stayed in touch."

LeDoux looked at her in confusion. "I'm not following you. Just what it is that you do?"

Amber took in a deep breath, "I run one of the largest escort services here in town, but more importantly I provide Dominatrix services upon request."

LeDoux could only look at the woman. "So that is why the story was so important to Cassie?"

"Detective there is something else that you should know. Cassie… Cassie…" As a mixture of grief and guilt overcame her, Amber found herself unable to finish the sentence. Captain Fontenot walked over to Amber, pulling her into his arms.

"It is okay. Take your time."

Wiping her eyes, she looked over at Detective LeDoux, "I believe I know who did this. She was going to talk to Frank Marcel and Mike Johansen to see if either man had any idea as to who was murdering these women."

All three men looked at Amber and Captain Fontenot let out a muffled curse. "Are you telling me that she was going to confront Frank Marcel about being involved in any of this?"

Forcing back a sob, Amber replied, "She wouldn't listen to me. She was determined to find out who was killing the women."

LeDoux slammed his fist on the table, causing Amber to jump. "Damn, I knew that woman was up to something. Why couldn't she come to me?"

Amber reached out and grabbed his hand, "She was falling in love with you. At first she was only after the story with regards to you, but she told me that she didn't want to ruin any chance she may have with you by discussing the case. Now I wish she had."

LeDoux grimaced, "I do too."

As LeDoux made his way to the door, Captain Fontenot stopped him, "Son, I know exactly what you have planned and before you do that let me talk to the man."

"Captain, this is still my case and I want to be the one to look the man in the eyes and find out if he is lying."

Shaking his head, "No, just talking to this man could end your career. Let me handle it. I have some leverage I can use with this man." Looking LeDoux directly in the eyes, "I promise you, son, that I will let you know something as soon as I talk to him."

Chapter 84

Just as Neil was calling his wife to see how she was his phone rang, "Hi honey. I was getting ready to call you. How are you?"

Rubbing her swollen stomach, she smiled, "The twins are really active right now. I need you to do me a favor. Shelley just called. Joshua Guidry is causing trouble at the shop."

If only she wasn't too big, then she would have driven directly to the store when Shelley called her. Unfortunately, she no longer fit behind the wheel. Neil let out a sigh. That man was becoming a royal pain in the ass. "Look honey, I don't want you to worry about this."

"I swear he really needs to find something else to do besides bother me about books."

"I'm going to call Derrick LeDoux; maybe he can scare some sense into him."

***

LeDoux looked at the caller ID on his phone and wondered why Neil Chaisson was calling him, "Mon ami, how are Lisa and the twins?"

Neil sighed, "If it weren't for Joshua Guidry, she would be doing a lot better. Listen, mon ami, I know you have your hands full right now, what with the murders and all, but I need a favor. Joshua is causing problems at the bookstore again. I was wondering if perhaps you talked to him you could scare some common sense into him. This is the last thing that Lisa needs right now.”

“What has Joshua riled up this time?”

Letting out a low moan, Neil said, “Some new book the book club is reading this month. He swears it teaches these girls to be promiscuous. If that man would only get laid perhaps he would leave us alone.”

Stroking his goatee, he contemplated what his friend was saying, “I will go down there and talk to him for you.”

“Thanks, mon ami. I will tell Shelley to have your usual prepared for you.”

 “You don’t have to do that.”

“Mais oui, I do. When dealing with Joshua Guidry you need something stronger than caffeine, but, unfortunately, that is all I have to offer right now.”

Riley just kicked his feet up on his desk when LeDoux knocked them down, “Don’t get too comfortable. We are going for a ride.”

“Mon Dieu, please don’t tell me that there has been another murder.”

“Mais non, we are going to go get a cup of coffee.”

Shaking his head, Riley started, “But there is coffee here…”

LeDoux cut him off, “But this coffee is free and comes with the opportunity to ruffle some feathers.”

Adjusting his belt, Riley asked, "Oh yeah, are we going to play good cop/bad cop?"

"Mais, perhaps. Joshua Guidry is over at Lisa Chaisson's bookstore picketing a book she has for sale."

"You owe me for this one mon ami. That man could try a saint's nerves. If ever a man needed to get laid, it would be him."

On the ride over to the bookstore, LeDoux stated, "We can use Joshua Guidry's disturbing the peace as a reason to bring him in and talk about the murders."

Riley looked over at his partner, "Just what are you thinking?"

"Well, if he can get this upset about a book with sex in it, what do you think he would do if he found out a good citizen here was selling her body for sex."

"You may be onto something."

***

Joshua Guidry clasped his hands together beneath the scarred wooden table. His patience was wearing thin with these two detectives. They kept asking the same questions over and over again. He was beginning to understand why someone would confess to a crime they didn't commit, they wanted to put an end to the interrogation.

He glanced over at the one way window, wondering who was behind there watching him. He wondered if Neil

Chaisson was behind there, gloating. He knew that man was behind this.

What was worse was that neither detective believed his story. "Mr. Guidry, would you please answer the question."

He looked at the coffee cup next to the detective longingly. His mouth was dry from all the useless talking. Drawing a deep breath, he answered, "I don't understand how picketing a bookstore leads to questioning me about some murders. I have never killed anyone. Murder is not only a crime, but it is a mortal sin."

Joshua Guidry let out a sigh of relief as a knock on the door stopped the detectives' line of questioning. Captain Fontenot opened the door and informed the occupants, "Mr. Guidry's attorney is here."

While Joshua Guidry talked to his attorney the detectives and Captain Fontenot met in his office, "Well, what do you think? Do you think he is our killer?"

"I'm just not sure. There is a part of me that says the man doesn't have the balls to commit these murders, but then when I saw the rage he felt for the book, I am not so convinced."

Riley interrupted, "Captain, I never saw anything like it before. He was spitting fire and brimstone about sex in a book, and I can just imagine what he would do if he found out a good citizen here was selling her body for sex."

"Do you think you have enough to justify holding him for forty-eight hours?"

LeDoux nodded his head, "I am going to ask Neil and Lisa Chaisson to press charges."

"That should give us enough time to look into Mr. Guidry a little deeper. "

Riley nodded, "I say if he makes bail we keep a tail on him. That way, if he goes to her, we got him."

Chapter 85

Captain Fontenot walked into the Petroleum Club and looked around. If it weren't for the fact that he came to see an elite member of the club, he would never be allowed in these doors.

Even now Captain Fontenot didn't feel as if he belonged here. This place screamed wealth and lots of it. The floors of the entrance were dark marble and in the dining room they were highly polished wooden floors. The walls were dark oak paneling adorned with paintings of the founders.

A hostess stood behind the desk leading to the dining room. She was a tall, thin, attractive woman with flowing auburn hair and the bluest eyes. The mandatory outfit they wore here did nothing to show off her feminine curves, which was such a shame.

Looking Captain Fontenot over, "Can I help you, sir?"

"I'm here to see Mr. Frank Marcel."

"He is at his table, but he left strict instructions not to be bothered. May I take a message?"

An older man came up to the hostess, "Excuse me, sir, but Mr. Marcel saw you out here and instructed me to walk you back."

Suddenly a scream echoed through the dining room. Drawing his gun, Captain Fontenot ran toward where the scream came from.

He called out, "Call 911 immediately. Do you have security to secure all the exits?"

The man beside him could only stare at the body, "No… No… No sir we don't."

"Damn, do you know where his security detail is?"

Shaking his head, he replied, "No, he usually comes here without any companionship. They are more than likely waiting somewhere outside." With a shaky voice, he added, "I just don't understand how this could have happened here."

Taking out his phone, Captain Fontenot called LeDoux, "I won't be able to ask Frank Marcel if he had anything to do Cassandra's death. Someone got to him before I could talk to him."

"Son of a bitch. Where is he?"

"I'm at the Petroleum Club. There is no security here. I have sent someone out to look for his security detail, but it is more than likely the killer has left the building."

LeDoux let out a muffled curse, "I'll call it in now. Who the hell do you think killed him?"

"If I was a betting man, I would say your killer. I'm sitting here looking at a man whose throat has been slit." Lowering his voice, he added, "You should know that our guest last night confirmed Frank Marcel liked it a little rough at times."

Captain Fontenot canvassed the room. There were no signs of a struggle. He asked the manager, "Who all knew that he came in here without his security detail?"

"Pretty much anyone who eats lunch here. I'm also sure that anyone who worked for Mr. Marcel as well."

"Damn. Damn. Damn." Captain Fontenot couldn't believe his luck. He planned on asking Frank Marcel if he found out any information. Now it appeared that perhaps he did find some useful information; that or the killer felt he needed to be disposed of. Either way, if the press got wind of this the shit would hit the fan.

Captain Fontenot watched as the medics quietly removed the body from the dining room. The way they rushed about you would believe that he was still alive. He had to admit LeDoux was smart in working this the way he did.

LeDoux walked up to Captain Fontenot, "Crime scene techs are finishing up, but it doesn't look as if they will find anything useful. This place is just as bad as a hotel room with all the fingerprints."

"So it looked as if the killer struck again?"

LeDoux nodded his head, "Dr. Chauvin will have to confirm it, but that's what it looks like right now."

"Son of a bitch, right under my nose too." Looking back at the hostess he angrily said, "Perhaps if she hadn't given me a hard time then I could have saved him."

LeDoux patted the man on the back, "Relax, she was just doing her job. What I want to know is who all knew that this would be the best place to get to Frank Marcel."

Captain Fontenot drew a deep breath, "Apparently, the list is fairly long. Hell, even I knew he took his lunch here."

"Yeah, but you didn't know that he would be without his goons did you?"

"No, no, I didn't."

"I can't help but wonder if our killer didn't like the fact that he tried to copycat his killings."

Looking at LeDoux, the Captain replied, "You should know that rumor on the street is Frank Marcel was offering a reward for information leading to the identity of your killer."

Now that did surprise LeDoux. "Let me guess your friend from last night informed you of this as well?"

"Yes. She doesn't believe he had anything to do with the murders, but she isn't certain that he is innocent when it comes to Cassandra's death."

LeDoux could feel the anger of Cassie's death moving through his body once again, "Now I wish I went to Marcel's house last night."

Shaking his head, he said, "It wouldn't have gotten you anywhere son. At least we know Guidry didn't kill Marcel. He hasn't left his house since he made bail."

***

On the way home, he picked up the phone to call his beloved Bree. He wanted to let her know that Frank Marcel would no longer be able to threaten her or her livelihood. But something deep inside of him kept him from making the call.

On the one hand, if she were to find out he rid her world of this despicable man, she could fall into his arms. Then again, if she knew that she no longer had to worry about him threatening her life she may not feel the urgency to stop doing what she does.

Could he take the chance that she wouldn't see this as an opportunity to keep the business going? He could no longer watch another man worshipping her body.

It was such a rush to kill the man there, a place where he truly felt safe. If he closed his eyes, he could still see the blood gushing out of his wound.

Chapter 86

Jonathan LeFleur looked at his best friend Brady Segura. He saw red as he watched the computer screen in front of him. There was no way that woman in the video was HIS mom. As much as he wanted to believe that the woman on the computer screen wasn't his mom, he began noticing small things around the room. The pillows on the bed were the ones he saw his mom pulling from the washing machine the other night. The bed was the same as the one in his mother's room as well as the layout. As he continued to look around the room, he noticed knick knacks his dad used to complain about. Little things that he said were merely dust collectors.

Watching his mother performing these whorish acts filled him with an overwhelming anger. His dad would roll over in his grave if he saw his beloved wife doing these horrid acts.

Without stopping to think about what he was doing, he took off from school. He must confront his mother; tell her that she had brought nothing but shame to his father's good name. That she had made him and Gracie the laughing stock of the school.

He would catch her in the act, humiliate her the way she humiliated him.

Chapter 87

Excitement built as he followed her into the room. "You have no idea how much my time with you means to me." Pulling her into his arms, he said, "You are the love of my life. I want to be with you and you only."

Bree looked at the man dumbfounded. She never thought any of the men actually saw her as a lover. She exclaimed, "This is in no way a relationship!" Her stilettos paced the bedroom as she contemplated her next move.

Grinning at her, he said, "Cher, this is a relationship. I so look forward to our time together." He could tell by her cool expression that she didn't feel the same way about him. He had to convince her that she meant the world to him.

She stared at him with a completely detached air, no sign of emotion. "This is simply a business arrangement."

He ran a finger up and down her arm and replied, "You and I both know that this is so much more than just a business arrangement." With a boyish grin, he pulled her into his arms.

She pushed him away. "You know the rules; you agreed to them. If you can't abide by those rules, then you can leave."

As she turned towards the door, he yelled out, "Wait! You must know that I worship you. You are a temptress who drives me wild with desire. I think about you all the time, even while I am working. I will do anything you say."

A smile played at the corner of her mouth as she turned back towards him, "You will abide by the rules."

 "Just the mere thought of you makes me hard." He ran his fingers through his hair and said, "I don't want to leave. Let me show you how much you mean to me."

She made her way over to him, stopping so close that he could smell her perfume. She tapped one of her four inch black stiletto heels on the floor, "And?"

He stared at her pedicured toes, dropping to his knees, "I will be your worthless slave to use and abuse as you will. I will abide by your rules. Do with me as you please, just do me please my Mistress."

He looked up to meet her eyes. Her expression didn't change. "Abiding by the rules isn't an option. If you want to please me, you must obey my every command."

Kissing her feet, he whispered, "Oh, Mistress tell me what you desire of me."

As he went to touch her once again, she stepped back. Waving a finger in the air, she taunted, "Nuh-uh, you didn't ask, did you?" Her glossy red lips curve into a smile. "Now you must be punished you bad boy."

Anticipation of what she would do to him snaked up his spine. "Punishment, Mistress? What kind of punishment?"

She pushed him to the floor with the toe of her shoe. "Whatever punishment I choose. I am the Mistress of your desires."

"You are the Mistress of my heart as well as my desires."

She raised a perfectly arched eyebrow, "You dare to correct me?"

"I didn't mean to offend you Mistress. It is nothing more than a fact."

With a sultry laugh, she said, "I think you should beg for my touch a little more."

Licking his lips, he replied, "As you wish, my Mistress." Staring up at her, he asked, "Mistress may I please kiss you?"

"You may."

He started lavishing kisses over her foot, slowly making his way up her leg.

She moved over to the bed and ordered, "Crawl over to me on your knees."

"As you wish Mistress."

As he made his way over to her, his eyes were at eye level with her long, luscious legs. She slowly opened her legs, allowing him a gaze at what he desired, "Is this what you desire?"

Growling, he said, "Yes Mistress, very much so."

"Then come please me, you slave."

***

With a smirk, he called out, "Honey, I'm home."

In mid thrust, Bree pushed the man off of her. "Did you hear that?"

He let out a moan, "Come on honey, it was nothing. Besides, I'm paying you good money. You can't get Mr. One Eye at attention and then bail on me."

Bree played with his crotch, "Don't worry. You will get your money's worth. I plan on making Mr. One Eye very happy, okay? I thought I heard something."

Not wanting to stop, he continued playing with Bree's breasts. She slapped his hands away when she heard a noise right outside of her door. "Wait! Listen!" Bree listened, fearing maybe one of her children was home.

With a dangerous smile on his face, he turned the door knob only to find it locked. The stupid woman thought a locked door could keep him out.

Before either could make a move the master bedroom door splintered open. The two jumped as Tom stood before them with dead eyes. He grabbed Bree in a tight grip and pointed the gun at her client.

"Did you miss me honey? I see that it didn't take you long to find someone else to warm your bed, though." Laughing menacingly, he said, "Oh wait, I believe that you had someone warming your bed for a while now though, haven't you my love?"

Bree looked at the gun, then her supposedly dead husband. Tom's sudden appearance had scared the life out of her. Unsure of just what kind of game he was playing, she felt the terror building up inside of her.

She felt as if she were looking at a stranger rather than a man she shared her life with. What was even scarier, he no longer attempted to act like a loving husband.

With his voice low and calm, he said, "I'm disappointed in you Bree. You have not been acting like a very good wife. I thought you loved me only to find out that you were handing out your goods to men while I was at work."

Crying, she tried to explain, "I never meant for you to find out Tom. I promise. I only did it to help pay the bills."

With a cold expression, Tom ordered the two of them, "Back on the bed both of you!"

Eyes focused on the gun the two moved to the bed. Tom moved his hand to Bree's throat and squeezed as he stared at the man. He ordered the man, "Open your mouth."

Fear clearly heard in his voice as he pleaded, "You don't have to do this. Let me go man. I promise not to breathe a word of this to anyone." Pointing to where his pants were, he added, "I can even pay you to let me go."

Tom had carefully planned this out. He listened to the news and read the papers since his "death". The press had released enough information for him to pin the murder on the serial killer that preyed on women just like his beloved wife. Once the gun was inside of the man's mouth, he fired.

Bree squirmed, trying to free herself from Tom's grasp. Slapping his hand hard across her face, "Oh no my dear. I want you to watch as I kill you. I want you to feel as the knife blade cuts into your skin. A bullet to the head is too good for you. Besides, it will look as if the serial killer the police were searching for killed himself once he realized he had killed the wrong woman." The anger was evident in his voice as he spat out, "You disgraced me and our kids. What do you think they will say when they find out their mother is a whore?"

Without warning, he let go of her. It was as if he was too disgusted to touch her. Her tears left trails down the sides of her face.

She looked up at him pleadingly, her fear showing in her eyes. "You are not fit to be a mother. I thought you loved me as much as I loved you. How wrong I was. We took vows to love each other for better or worse."

She watched in horror as he swung the knife through the air. At that moment, as she looked into his eyes, she knew that she was going to die. What was worse, she would be killed by the hands of the man whom she had loved. "Please Tom don't do this. Think about our children. I am so sorry. I did all of this for you. I will give it all up. You can have all of the money. Please just don't kill me."

***

Rage consumed him as he held the knife to her throat. All he felt was a release as blood poured from the gaping wound. He found himself marveling at the color of blood. He never noticed before just how much it resembled a precious jewel. It was somehow ironic that his lovely wife should look just as beautiful in death as she did in life. Revenge was sweet. As he looked down at the dead bodies, he felt a surge of not only power but satisfaction. He knew that what he did was right and necessary.

He quickly arranged the crime scene to look like that of a murder/suicide. Before leaving the house, he packed each of the children a suitcase. He prayed that the sight of him at school would not be too much of a shock for them, but he could not allow them to find their mother in this setting.

He may be a cold hearted bastard, but he did love his children. Together they would start a new life far away from here. He had to explain that he hadn't meant to cause them pain, but that he needed to start a new life for them, away from this town.

As he headed down the stairs, the front door burst open, and Jonathan bolted inside. Tom froze in place, "Dad… Dad, is that really you?"

Tom could see the uncertainty in his son's face, "Jonathan, I'm so sorry to cause you any grief over my death. I never meant for any of this to happen."

"Dad, is that really you?"

Putting his hand on his son's shoulder, "Come on son. We need to get out of here."

"But where is mom? I need to talk to mom."

Shaking his head, he said, "No, you don't son. I'm sorry, but she is gone."

"Did she leave with one of those men? I know what she has been doing; I saw it. My friends were watching her this whole time."

"You don't have to worry about her embarrassing you in front of your friends anymore." Escorting him out the back door, he said, "Let's go get your sister. I have everything ready for us to start a new life."

***

He watched in disbelief as the man entered the room. Tom LeFleur should be dead. Bree was his and his only. Now this man took her away from him. He never had the opportunity to show her that he was the only man for her.

Rage filled him as he watched his beloved's blood spill from the open wound. Tom would pay. His fingers ran over the photo on his desk. He now knew what he must do. He would have her all to himself. He would take something from Tom that meant the world to him.

She would be perfect, untouched by any other man. Why didn't he see her before? She had never degraded herself by selling her body to a man. She was pure.

He could already imagine what was hidden beneath her clothes, -rosebud nipples, virgin skin, and an untouched treasure just for him.

Yes, she was what he had been looking for. She would be the one woman who abided by his rules. If she did as he pleased, she would want for nothing. In the process, Tom would always be wondering what happened to his daughter. However, he must act fast for this plan to come to fruition.

He would hurt this man just as he hurt him. Tom thought of this girl as his princess. She was his pride and joy. She was the perfect athlete, perfect student, and perfect daughter. Yet Tom didn't see what he saw, she was also rebellious. He saw it in her, heard it in the way she talked to her mother.

He could already imagine just what she would do with the right sort of prodding. His body responded immediately. He was already hard, throbbing.

Soon Tom would feel the pain of losing that which he held dearest.

Chapter 88

After weeks of planning, Officer Bruni was finally able to make his move. This would be the largest sting operation he had ever been a part of. The surveillance had paid off big time. He would have never suspected a brothel was in this neighborhood.

Bruni couldn't help but wonder just which of her clients would be there this morning. However, what they found was not what any of them anticipated. On the bed were Bree LeFleur and Eric Stevenson.

"Son of a bitch. How the hell did this happen? We were watching the house and never once heard gunfire."

Carefully picking up the gun Captain Fontenot exclaimed, "Looks like our lover boy thought of everything. There is a silencer on the gun."

"But it doesn't make any sense. If he is the killer, why kill himself now?"

"Who knows, perhaps he couldn't take the loss of the woman. It appears that the town will be able to close two cases today."

Captain Fontenot called Detective LeDoux, "I believe your killer has been found."

LeDoux found himself speechless at the moment, "I'm sorry, what did you say?"

"The bust that Office Bruni had scheduled for today, well it revealed more than just a prostitution ring. We walked in to find a murder suicide."

By the time LeDoux and Riley arrived at the crime scene, it was alive with activity. Not only was the medical examiner's van in the driveway, but the crime scene techs were busy collecting evidence.

LeDoux looked at the scene and couldn't shake the gut feeling that something wasn't right. It looked too staged. Why would the killer even bring a gun with him? He'd never used one before.

***

No sooner than the two detectives walked into the murder suspect's house did they have the answers to all of their questions. Everywhere they looked were pictures of Bree LeFleur. There were hundreds of pictures of Bree and her family.

Sighing LeDoux said, "It looks as if he has been infatuated with the victim for a long time now."

"I wonder what finally sent him over the deep end."

"Maybe she told him she wouldn't give up her profession?"

Shrugging his shoulders, Riley replied, "Well the gun was registered to Tom LeFleur, so we know that he didn't bring it with him. We may never know all of the answers."

"At least we have a cold blooded killer off the streets."

Nodding his head, Riley agreed, "Now comes the hard part. We have to go to the school and let the children know that they have lost both parents."

***

Riley let out a soft whistle as LeDoux parked the cruiser, "This is one fancy school. I'm surprised they don't have valet parking here."

Nodding his head, LeDoux agreed, "It's not a place I will ever be able to send any of my kids that's for sure."

After being buzzed into the school, the secretary asked, "I'm sorry detectives, but who did you say you need to see?"

"Jonathan and Gracie LeFleur."

The school secretary looked at the two detectives, "But, sir, you already sent an agent here to pull Gracie LeFleur from school. As far as her brother, Jonathan LeFleur, he did not answer his page. The teacher said he wasn't in class."

LeDoux let out a muffled curse, "Exactly what did this agent look like who checked out Gracie LeFleur?"

The school secretary looked at the detective, "I can do one better than giving you a description, I can let you see his actual face. We have extensive security monitors around the school. After all the school shootings around the United States, the parents here were more than happy to pay for an upgraded system."

As LeDoux watched the man check out Gracie from school, he tried to place just where he knew him from. He had seen his face somewhere, but for the life of him, he couldn't remember where. "Can you please print me a picture out of this man? Also, would it be possible to get copies of all the security tapes?"

As the picture printed she replied, "Yes sir. It shouldn't take too long to get you the copies of the security tapes." Handing him the picture, she asked, "Did you want to wait for them?"

Not wanting to waste a minute of time he handed her a business card, "No, just call the precinct when they are done. An officer will come by to pick them up." With time being of the essence, he wanted this photo run through all the facial recognition software that the department had. They also needed to get an Amber Alert out on the missing child.

Riley looked at the picture and said, "That is Owen Leger. I worked with him on a few cases when he was with the FBI. He is now a private investigator here in town."

LeDoux looked over at Riley, "Son of a bitch. That is why we could never find any evidence. The damn killer knew just what we would be looking for."

"Wait, you don't suspect that he is the killer?"

"Why else would he come check out Tom LeFleur's daughter?"

"I don't know, but if he is the killer this little girl is in serious trouble."

***

Tom LeFleur stared down at his phone in complete disbelief. An array of emotions ran through his body at this moment. If whoever had his daughter hurt one hair on her head, he would wish he was dead. He would not rest until he found his precious Gracie.

Chapter 89

"Detective LeDoux, the vehicle you put out an APB on has been located."

"What? Where?"

"The vehicle is on I-10. The officers have confirmed that there are a man and young girl in the car."

Letting out a sigh, he said, "Please let them know to proceed with extreme caution. This man is dangerous and more than likely armed."

"Yes, sir."

LeDoux looked over at Riley and said, "Let's go. They have Leger in their sights."

"The girl?"

Nodding his head, he explained, "She was spotted in the car."

Neither detective could believe their luck. Still, everything that could possibly go wrong kept going through LeDoux's mind. There was a chance Leger would realize that they were on to him and make a run for it. The last thing they needed was a high speed chase with a young girl as a hostage.

***

Gracie looked at the man driving, wondering what was going on. Where was Jonathan and why did this man keep mumbling something about her dad? "Um, sir? You just passed the exit to my house."

Smiling over at the girl, he said, "I'm taking you someplace safe Gracie."

A chill of apprehension washed over her. Something was wrong, seriously wrong. She didn't like the way this old guy kept looking at her. She had to find a way to get in touch with Jonathan, and fast.

While pretending to be searching through her purse, she sent Jonathan a text, "What is going on? Why did this policeman come get me from school?"

Jonathan heard the text message alert, "Dad, Gracie just sent me a text. She says some man has her."

Tom felt the ground open up underneath him. Dear God, please let me get to her in time. "Ask her where she is, and hurry."

Jonathan sent a text back, "Where r u?"

Gracie looked at her captor before replying, "On I-10. Just passed exit to house. In a black GMC SUV."

Jonathan could feel his heartbeat start to race. "Dad, she is behind us. They are on the interstate."

Tom couldn't believe his luck. This may be his only chance to save his daughter. He slowed down, almost to a crawl. If they were behind them, Tom would find them.

Jonathan sent one more text, "Dad says b careful. Man is dangerous."

Gracie felt the tears building in her eyes. She had to have misread the message because her dad is dead. "Dad?"

"He's alive."

Before Gracie could respond, the SUV was surrounded by cop cars. As Tom watched the scene play out before his eyes, he knew that he had to leave. Gracie was safe, and he knew that Bree's parents would take her in. When the time was right, he would come back for her.

It had been ingenious of him to fake his death. Not only did that allow him to kill his adultering wife, but Frank Marcel would no longer hound him for the money he owed him. Plus, with all the money he embezzled, he and Johnathan would live very comfortably.

***

Gracie didn't even give the man next to her a chance to react. She jumped out of the car just as he reached for her. Gracie ran directly to one of the police officers, tears streaming down her face. "Where is my Daddy? I want my Daddy!"

Officer Harvey took the distraught girl in his arms, letting her bury her face in his neck as she sobbed. "Shh, cher. It will be okay. Did he hurt you?"

Shaking her head, she said, "No, but he said something happened to my mother. Please what happened and where was he taking me?"

Officer Harvey looked at the young, distraught teenager unsure where to begin. He was just thankful that they were able to rescue her before anything bad happened. Through sobs, she continued, "Jonathan told me that my Dad is alive. Where is he? When can I talk to him?"

Officer Harvey shook his head, unsure of just what to tell the girl. Before he could respond, though, Detectives LeDoux and Riley were at the young girl's side, Detective LeDoux asked, "Gracie?"

Nodding her head, she answered, "Yes, sir."

LeDoux escorted her to his car and said, "We are going to take you back to the station. There is a lot we need to tell you okay?"

As glad as LeDoux was to have Gracie safe and sound he dreaded telling her that her mother was killed. Worse, LeDoux was confident that Leger did not kill Bree, but that it was Tom LeFleur who killed the woman.

***

Sitting across from Leger in the interrogation room, LeDoux could no longer control his anger and grabbed him by the collar, "Did you kill Cassie?"

Leger gave him a wicked grin, "She wasn't a woman, but a dirty whore who sold her body for money. All of these women were whores. They were supposed to only care for me, and not those other men. I would have given them the world if they had only let me be their Master."

"I don't buy that. Her friend told me that she had gotten out of that business."

"Once a whore, always a whore."

Bill Ingaldson, Leger's attorney, placed a hand on his shoulder, "Detective LeDoux, if you don't let go of my client I will make sure that you are arrested for police brutality. Now, I need to speak with my client for a few minutes." Turning to Owen, "And I told you not to say anything, didn't I?"

Leger glared at his attorney, "I don't need to take any advice from you!" Focusing his eyes on LeDoux, he stated, "I didn't kill that whore Cassie, but I did take care of the man who did. Not only did Frank Marcel have her killed, but he also forced himself on Bree LeFleur. The world is better off without him."

Leger sat there looking at the detective smugly, while he thought about everything he had just told him, "You are a pathetic excuse of a detective, you know that? You never even figured out that it was Ben Taylor raping all of those women, but I did. I also made sure that he couldn't hurt another woman ever again. You should be kissing my ass for saving this town money by not having to convict the man."

Ingaldson abruptly stood up, "Owen, that is enough! Detective, I am ordering you to leave so that I can have a few minutes with my client."

Riley pushed LeDoux towards the door, "Come on, mon ami, let's go get a cup of coffee while these two talk."

Chapter 90

Detective LeDoux was about to head out to lunch when a messenger walked into the precinct, "I have a delivery for a Detective Derrick LeDoux. It is marked personal and confidential."

LeDoux signed for a large package, forfeiting protocol, and immediately tore open the package curious as to just what it was. Taped to the laptop was a note, "Thank you for finding my daughter!"

After booting up the computer, he let out a surprised gasp. It was the deceased Bree LeFleur's laptop. As he looked through the various files, he couldn't believe what he was seeing. The woman was one hell of a shrewd business woman.

She had a detailed list of all her clients, their fetishes as well as dislikes. It also had the various charges for each client. He felt his heart skip a beat as he reviewed the names.

What he had in his possession could be very dangerous for him if anyone were to know of its existence. He would have to keep its information well hidden.

As Riley walked up behind him, he closed the computer. "What are you so deep in thought over," Riley asked.

"Nothing, just thinking about how nice and tidy Owen Leger thought he wrapped this case up for us."

Riley looked down at the closed laptop and asked, "Who sent you a computer?"

Shaking his head, he replied, "Someone who was grateful. This computer, though, holds some very powerful secrets."

"Bon ami let me buy you a drink." Slapping his partner on the back Riley continued, "I think after the week we HAD we both deserve it."

"I still can't help but think of Gracie LeFleur. Her dad will come looking for her."

Riley was certain of that as well, but at least the young girl was safe for now. They could only pray that her dad decided to let her heal and stay out of her life. He was certain that if Tom or Johnathan contacted Gracie, Bree LeFleur's parents would let him or LeDoux know immediately. Bree's father had already informed all of those involved in this case that he would not quit looking for his grandson.

As LeDoux gunned his Saxton down the road, he thought back to all the names he saw on the computer monitor. Mrs. Bree LeFleur was a very busy lady and someone would soon take her place. Her client list read like a Who's Who of Louisiana. There were some very famous sports figures, politicians, and prominent members of society. Even more interesting, she wrote down each of their fetishes next to their name. There were a few judges he could never look at the same when he was in their courtroom.

For the life of him, he didn't understand why a grown man would be into infantilism. Why would a grown man want to wear diapers and have a woman like Bree LeFleur change it? Although he could see how it would be rather embarrassing if that little fact did become known.

***

Mike Johanson watched the nine o'clock news in disbelief. Not only was he finally free from Frank Marcel's powerful grip, but the man who had been killing his employees had also been captured.

Now with everyone out of the way, he could go back to doing what he did best- making money and lots of it.

www.ingramcontent.com/pod-product-compliance
Lightning Source LLC
Chambersburg PA
CBHW070739190726
48292CB00002B/333